MAFIA III

PLAIN OF JARS

MAFIA III
PLAIN OF JARS

JEFF MARIOTTE AND
MARSHEILA ROCKWELL

TITAN
BOOKS
London

Mafia III - Plain of Jars
Print ISBN: 9781785657290
E-book ISBN: 9781785658624

TITAN
BOOKS

Published by Titan Books
A division of Titan Publishing Group Ltd
144 Southwark Street
London SE1 0UP
www.titanbooks.com

⬛Find us on Facebook: www.facebook.com/Titanbooks
🐦Follow us on Twitter: @titanbooks

Published by arrangement with Insight Editions, PO Box 3088, San Rafael, CA
94912, USA. www.insighteditions.com

First edition: November 2017

10 9 8 7 6 5 4 3 2 1

A CIP catalogue record for this title is available from the British Library.

Printed and bound in Great Britain by CPI Group (UK) Ltd.

Did you enjoy this book? We love to hear from our readers.
Please email us at readerfeedback@titanemail.com or write to us at
Reader Feedback at the above address.

www.titanbooks.com

THIS BOOK IS RESPECTFULLY DEDICATED TO ALL THE VETERANS
OF THE VIETNAM WAR AND TO THOSE WHO DIDN'T MAKE IT HOME.

1

Vietnam, December 1965

The man walking point went down first.

Next was a kid from Springdale, Arkansas, nineteen years old. Two nights earlier, he had tried to interest Lincoln Clay in a reel-to-reel tape of a country and western singer named Porter Wagoner. Lincoln hadn't heard anything in Wagoner's tunes that spoke to his life and asked the kid if he had any Marvin Gaye or James Brown.

Now Lincoln was flattening himself on the muddy path, wearing the kid's blood on his face.

Sustained fire erupted from the jungle darkness to his left, the south side of the pathway. At the first burst, everybody had hit the dirt, but some, like the kid whose name Lincoln couldn't remember, hadn't dropped fast enough. The heavy, continuous thumping sounded to Lincoln like BARs, no doubt stolen or bought from the ARVN soldiers to whom they'd been issued. American advisers and South Vietnamese troops returned fire, some of the Vietnamese pumping grenades at the ambushers from their M7 grenade launchers.

"Where's that mortar?" someone called. "Thompson!"

"Thompson's hit!" someone else shouted back.

The mortar crew had been a couple of men behind Lincoln in the line. Lincoln emptied his M16's magazine, ejected it, slammed another one in, then slithered through the mud. He found Thompson there, with the lower right quarter of his face shredded. Behind him, a skinny black guy cowered, tears glistening in the flickering light of the illuminating rounds, his arms wrapped around the mortar.

"Jenks," Lincoln said. "We need that mortar."

"Thompson's hurt b-b-bad," Jenks said.

"He's dead," Lincoln said. "Come on, give it here."

The mortar crew's third man was just called Breeze, for reasons Lincoln had never known. He was a white kid from Oregon or Washington, someplace like that, and he was just about always high. He was facedown in the mud, his arms thrown over his head. Alive, Lincoln figured, but checked out.

"Come on, Jenks," Lincoln said again. "I'll handle it."

Jenks stuttered something unintelligible, but he let Lincoln pry the mortar from his hands. Lincoln slipped off the path with it, jammed the base against a tree, and slotted the mortar tube into the base plate. "Give me your towel!" he said. Jenks shoved a rag into his hands. Lincoln wrapped it around the tube.

"Round," he said.

With quivering hands, Jenks passed him one. Lincoln shoved it into the tube and directed the tube more or less at where the fire was emanating from. He triggered it, then shielded his eyes from the explosion that followed. Jenks handed him another round, and Lincoln rammed it home, only the towel protecting his hands from the heat of the tube.

By the fifth mortar round, the gunfire from the jungle seemed to have tapered off. "WP," Lincoln said.

Jenks fumbled in Thompson's pack for a few seconds, then came up with a white phosphorous round. Lincoln triggered it, and a wall of white heat sprouted where the ambush had originated, illuminating the jungle to near-daylight levels. Heat and the mingled smells of burning flesh and foliage washed over him.

"That's some good mortar work, Private," someone said from behind Lincoln. He turned to see Captain Franklin standing there, his hands on his hips and a big grin on his ruddy, open face. "Where'd you learn that?"

Lincoln didn't want to admit that he'd been practicing with homemade explosives since childhood, alongside his adopted brother, Ellis. Wilson Tubbs was their father's explosives genius, back home in New Bordeaux, and Sammy Robinson didn't object to Wilson's giving the boys lessons in the finer arts of making things go boom.

"I just pay attention," Lincoln said. "Guess I got lucky."

"Luck, hell," Franklin said. "You're my mortar man now."

Lincoln jerked a thumb over his shoulder. "What about them?"

"Thompson's history. Breeze is stoned out of his gourd. Jenks can work with you."

"Long as he carries the mortar," Lincoln said. Making demands of officers was a good way to wind up on the wrong side of the people who could order you into a world of hurt. Still, if he was going to get anything out of the captain, now was the time. "I need my hands free for my weapon."

"Deal," Franklin agreed. "Just stay close to Jenks. He's pretty shaken up."

"He ain't the only one," Lincoln said, but the officer had already walked away.

• • •

"It don't make sense," Lincoln said. He was sitting in a circle with Jenks and four other guys, chowing down on C rations. Breeze was there, too, but only physically. In his head, Lincoln figured, he was off in Tibet or Timbuktu or some damn place. "We're, what, four clicks from our objective? Why ambush us here? Why not concentrate their forces around the village? They gotta know that's where we're headed. And they gotta know we're comin' from three directions at once."

"How would they know that?" The questioner was Ramos, a Puerto Rican kid from Spanish Harlem, someone Lincoln respected as a hard case who would give as good as he got in a fight.

"Man, ain't nothing happens in this jungle the VC don't know about. A lizard pisses under a bush, old Victor Charlie's watching him. How do you think they knew where to set that ambush?"

"I didn't think about that," Jenks said.

Lincoln nodded toward the South Vietnamese strike force traveling with the platoon. "You got to figure at least a quarter of those guys are Vietcong sympathizers," he said. "Back in camp, there's more. The girl who does your laundry might have a boyfriend in the VC. The Buddhist priest who sits near your hut. You can't trust anybody in this fuckin' country."

He tore into his second carton of rations. He had traded a favor, to be named later, with the guy who'd been the first to grab Thompson's box. He figured it was a safe trade, because the chances that the guy would still be alive at the end of the mission were probably fifty-fifty at best, and if they both survived, Lincoln could simply deny any memory of the exchange if he didn't want to do it. It wasn't like the guy would be able to take the meal back later.

"Point is," he went on, "if they know the village is being attacked from three sides, why not spend their time setting up defenses there? Booby traps and such. Then meet the attack with all they got, instead of sending out little ambush teams to get slaughtered?"

"I don't know," Ramos answered. "That makes sense to me."

"If it was me," Lincoln said, "I'd only do it to buy time."

"How you mean?" Jenks asked.

"Look, they know we're comin', right? From the north, east, and west? So if they run anywhere, it'll be toward the south, where we got most of our forces."

"Right," Jenks said, clearly not catching on.

"So maybe they just want to delay us a little. Give them time to get something out of the village they don't want to be there when we show up."

"Like what?"

"A weapons cache, some high-up VC muckety-muck, I don't know."

"You think they already moved whatever it is?" Ramos asked.

"Only one way to find out." Lincoln abandoned what was left of his rations and went to find Franklin. The captain was sitting on the tree stump with a map unfolded across his knees, a flashlight in one hand and a pencil in the other. Lincoln waited until the man looked up, acknowledging him, then explained his theory.

"You could be right," the captain said when he was finished. "But that doesn't change our mission."

"We're coming in from the west," Lincoln said. "Let me have a few guys and we can hook south, maybe cut them off before they *di-di.*"

"Lincoln, I need you. You're my mortar guy."

"I can leave you Jenks and Breeze."

"They're worthless."

"Sir, if the VC are trying to hustle something out of that village, don't it make sense that it's something we want? They'll boogie south for a while, then shift east or west until they're clear of us, before heading north with it. We don't have a big window here, and it's gettin' smaller all the time."

Franklin studied him. "Now you're a mortar genius *and* a tactician?"

Lincoln shrugged. No need to tell the officer that he just figured the Vietcong would do what he had done dozens of times back home. If the police—those who hadn't been properly compensated ahead of time—showed up at your door, you did whatever you could to stall them while product was flushed or weapons were hidden or whatever they were looking for was otherwise made to disappear.

That VC ambush hadn't been meant to eliminate the threat—they'd have used considerably more men for that. It had been a delaying tactic, nothing more.

And you didn't delay the inevitable without a good reason.

Franklin bit down on the end of the pencil, then gave a nod. "Okay, Private Clay. The name of the game here in Vietnam is going to be unconventional warfare, and I guess there's nothing more unconventional than letting an untested infantryman lead a task force on an entirely unauthorized side mission. Just remember this—if it goes south, you didn't have my permission. You deserted. You okay with that?"

Lincoln considered only briefly. He could get with the program, stay with the platoon, and take part in the clearing of the village—ultimately, he suspected, to no purpose. Or he could take advantage of this rare opportunity to go off on his own, to risk his life but maybe accomplish something.

When it had come time to register for the draft, Sammy had taken him aside and said he could fix it so Lincoln didn't have to go. Lincoln had appreciated the offer, but he knew most young men didn't have that advantage. Something stirred in him when he thought it over—patriotism, maybe, some sense of duty to country and flag. Sammy had drilled into him from boyhood that the only loyalty that really mattered was to family, which in his case meant Sammy, who'd made a man of Lincoln; Sammy's late wife, Perla; and his brother, Ellis; and beyond that, to the mob that Sammy ran.

Lincoln understood that, accepted it. But Sammy, Perla, and Ellis had been a tight-knit family. He had been an orphan, taken into their family but still somehow apart from it in small but genuine ways. The army, he'd hoped, would be someplace he would really belong, for once.

Anyway, he couldn't bring himself to take the easy way out that Sammy offered. Besides, he had justified, maybe he would learn something in the jungles of Southeast Asia that he could use back home, in the swamps and alleyways of Louisiana.

Here, faced with a decision to bow to authority or to flout it, he made the obvious choice. "I'll see if I can round up a few volunteers," he said. "Ones who don't mind bein' called deserters if it turns bad. Or gettin' killed, either."

"You going to take some of the ARVN strikers?" Like everybody else Lincoln had met here, he pronounced the acronym for the Army of the Republic of Vietnam as "Arvin."

"Rather not."

"It's their war," Franklin reminded him. "We're just advisers."

"Then I'd advise 'em to stay out of my way when my finger's on a trigger."

"Clay," Franklin said, something like admiration passing briefly across his face, "you're a shitty soldier, you know that? But you just might make one hell of a warrior."

• • •

Ramos had been the first to hop on board with what Jenks was calling Lincoln's "suicide mission." Then O'Malley, a broad-faced Irish kid from outside Boston, had declared that it sounded like a good time to him. Rutt and Fisher had been next, and then, as if afraid of being left behind, Jenks agreed. Seeing that the rest of his "mortar team" was going, Breeze declared that he was in, but Lincoln told him the squad was full and he would have to stay with the platoon.

They left the mortar with Breeze so they didn't have to carry it and took off at a steady trot. The streets of New Bordeaux generally made sense, but the swamps outside the city were without signposts or landmarks, and Lincoln had always managed to find his way through those, so he wasn't worried about getting lost. He knew which way was north, and knowing that kept him on course.

The jungle held plenty of dangers that weren't posed by the enemy—snakes, poisonous insects and plants, even the occasional tiger among them—but Lincoln didn't have time to worry about those. If they were going to intercept whatever the VC were hustling out of the village, they had to move fast.

The worst part was that the regular din of the jungle—the birdcalls and monkey screeches, the constant rustling of huge leaves against rough bark—would have drowned out their progress, except that the sound of their movement alarmed those creatures sentient enough to know it signaled man, causing them to go still. In that way, sudden silence announced their presence more than anything else would have.

Lincoln guessed it would do the same for the enemy, though. His hearing was acute, and as he listened for the expected silences surrounding his own group's progress, he also kept an ear out for any other gaps in the jungle's night noises.

After about forty minutes, Jenks slammed his palms against a tree. "This sucks, man," he said. "We're runnin' our asses off out here for nothin'!"

"You didn't have to come," Lincoln reminded him.

"I thought we was gonna shoot somebody," Jenks said. "Ain't nobody out here but us."

"Shut up." Lincoln was already sorry he'd brought the kid along. "I'm listening."

"Listening to what?"

Lincoln shot him a withering look. Jenks closed his mouth and looked down toward the tops of his boots.

Listening to what? Lincoln thought. *To nothing. No calling birds, no nighttime screeches.*

Someone was on the move, and it wasn't friendlies.

He held up a hand to keep anyone else from speaking. Concentrated. He heard night noises in the distance and focused on the direction, listened to where they stopped, where they started up again.

Convinced he knew where the unseen men were traveling, and how fast, he said, "Time to boogie."

They double-timed, cross-country through dense foliage where every plant seemed designed to block their way, trip them, or snag them from above. Lincoln set an interception course, and soon the roving silences merged into one.

Lincoln held up a fist to halt his tiny squad, then motioned the men to squat in the brush, at the edge of a small clearing. "Just a couple minutes," he said, his voice low and calm.

It took even less. Barely a minute later, he heard the distinctive rustle of men pushing through the jungle. He raised his M16 and waited. Only scant moonlight penetrated the overhead canopy, but there was enough to limn the VC soldiers, in their traditional black pajamas, as they broke into the clearing.

Using hand signals, Lincoln let the others know to hold their fire, even though he itched to squeeze his own trigger. His patience was rewarded; after a few moments, the entire party was visible. They were fourteen in all, and only one of them didn't look Vietnamese.

He was the tallest of the group, a white man with short, swept-back hair, wearing fatigues with no visible insignia.

"Just target the VC," Lincoln said softly. After nods indicated acknowledgment of his order, he sighted on the last man in the line and opened fire.

Taken by surprise, only a couple of the Vietcong were able to return fire at all, and that without effect. The white man they had been escorting tried to run, but Lincoln stopped him with a single shot to the back of the knee. The man dropped, cursing.

In a language Lincoln didn't know but could only assume was Russian.

2

Ramos knew some basic first aid, though he was no medic. He wrapped the Russian's wound sufficiently to stanch the bleeding, while Lincoln cut him a crutch from a tree branch. Moving at a considerably slower pace than they'd come, they made their way back to the village that had been the search-and-destroy mission's original objective. It was reportedly a local haven for VC activity, and with the sun rising in the eastern sky, it was easy to find by the smoke billowing from burning huts.

When they arrived with their prisoner, Captain Franklin was overseeing the digging of an enormous hole in the center of the village. Stacked around it were the explosives that would go inside once he was satisfied with it. He saw Lincoln coming and stepped away from the men with shovels.

"We found a whole warren of tunnels," he said. "Killed or captured more than a hundred VC. We're going to blow the place."

Lincoln ticked his gaze toward the women and children standing to one side, under armed guard. "What about them? Where will they go?"

"I guess they'll have to find new digs," Franklin said. "Maybe next time they won't let Charlie move in with them." He eyed Lincoln's prisoner. "Who's that?"

Lincoln grinned. "Brought you a present. I don't know his name—haven't bothered to ask—but he's a Russian. We found him being escorted away from the village by a dozen or so VC."

"A Soviet agent, this far south?" Franklin sucked air through his teeth. "Washington's gonna have a field day with this. They're not supposed to be anywhere near here."

"Are we?"

"We're just advising the army of our host nation. They asked for our help."

"They pay for all those explosives?"

"We've been paying for this war since the 1950s, when the French were fighting it," Franklin said. "Now we're just more up front about it. Slightly more up front, anyway."

"We have? I didn't hear about that in school."

"You didn't hear it from me, either, Clay. Some things they don't teach."

"Maybe they should. I pay taxes like anybody else. Be nice to know how they're bein' spent."

"What are you looking for in the military, Private?"

Lincoln dug the toe of his boot into the dirt. "Just, you know, doin' my duty. Tryin' to make it through each day."

"You're setting your sights too low. Man like you? You should be Special Forces. You want to be where the action is, right?"

"Special Forces? I don't think I'm cut out for that. Don't you need a diploma for that?"

"Just high school. You have that, right?"

Lincoln nodded. He had never considered the possibility of wearing the Green Beret. Even having this conversation felt like some strange dream. "Yeah," he said.

"That's what I thought. You could have a great military career ahead of you, Private Clay, but you've got to make the right moves. It doesn't just happen—you've got to make it happen."

Lincoln shook his head. He knew, from hard experience, how this went down. Guys like him, poor kids from Delray Hollow, were offered all kinds of things, only to have those chances vanish as soon as they got their hopes up. "I just don't see it."

"Clay, I'm not in the habit of blowing smoke up people's asses," Franklin said. "I think you could have a shot at it. If you want it. That's the key. You've got to want it first."

There had been plenty of things in his life that Lincoln had wanted.

Some he had acquired; others had remained forever out of reach. But there was something about this idea he found appealing. "I've heard some stories about the Green Berets. They get to make their own rules. Go in where it's hot and heat it up some more. Sounds all right to me."

"Now you're talking," Franklin said.

"But I'm here. Doesn't it take a year of training stateside to earn the beret?"

"Ordinarily, yes. But these aren't ordinary times, Clay. This war's going to ramp up fast, and we're going to bear more and more of the burden, despite whatever Johnson and McNamara are saying on the evening news. We're going to need good men. Let me see if I can pull some strings."

Lincoln figured the man had some kind of angle, but he couldn't imagine what it might be. People didn't just offer to help each other out that way, not unless they got something in return.

"For me?"

Franklin put a hand on Lincoln's broad shoulder. He had to reach up to do it. "Clay, you just found a Soviet agent ninety clicks from Saigon. If you're not careful, you might get called to Washington so LBJ can pin a medal on your chest. And believe me, you don't want to come to the attention of anybody in Washington. I'll see what I can do to make sure your future is as a fighting man, not as a wooden Indian with a chestful of ribbons."

• • •

Lincoln didn't expect anything to come of the promise. He was just an infantry private who'd had a lucky break. And he still couldn't see what Franklin would get out of it.

So he was surprised to find himself, two weeks later, on an airplane back to the World, as everybody stationed in Vietnam had taken to calling the US. As soon as Vietnam fell away below him, he was joined by a lean, rangy colonel whose raw-edged features could have been chopped from a log with a hatchet. He wore his beret at a rakish angle; bare scalp gleamed beneath it. He introduced himself as Philip Giunta. Lincoln could hear some Brooklyn in his accent, though it wasn't strong.

"Thanks for agreeing to this assignment," Giunta said, once the introductions were done.

"Did I agree to something?"

"According to Tom Franklin, you did. He made a strong case for you. It's unusual, to say the least, but Tom has friends in high places."

"Where exactly am I goin'?" Lincoln asked.

"Fort Benning, Georgia."

"What's at Fort Benning?"

"Jump school," Giunta replied. "You'll spend a week there, jumping out of airplanes under every condition you can imagine. Then it's off to Fort Bragg for an abbreviated session of Special Warfare School. I understand you've already improvised some guerilla combat techniques, but they'll teach you how it's really done."

Lincoln was confused. "Don't I have to try out? Pass some kind of test and a background check?"

"You've already tested in, Private. And passed your background check. There were some findings that were, let's say, concerning, but like I said, Captain Franklin was pulling for you, and he's got connections I don't even have. I'll be honest—I don't like ignoring protocol this way. I feel like if rules have been established about these things, it's probably for good reason, and we ought to follow them.

"But the truth is that we're going to need good Special Forces operatives faster than the school can turn them out. Every indication is that we'll be in Vietnam for a while. The president sees Southeast Asia as a tipping point. If it falls to the commies, then we've lost Asia altogether. And he doesn't want that to be his legacy."

Lincoln knew that President Johnson had passed civil rights legislation, but he had thought it mostly applied to black folks like himself. He hadn't given much thought to the president's relationship with Asians, and he wasn't sure Johnson had, either. "So now he's concerned about the yellow man?" Lincoln asked.

"I can't say for sure what's driving him," Giunta answered. "He's a politician, so I'd guess he's worried about being reelected, like the rest of them are. All I know is that we're going to be committing more Special Forces to the region for the indefinite future."

Lincoln wondered how in-depth the background check had been. His mother had abandoned him when he was two, and he'd been raised at Saint Michelle's Home for Colored Boys until he was thirteen, when the city had decided that foster families were a better way to bring up orphans. Little black kids always seemed to be the last to be fostered, and he had occasionally doubted that he would ever have a family until Sammy and Perla Robinson had taken him in.

He had been in trouble with Father James at the orphanage now and again—fights, the occasional theft, drinking, a little pot. He'd been big for his age even then, and small kids weren't the only ones bullied and picked on. And there was the fact that he was a black kid, growing up in the 1950s American South. Using the wrong water fountain or trying to swim in the wrong pool could earn a kid a beating, or worse. Father James had protected his charges from that sort of abuse, as much as he could, but he wasn't always around when Lincoln was tearing about the city.

And even the most cursory background check would have revealed Sammy's history. He came across as a successful businessman, but one didn't have to dig very deep to see that much of what he earned came from running numbers, selling dope, pimping, and worse. Franklin's contacts must have been impressive, indeed, to make the authorities overlook Lincoln's role in those enterprises.

"So, what's my security clearance?" he asked.

Giunta grimaced a little but tried to hide it. "Top Secret," he said. "That's standard for Green Berets." He shifted in his seat, turning to face Lincoln. "Tom Franklin put his ass on the line for you, Clay. So did I, for that matter, by backing Tom up. I trust his judgment, and if he thinks you're fit to wear the beret, then so do I. But I need to know you'll honor it—honor the trust Tom and I put in you, and that the nation will put in you. We've got about twenty more hours before we land at Fort Benning, so you don't need to answer me right now. But by the time we touch down, I'll want to know if you're in or not. If not . . . well, there's always another plane heading back to 'Nam."

He left Lincoln sitting alone and disappeared toward the front of the aircraft. The plane was largely empty—Lincoln had the impression this wasn't a regularly scheduled flight, rather something that had been put together for his benefit. A few other GIs were scattered around, most lost in their own thoughts but some engaged in quiet card games or conversation. There wasn't much else to do except sit, listen to the roar of the propellers, and think.

Truth be told, although he didn't mind thinking, he thought doing too much of it was overrated at best and maybe harmful. Instead, he moved around in his seat until he was as comfortable as he could get, closed his eyes, and drifted off to sleep.

• • •

The evening air on the tarmac at Lawson Army Airfield was heavy and damp and smelled of diesel and exhaust. Lincoln was used to humidity; it was a staple of New Bordeaux summers, and Vietnam was more of the same. Despite the heat, he was hardly sweating as he walked toward the waiting trucks with his duffel bag in his hand.

Colonel Giunta strode up beside him. "What's it going to be, Lincoln?" he asked. "There's a Jeep over there that'll take you to your barracks, if you're staying. If not, there's a plane sitting on the tarmac waiting to take off. Your call."

"I'll stay," Lincoln said. "Might as well, right?"

"That's one way to look at it, I suppose."

"I mean, the food here's got to be better than the C rations I get back there."

"You should spend some time in Saigon," Giunta said. "The French taught those people how to cook. You can get some delicious Vietnamese food, and their French restaurants are as good as any in the world."

"I'll get there one of these days, Colonel. For now, I think I'd rather be where the action is."

Giunta looked at him searchingly. Lincoln got the feeling he was waiting for something else—maybe some sort of declaration of patriotic altruism. But he'd gotten all Lincoln was going to give him, and he'd have to be satisfied with it. Giunta seemed to figure that out after a moment, because he gave a little half-shrug and turned away.

"Trust me," he said, leading Lincoln toward a waiting Jeep. A soldier sat behind the wheel, one arm dangling casually outside. "You'll definitely see some action after you earn your beret. Maybe more than you're banking on."

And Lincoln wondered, not for the first time, just what he was getting himself into.

3

Jump school was pure hell.

Despite Father James and the sisters at the orphanage, Lincoln mostly made his own way on the streets of New Bordeaux during his childhood. Physical exertion and punishment weren't new to him, but this was punishment on a different level. It was compounded by the fact that he had to squeeze a three-week course into a week, which meant that when others in the morning session got to use the afternoon to recover, Lincoln had to attend another session. After that, he got an hour for dinner and "recuperation," then another four hours of individual instruction from the jumpmaster. He spent the first few days learning the principles of jumping from airplanes and performing practice jumps—seemingly hundreds of them—from platforms of varying heights. Once he had demonstrated that he knew how to pack a parachute, how to land, how to roll, and how to disentangle himself, he started going up in planes for the real thing.

His first jump was at the comparatively low altitude of 1,500 feet, barely allowing enough time for the chute to open—but plenty of time to worry about what would happen if it didn't. He survived, so the jumps became higher and more challenging—he was weighted down with ever more gear, and he had to jump at night and into forests, swamps, mountainsides, and other difficult terrain.

Despite his doubts, he lived through it all and was declared a paratrooper. Then he was flown to Fort Bragg, North Carolina, for the next step in his sudden advancement: three classes offered at the John F. Kennedy Special Warfare Center and School. He had most of a day off between landing at Bragg and starting school, and he had arranged for Sammy and

Ellis to travel up from New Bordeaux for the occasion.

The men were escorted to the barracks Lincoln would occupy for the duration of his training. The building was empty but for Lincoln. Dust motes danced in sunlight slanting in through the windows, and despite regular cleaning, the air was thick with the smell of sweat from men who worked hard, then slept in hot, humid conditions.

Lincoln rose from his bunk when he saw his father and brother enter. The first thing Sammy did was hold out his arms and wait for Lincoln to come into them. After a long embrace, the old man backed off, patted Lincoln's upper arms, and said, "You're looking good. Strong."

"I think I'm just shorter. All the jumping I've done the last few days has compressed me by at least three inches."

"He's right, Lincoln," Ellis said. "You do look different."

Lincoln hadn't really noticed the changes, but looking at Ellis now, he realized his face was leaner than it had been back home, his stomach flatter, more cut.

"Guess it's all that shitty food," Lincoln said with a laugh. "I tell you, there's no food like New Bordeaux food. I haven't had dirty beans and rice or a po'boy in months."

"They said we could take you out," Sammy said. "Fayetteville's no New Bordeaux, but they got to have some decent restaurants, n'est-ce pas?"

"You've always been able to pick 'em, old man," Lincoln said. "I'll follow your nose." He turned to Ellis. "How you doin', man? You got a girlfriend yet?"

"So many I can't keep their names straight," Ellis shot back.

"Any keepers?"

Ellis shrugged. "You know, just chicks from the Hollow."

"Man, if it's left up to Ellis," Sammy said, "I'll never be a grand-père. That's another reason you got to hurry home from this war, Lincoln."

"One of these days, brother," Lincoln said. "One of these days, you'll meet the right girl."

"With any luck," Sammy added, "she'll be blind."

Ellis's jaw dropped open and he started to frame a retort, but Lincoln burst into laughter that precluded any response. "Come on," Sammy said. "We got to find us some sustenance. Growing boys got to eat, *non*?"

• • •

"Business is okay," Sammy said after the dinner dishes had been cleared and drinks poured. "Same ol', same ol', you know?"

"Business is in the shitter," Ellis countered.

"Hush, you!" Sammy snapped.

"No. Why you want to hide the truth from Lincoln? He's a part of this family; he ought to know the real deal."

"Lincoln has bigger things to worry about." Sammy sipped his brandy, made a face, drank some more. When he put his glass down, he said, "Boy's going to be a hero."

"I don't know if there are any heroes in this war," Lincoln said. "Not me, anyway." He fixed Ellis with a steady gaze. "What's going on at home?"

"Lot of heat from the Haitians," Ellis said. "Feels like they're thinkin' about makin' a play for some of our turf."

Sammy wagged a finger at him. "Now, you know we put that down, Ellis. Don't be telling tales out of school."

"Put it down for now," Ellis admitted. "But for how long? Seems to me when it takes a show of force to get someone to back off, eventually they forget what you showed 'em and they come back for more. Plus the Dixie Mafia's been making noises about expansion, too."

"Turf wars are always gonna happen," Lincoln said. "That's all Vietnam is, really. A turf war, just on a bigger scale."

"I don't want you to worry about us, Lincoln," Sammy said, banging his brandy snifter on the table for emphasis. "You got to have a clear head out there. We're fine, really."

Ellis made a scoffing noise, but a glare from Sammy silenced him. Lincoln didn't like it. Sammy had always been straight with him, whether the news was good or bad. There had been plenty of the latter, from Perla's death to the ins and outs of the family "business."

He had never tried to hide the nature of that business from Lincoln, or apologize for it. Yes, he admitted, he was a crime boss. But the reasons for that were complex, and mostly beyond his control. In the American South in which Sammy had grown up, opportunities for men of color had been limited at best. He could have toiled at a menial blue-collar job like a janitor or garbage man, or worked in some white farmer's fields, or he could have joined the crew of a fishing boat.

But Sammy had been born just more than a half century removed from slavery, and his own father had been a sharecropper. He wasn't interested in an occupation that smacked of that evil institution in any way. The occupations whites had decided were good enough for the descendants of slaves were meant, he believed, to keep black men in their "proper" place and to limit economic advancement and the choices that came with it—choices like where to live and with whom to associate.

Sammy didn't want to be limited in those ways. He wanted to take what he could, and if it meant breaking the white man's laws, that was a bonus as far as he was concerned. So he had turned his back on those "acceptable" professions and instead used his wits and his cunning and an occasional ruthless streak to make his own way in the world. Now he was one of the wealthiest black men in New Bordeaux, with legitimate businesses—like Perla's Nightclub, the jazz club he owned in the Delray Hollow district—that he ran alongside his illegal ones.

Lincoln remembered the first time Sammy had explained these things to him, with a solemnity resembling that with which Lincoln had heard some parents explained the mysteries of sex. He had taken Lincoln into his study and sat him down in a chair that dwarfed the boy, and he'd explained that there were activities, like lotteries, that were frowned upon by white society, even though when nobody was looking just as many white folks were drawn to them as black folks. The Robinson family fortune had, Sammy explained, been made by catering to those desires. He was quick to stress that there was nothing wrong with that. "We don't have anything to do with products that hurt our own," he'd said. "Putting down a dollar in hopes of making a thousand, well, that's not gonna deprive a family of a roof over their head or food on the table. Might just put more food on the table, in fact, and patch some holes in that roof in the bargain. Some men got the urge to gamble; some got the urge to cat around. As long as none of our own folks are getting hurt, we help them enjoy those things they're gonna do anyway."

Lincoln had learned, as the years passed, that the business was a bit more complicated than that. In that first conversation, Sammy hadn't said anything about taking a competitor who'd dared to tread on Black Mob turf into a neighborhood slaughterhouse and feeding him through the meat grinder. Then again, those parents describing the wonders of human reproduction never went into detail about the nuts and bolts of it, either.

When the evening ended, Sammy and Ellis dropped him off at his barracks. Special Warfare School would begin the next day. He would take abbreviated classes in unconventional warfare, psychological warfare, and counterinsurgency—classes designed to make him the kind of soldier the Army needed in the decidedly unconventional landscape of the Vietnam conflict.

But that night, he hugged the only father and brother he had ever known. Both squeezed him tight, and Lincoln saw a tear in Sammy's eye when he said, "You take care over there, Lincoln. Like I told you from the start, we need you back home. If wearing that Green Beret means you make a little more money and get back sooner, that's okay, but I don't want you taking any foolish chances. I hate having you over there in the first place."

"Don't worry about me," Lincoln said with a chuckle. "I'll get home just as soon as I can."

"In one piece, I hope," Ellis added quietly when he embraced his brother. "I'm not worried about you, but he frets like an old lady."

"Don't let him hear you say that," Lincoln muttered. "He'll whup you just to prove you wrong."

Ellis and Lincoln had laughed at that, and then Sammy and Ellis were gone and Lincoln turned to walk into a barracks full of men he'd never seen before and who might well resent the fact that he was there for a few months instead of a full year.

4

Because he was traveling solo instead of with his unit, he flew back to Vietnam on a commercial flight, aboard a Pan Am jet that landed at Saigon's Tan Son Nhat Airport on a hot evening with a steady rain. He crossed the tarmac with his gear in his arms, feeling the rain splash against his face and breathing in the unique blend of jet fuel, garbage, and night-blooming flowers that would always say Vietnam to him.

He had left Vietnam as Private Clay, but when he returned, he was Corporal Lincoln Clay, assigned to Detachment A-101, C Company, 5th Special Forces Group. Instead of returning to his unit, he was sent to a Special Forces Operating Base—an SFOB—near the 17th Parallel, which was the line that had been drawn to divide North and South Vietnam. The Special Forces troops at the SFOB were an A Team—officially advisers, not combatants, under the command of a B Team headquarters situated in Danang. He hitched a ride there on a helicopter carrying two government bureaucrats from Washington who, Lincoln guessed from their manner, had enjoyed their few days in Saigon a bit too heartily, and a reporter from the *New York Times* who ignored Lincoln in favor of badgering the hungover guys in suits.

Three days after landing in Saigon, he was on the ground at the Lang Vei Special Forces Camp in Quang Tri Province, seven kilometers down Route 9 from where the Marines were busy building a major base at Khe Sanh. The terrain was mountainous, and the blades of the helicopter that had brought him there whipped dense fog into a funnel as it ascended again.

The camp was a chaotic-seeming assemblage of thatched huts and concrete bunkers. The dominant feature was a two-story concrete tower that Lincoln would learn was the TOC, the Tactical Operations Center.

27

Lincoln stood there as a second lieutenant greeted the bureaucrats and led them toward the TOC. A sergeant did the same with the reporter. Finally, after several minutes alone, a corporal emerged from the fog.

"You lost?"

"I'm Corporal Clay." He patted the pocket containing his orders, as if that would mean anything to the other soldier. "I've been assigned here."

The corporal eyed him. He was a white guy who hadn't shaved in a week or so and maybe hadn't bathed, either. His shirt hung open, and a scar that Lincoln thought looked as though it had been made by a knife puckered the flesh of his sternum. "Sorry to hear that," he said. "You can still run, and I'll pretend I didn't see you."

"Run where? All the way back to Saigon?"

"All the way back to Fort Bragg, if you know what's good for you. Lang Vei is the shithole of Vietnam." The corporal pointed north, then west. "Go any farther north and you're in North Vietnam. Laos is just two clicks over there. It's been pretty quiet lately, but that could change any time."

"I guess I'm here to stay," Lincoln said.

The other man shrugged. "I'll show you the team house. Captain's in the TOC, but he's got guests so you can meet him later."

"I flew in with them. They were looking pretty green."

"Saigon will do that to you. Lincoln, huh?"

"That's right. Lincoln, like the president."

"I'm Stephens," the man said. "Duncan, like the yo-yo."

On the way to the team house, they passed more indigenous faces than American ones. Stephens explained that there were only twenty-four Special Forces soldiers at the camp, but the force included a whole company of Montagnard tribesmen and three South Vietnamese rifle companies.

"Twenty-three now, actually," Stephens corrected himself. "Well, you make twenty-four, I guess. You're replacing DuPage."

"What happened to him?"

"He threw a grenade."

The answer confused Lincoln. "He *threw* it?"

"It hit a tree and bounced back. Everybody scrambled, but he was too slow. Surprised that it came back at him, I think. Anyway, he was still standing there when it went off."

"That's some shitty luck," Lincoln said.

"Bad luck for him, bad luck for you."

"Me?"

Stephens shrugged again. "Everybody liked DuPage. You live long enough, maybe they'll like you, too."

"Or maybe not?"

"Chance you take," Stephens said. "Sure you don't want to run?"

"I'll stay," Lincoln replied. "I'll take that chance."

• • •

There were a half dozen guys in the team house. A couple were smoking on their bunks, one reading a paperback book. Three others played cards around a table laden with ashtrays and soda cans and a few beer bottles. One sat on his bunk in his underwear, strumming an acoustic guitar and mumbling the words to some song Lincoln didn't know.

Lincoln suppressed a smile when he saw the table. Where there were booze, smokes, and gambling, there was money to be made. He would just have to figure out what the supply lines were and take them over for himself.

Everybody except the guitarist looked up when Lincoln trailed Stephens inside. Stephens pointed to an empty bunk, and Lincoln dropped his duffel onto it.

"That's DuPage's bunk," the guitarist said. He hadn't raised his eyes.

"I guess it's mine now," Lincoln said.

The guitarist shook his head slowly. "No respect for the dead."

"What do you want me to do, sleep on the floor?"

"Or outside. It don't make any difference to me."

"I'm pretty sure DuPage won't care."

"You didn't know him," the soldier with the book said. He set it down on the bunk, pages down, spine up. "He was from Alabama. He didn't much care for colored folks. Having one sleeping in his bunk—he might just come back to haunt you."

"I'm not too worried about ghosts," Lincoln said.

"This here's Lincoln Clay," Stephens said. "Lincoln, like the president."

The guy with the book barked a laugh. "Anybody DuPage hated worse than colored people, it was Lincoln."

"He sounds like a charming dude," Lincoln said. "Too bad he's gone; we'd probably be best friends."

The men all laughed at that, except the guitarist, who picked a mournful-sounding dirge.

• • •

Captain Prato appeared not to have an ounce of fat on him. His skin was tanned and tight and seemed to cling directly to his musculature. The other soldiers Lincoln had met here were casual about their uniforms and their hair—it was hard to be otherwise when both were constantly coated with dust that thickened into mud when the men sweated in the oppressive heat between their too-irregular field showers—but Prato was crisp and military to the core and somehow clean and shaved. Ushered into his presence, after the civilians from D.C. had been picked up by some marines from Khe Sanh, Lincoln whipped off his beret, snapped off a salute, and stood at attention while Prato studied him. After several long seconds, the captain said, "At ease, soldier."

Lincoln spread his legs and clasped his hands behind his back, still clutching the beret.

"Welcome to Lang Vei, Corporal," Prato said.

"Thank you, sir."

"I read your file. I gather you're . . . new . . . to Special Forces."

"That's right, sir."

"Abbreviated course, it said."

"Yessir."

"You know which end of a gun to point at the enemy?"

"Yessir."

"That's something, I guess."

"I won't let you down, sir."

"You'd better not. There aren't enough of us here for anyone to not pull his own weight. The Montagnards are brave, and they hate the communists. The South Vietnamese regulars, I'm not always so sure about. Sometimes I think they'd sell us out for a few bucks and a bottle of wine. Other times I think it'd only take the wine. But it's their war, so we've got to let them stay and fight it."

"I understand, sir," Lincoln said.

"Do you speak Vietnamese?"

"No, sir. I mean, just a few words."

"What can you do?"

Lincoln considered for a moment. "Well, sir, I guess not much. All I know for sure is I'm pretty good at killin' people."

Prato cracked a smile, which looked like it hurt. He took it back in a hurry. "Well, that's a start, I guess," he said. "You're dismissed, soldier."

5

Ellis parked Lincoln's Samson Drifter a few blocks away from Heritage Square. The LaValle Street sidewalks were busy with people headed toward the rally, though whether to participate or just to gawk, Ellis couldn't tell. Maybe, like him, they were going there hoping to score, one way or another.

Oh, the ones with signs were easy enough to figure. "Equal Rights for All," "End Segregation," "I Am a Man." Even a few "Make Love, Not War" placards scattered about. And more humorous ones like "This Is a Sign"—that one was carried by a long-haired white kid, probably from one of the local colleges. Ellis wasn't surprised to see white college students in the crowd streaming toward the park—what better way to rebel against society than to support the burgeoning civil rights movement? He *was* surprised by the number of older white people he saw, many of them pulling along elementary school–aged children. Somehow, he didn't think they were gawkers, or counter-protesters, but they looked more like Southern Union supporters than Freedom Marchers. Still, Ellis wasn't one to judge a book by the color of its cover. Maybe because he was sick and tired of being judged all the time himself.

That was part of the reason he was here today. These rallies were a good place to pick up chicks, and after all the ribbing Lincoln and Sammy had given him up north about not having a girlfriend, he felt the need to prove to himself—and everyone else—that Casanova Clay was not the only smooth operator in the family.

Getting laid was easy for the son of a mob boss. At the rally, though, the girls wouldn't be in the life, so getting in one's pants would require a bit more finesse. He was sure he had the goods, but it didn't hurt to exercise them once in a while.

He took a deep breath, checked his hair in the rearview one last time, and climbed from the car. He blended seamlessly into the sidewalk traffic, sizing up the women around him as he did. Most of them were not what he'd call prime pickings—chubby girls in tight bell-bottoms and multicolored striped shirts that accentuated their curves in all the wrong ways, thin girls in short shorts all but swallowed by long cotton tunics. Too short, too tall. That one was pretty until she opened her mouth—practically all gums—to bray out a laugh like a horse that smoked a pack a day.

Part of him wondered if this was why he didn't have a girlfriend—because he was too damned picky. Another part wondered if it was just one more way of keeping them all at a distance. If none of the women he met were ever good enough, then no one could blame him for not being in a relationship, could they? And if he was never in a relationship, he didn't have to worry about screwing it up. You couldn't fail at something you never tried.

Then again, maybe fail was all you could hope to do in that case.

He shook his head. This much introspection couldn't be good for him. He doubted he'd find a beer at the park, but maybe he'd get lucky and find someone dealing. Nothing hard—Sammy would freak—but a little weed couldn't hurt. Might make finding a girl easier, too. Being high tended to lower his standards.

He saw a group sporting tie-dyed shirts and flowers in their hair and made a beeline for them. Today was his lucky day; peaceniks and pot went hand-in-hand.

But he'd wormed his way only about halfway through the crowd toward them when a gap opened up ahead of him and he saw her.

God, but she was beautiful.

Hair worn in a curly Afro that framed her face like a midnight halo, heavily lashed eyes that a man could drown in, lips so full and lush he felt an instant reaction below his belt. And then his gaze traveled downward.

She had a rack a Playboy Bunny would envy, even buttoned up behind the prim-and-proper dress she wore. But not too prim—the light blue muslin hugged her hips like a lover's caress, then fell, cascading, just below her knees. The sight of her bare calves, shining like polished ebony in the sunlight, made Ellis's mouth go dry.

His feet adjusted course, heading straight for her, peaceniks and their probable weed forgotten.

She caught sight of him when he was a few feet away and watched him approach curiously.

"Do I know you?" she finally asked, after he'd stopped and stood there speechless for several agonizingly long moments.

Ellis shook his head.

No, but you want to, he thought, knowing it was the kind of line he would usually use. Also knowing there was no way he could pull it off now, not with this one; he'd sound like an arrogant ass at best, a second-rate pickup artist at worst.

Instead, he thought the sincere, humble approach would be his likeliest play. "No, I don't think we've met before. But you seem to know what's going on here, and I was hoping you could explain it to me."

He had no idea where *that* had come from, but he'd take it. Especially since it elicited a friendly smile and an outstretched hand.

"Well, you've come to the right place. I'm Vanessa Dautrieve, with CORE, and I helped organize this rally."

"I'm Ellis Robinson. What's CORE?"

"The Congress of Racial Equality. We seek to bring about equality for all people, regardless of race, creed, sex, ethnic background, what have you. Our methods are nonviolent, patterned after Gandhi's. We believe civil disobedience can effect real change. That's why we're here today. To show them we're not going anywhere, no matter what they do to us. We won't give up until we get what's rightfully ours."

All Ellis really knew about Gandhi was that he'd gone on a hunger strike in India. He wasn't even really sure why, or if it had been successful—though he supposed if civil rights groups in America were using the man's tactics, it must have been.

He had his doubts about the nonviolence part, though. Bullies were rampant in his world, and turning the other cheek meant only that you'd get hit harder the second time than you had the first.

Still, he didn't think admitting his ignorance—or his doubts—to Vanessa was going to win him any points, so he just nodded in what he hoped was a sage fashion. Then he remembered something.

"Weren't you guys part of the Dryades Street boycott? 'Don't buy where you can't work' and all that?" Dryades Street was where all the black people bought their clothes—up until 1960, that is. Then some civil rights groups—including CORE, if Ellis was recalling correctly—organized a boycott of the white-owned and -operated merchants who sold to blacks but refused to hire them. Faced with economic disaster, some of the stores had started hiring blacks—but just as many had picked up and moved away, and boarded-up storefronts had become a common sight. Ellis wasn't so sure the boycott hadn't done more harm than good. "And the Freedom Rides?"

Vanessa nodded. "CORE was; I wasn't. I didn't become involved with the group until more recently." She looked away then, as if she were embarrassed or ashamed. Ellis understood the look—he'd worn it often enough himself. It was the same expression he had when trying to explain why he couldn't do something his friends wanted him to do, because either Sammy or Lincoln would frown on it.

"Your parents aren't big supporters of the cause, I take it?"

Vanessa's gaze rose to meet his, startled and grateful. She nodded again, this time with a small, rueful smile.

"You can say that again."

Just then, another woman came up to them, and Vanessa introduced her as Oretha Castile, former president of the local CORE chapter.

"Oretha can tell you far more about the movement than I can; she's been active here with various organizations in New Bordeaux off and on since—"

"—Boundary Street!" Ellis interrupted, sticking out his hand to shake hers.

Oretha smiled.

"Yes, that was me."

Oretha and three other students had been arrested for staging a sit-in at the lunch counter at McCrory's on Boundary Street—the whites-only counter. It had made the papers, and their case wound up going all the way to the Supreme Court, where they actually won. Maybe there was something to this civil disobedience stuff after all.

"Pleasure to meet you," Ellis said, and meant it.

Oretha nodded at him.

"Likewise," she said, before turning to Vanessa. "We need to get started. We have a few speakers lined up. You going to pass out buttons while they talk or try to sign up new members?"

"Janet's doing membership this time; I'm on button patrol. I'll take Ellis with me." She looked over at him and winked. Ellis felt a thrill go through him.

"Sounds good. We'll meet up after, then head to HQ. You can bring him along if you like. The movement can always use more guys."

Oretha nodded at him again before striding off into the crowd.

"She likes you. That's a good sign."

"Glad to hear it," Ellis said, wishing the "she" in question were Vanessa. "So, what exactly does 'button patrol' involve?"

Vanessa laughed. It was a musical sound that made Ellis think of angels.

"Nothing to it, really. You just hand them out to people as they're listening to the speakers, or getting high, or whatever it is they're here in the park doing. The hope is that some of them will come across the buttons later and their curiosity will be piqued and they'll come look us up. Or, at the very least, that they'll wear the buttons and be free advertising for us. Passive recruitment, you know?"

Personally, Ellis thought if they wanted to get more members, all they needed to do was have Vanessa go around flashing that smile of hers and she'd have a whole line of new recruits following at her heels, like some kind of Pied Piper.

But then he'd have to share her attention, and he discovered he didn't much like the idea of that. Not at all.

"Buttons it is," he said, gesturing for her to take the lead. "After you, *ma chère.*"

And as he hurried to follow her through the crowd, he realized to his surprise that he was no longer interested in simply scoring. He'd found something—someone—worth far more than a conquest he could brag to his friends about, and he damned sure didn't want to be left behind.

6

The attack came on Lincoln's fourth night at Lang Vei.

He was on guard duty a little before midnight, walking the inner perimeter fence. Beyond that were three rows of concertina wire, then another chain link fence topped with barbed wire. Lincoln had been told that land mines would have been planted beyond that fence, but the locals objected, saying their water buffaloes walked past the camp to get to the river. Lincoln figured the beasts could be shot and eaten, but he guessed that wasn't the way to win hearts and minds.

A sergeant named James William Gregory III had come out to check on him and stopped to have a smoke. Gregory, the only other black man at the base, was broad through the shoulders and deep through the chest, and his close-cropped head was almost as round as a cannonball. They'd been chatting for a couple of minutes when the mortar rounds started dropping.

Lincoln heard the whirring rattle of incoming rounds—a sound he had taken for a flock of birds the first time he'd heard it, until the explosions started—and hit the dirt. Gregory did the same. Five rounds landed inside the wire, but over where the South Vietnamese strike force was. Several of the Vietnamese soldiers cried out, and one of the thatched huts burst into flames.

Then quiet fell again. Lincoln picked himself up, dusted himself off. The other Special Forces soldiers rushed out of the team house, pulling on boots and helmets. South Vietnamese strikers fired into the brush toward where they thought the mortar rounds had come from, and the Montagnards raced to their battle stations.

But there was no one to shoot at. Gregory yelled at the Vietnamese to stop wasting ammunition. After a few minutes, they obeyed.

"What was that all about?" Captain Prato asked. He'd been asleep, but his uniform was pressed and his jaw looked clean-shaven. He'd come seemingly out of nowhere, appearing as if by magic beside Gregory and Lincoln.

"Mortar attack, Captain," Gregory said. He waved an arm to the northwest. "From the hills over there, I think."

"Casualties?"

"I don't know yet. I think some of the Vietnamese soldiers were hit."

"How many rounds?"

"I counted five."

Prato looked at Lincoln. "That's right," Lincoln said. "Five."

"They're not done," Prato said. "They're not going to toss five rounds into the camp, then go back into a hole and take a nap."

"Nossir," Gregory said.

"If they don't sleep, we don't, either. Return mortar fire. And I want every man on the wire. They're coming, tonight."

"Yessir."

"I'll have Nilsson radio Khe Sanh for reinforcements." Nilsson was a burly commo man with bad teeth and a quick, booming laugh. He wasn't much to look at, but he was some kind of communications genius, according to Gregory. "Check on those 106s and the .50-cals."

"Yes, sir."

Prato spun around and vanished into the dark as quickly as he'd arrived. As soon as he was gone, Gregory turned to Lincoln. "What are you waiting for, Corporal? Get on those guns."

"Yes, sir," Lincoln said. The captain's words had been addressed to Gregory, not to him, but that was a distinction that didn't matter. He swallowed it down and headed for the nearest 106 bunker.

A gunner named McClure was already manning the big recoilless rifle. It primarily served as an antitank weapon, but the North Vietnamese Army and the Vietcong weren't known to have a lot of tanks. Still, it could make chop suey out of foot soldiers in a hurry. "You got enough ammo?" Lincoln asked.

McClure took a quick look, using a flashlight to illuminate the inside of the pit. "Looks like a few dozen rounds," he said. "Should be okay, depending on what they throw at us."

"I'll be back," Lincoln said. He raced to the other 106, manned by a soldier named Adelstein, along with two Vietnamese soldiers to help spot and load. Satisfied that they were set, he made off with the rounds of the Browning M2 .50-caliber machine guns.

By the time Lincoln returned, Gregory had some mortars operating. Someone had fired a couple of flares to light the area beyond the perimeter, and mortar rounds were thumping into the hills north of the camp. Vietnamese and Montagnard companies, bivouacked on the east and west fringes of the camp, stood at the wire, waiting for someone to kill.

Lincoln had barely dropped down into the last M2 pit, occupied by a single soldier named Ligotta, when a trip flare went off at the northwest corner. Light from that and the overhead flares illuminated thirty or so soldiers in dusky gray uniforms, throwing ladders over the concertina wire and scrambling across it.

"There!" Lincoln shouted. "Ten o'clock!"

Ligotta swung the big, air-cooled barrel around on its tripod, both hands on the spade handle grips, and pushed down on the trigger. Lincoln took up a position on his left to help feed the ammo belts. The gun made a metallic, ratcheting noise, compounded by the clinking of shell casings and clips as they ejected. Interspersed tracer rounds helped Ligotta aim, and in the flare's light, Lincoln saw them tear apart oncoming NVA soldiers.

Then another trip flare went off, this one nearer his position. He raised his M14 to fire, but the flare showed him a black pajama–clad VC hurling a grenade toward them.

"Incoming!" he shouted.

Ligotta, focused on bringing the .50-cal around to target the newcomers, didn't hear him or didn't react in time. Lincoln pressed himself to the cool earth in the bottom of the pit, where the hot brass of fallen shell casings burned his face and hands. A wave of heat passed over him at the same moment as a roar that felt like knives stabbing his ears, and he was pelted with earth and shrapnel.

As soon as it was over, Lincoln straightened. "Ligotta, you okay?" he asked.

But Ligotta wasn't in any condition to answer. He had been thrown to the back of the bunker. Half of his face was gone; his chest was smoldering.

The gun looked okay, and half of a belt still dangled from it. Lincoln grabbed it, swinging it into place, and pressed the trigger. The weapon's shake and stutter were satisfying, as was the sight of communist attackers being shredded by the big rounds.

Then he heard the boom of the 106-mm recoilless rifle on the camp's north side. Its shell exploded on impact and was followed quickly by another one. The range was short for that gun, but it was hard to argue with the effect.

Still, the attackers pressed on. They seemed to be limitless, threatening to overwhelm the little camp through the sheer weight of their numbers. Lincoln wondered whether his first Special Forces assignment would be his last. He fed another ammo belt into the .50 and kept firing, sweat slicking his arms and rolling down his sides.

Gradually, the VC onslaught slowed. All over the camp, the Americans and their Vietnamese and Montagnard allies were returning fire, giving as good as they got or better. Lincoln felt the tide of battle shifting. The attackers still tried for the wire but couldn't get there; bodies piled up on the concertina, their weight making it droop in spots.

He risked a look over his shoulder, to see where the defense might need to be shored up. Twenty yards away—a little less, maybe—Captain Prato stood tall, an M14 nestled into his shoulder, firing into the latest wave of invaders.

Another fifteen or twenty feet behind him, one of the Vietnamese soldiers aimed his AR-30 in the same general direction.

In the uneven light from multiple flares, Lincoln couldn't be certain, but it didn't look like the ARVN soldier was looking the same way his gun was pointed. His gaze appeared fixed on the back of Prato's head. Then he swiveled his own head this way and that, as if checking to see if he was observed. He was too far back to notice Lincoln—dark-skinned against the darkness of the machine gun pit—and, satisfied that no one paid him any attention, he inched the barrel of his gun over until it pointed directly at the captain.

If anyone else spotted the threat, Lincoln couldn't see him. In another few seconds, Prato would be a dead man. Lincoln couldn't bring the .50-cal all the way around in time, and a shouted warning would be pointless over the roar of battle. Instead, he snatched up his own M14, took aim quickly, and squeezed the trigger. The Vietnamese soldier's body twitched when the rounds struck home, and the AR fell from his lifeless fingers. Captain Prato stared, wide-eyed, at the Special Forces soldier who had just nearly shot him. Someone else pointed out the crumpled form of the ARVN soldier and presumably explained what had happened.

With no more time to spare on that situation, Lincoln returned to the machine gun, feeding in another belt and firing in short bursts to keep the barrel from overheating, until the NVA and VC attackers fell back and disappeared into the hills.

When they were gone, he drained his canteen in two huge swallows and climbed out of the pit, lacquered with sweat and grime.

Prato strode up to him. "Corporal, you damn near shot my ass!"

"Your nuts, sir," Lincoln countered. "Your ass would've been on the other side, where that ARVN motherfucker was aiming."

"You're positive he was gunning for me?"

"Absolutely, sir. No question about it. He looked like he was shooting toward the enemy, but his finger was outside the trigger guard. When he turned the weapon on you, that's when he went for the trigger."

Prato studied him, as if he could tell through visual examination whether Lincoln was telling the truth. Lincoln didn't figure he could see much but a soldier in desperate need of a shower and maybe a brew.

He seemed to accept Lincoln's version of events, though. His stance relaxed, and a rare smile flickered across his lips. "I guess I owe you my thanks," he said. "A lot of men wouldn't have noticed that, and if they had, they wouldn't have been able to stop it at that distance, under those conditions. I'm a little disturbed that you even tried that shot, but I'm glad you made it. You're one hell of a marksman."

"Just doin' my job, sir."

"You've been here, what, three days?"

"Four."

"Four, what?"

"Four days, sir," Lincoln replied with a quick grin.

"I get the feeling you're not used to following orders."

Lincoln wasn't sure what he was getting at. Anyway, everybody in Sammy's organization learned to follow orders, or he didn't last long. "I'm a soldier, sir. That's what I do."

The captain shook his head. "There's something about you, Lincoln. Something I don't see often. What am I going to do with you?"

"That's why you wear those bars, sir. You get to figure that out."

The tight muscles on Prato's jaw moved, but he didn't say anything. Then he shook his head again, turned, and walked away.

Lincoln watched him go. If there was an answer to the captain's question, he didn't know what it was, either.

7

A week passed before Captain Franklin came to Lang Vei. Twenty minutes after his helicopter landed, he was walking with Lincoln up the hill on the far side of the fence, picking their way through stands of bamboo.

"I hear you saved Prato's bacon," Franklin said.

"I got lucky is all," Lincoln said. "I just happened to look at the right time."

"You've used that 'lucky' line with me before," Franklin reminded him. "It seems to me Captain Prato's the one who got lucky. Lucky having you assigned here, and lucky you made that shot when you did."

"Maybe he should've been more careful about who he allowed in his camp."

Franklin stopped, blinked his brilliant green eyes a couple of times, and turned to face Lincoln. "You know he doesn't get to decide who serves in the Vietnamese army, right? That's up to them. If some people get in who are sympathetic to the communist cause, that's too bad, but it's something we just have to keep our eyes open for."

"Why enlist on the enemy's side? Why not just join the VC?"

"Because they're looking for opportunities to gum up the works, just as you saw. You have to remember the history of this place. Vietnam was colonized by the French in the middle of the nineteenth century. During the Second World War, Japan took it over for a spell. After the war, the French wanted it back, but the Vietnamese had other ideas. It took ten years of fighting to get rid of the French, but the 1954 Geneva Accords that finally did that also split the country in two—Ho Chi Minh's Communists in the north and the former French loyalists in the south.

"The split wasn't meant to be permanent, but when Diem pronounced himself president of all of Vietnam in '55, old Uncle Ho put on his fighting gear again. We backed the French for years, and then we came in to help prop up the succeeding governments in the south. That's where we're still stuck. So when you're surprised that someone living in South Vietnam might take up arms against his own 'side,' remember that every adult you see has lived with nothing but colonization and war for his entire life, and the lives of his parents and grandparents since the days of our own Civil War."

Lincoln nodded along with Franklin's description. When the captain finished, he turned away and started up the hill again, Lincoln following. "I'm not saying it's not in our strategic interest to stop the spread of communism, and that's what we're trying to do here. I'm just saying, don't underestimate the lengths a man will go to if he thinks he's fighting for his country's freedom."

Lincoln had never thought of the struggle that way. He had come to Vietnam because that's where the Army had sent him, and he'd enlisted because he was likely to be drafted anyway. Rich white kids who went to Harvard or Yale were exempt from such things, but not black kids from New Bordeaux—even ones who, thanks to their adoptive father's criminal activities, were better off than most.

At the crest of the hill, Franklin stopped. Lincoln came up beside him and cast his gaze over rolling hillsides, each one cutting a line across those behind. The landscape was green and lush, each line of hills a darker green than the one before it until finally it faded into black. It couldn't have been more different from the flat swampland around New Bordeaux, except where the rice paddies broke the foliage, looking almost as green as Franklin's eyes. The view made Lincoln think about fairy tales he'd been read in the orphanage, as if this were a mystical, magical place where anything could happen.

Franklin pointed toward the west. "See that hilltop there?"

Lincoln looked, saw a dozen hilltops or more, guessed it didn't matter which one in particular the captain meant. "Sure."

"That's in Laos. You see the borderline between here and there?"

Lincoln looked for it. From here, he couldn't see a single man-made structure, no sign that any human hand had ever made a mark on the landscape. "Nope."

"That's because borders are imaginary lines. They're not acts of God or elaborate constructions of the aliens that came before us—"

"Aliens?" Lincoln interrupted.

"You ever read *Chariots of the Gods*, Clay?"

"No, should I?"

"Don't bother. It's probably all bullshit, anyway. Point is, governments set borders. Like the line between here and Laos, or between North and South Vietnam. They're not set in stone; they're lines drawn on maps. They can be erased or moved at the whim of fallible humans."

"Okay," Lincoln said. He was confused by the captain's philosophical musings and by the way the man jumped from subject to subject. If there were threads connecting them, they were as invisible as the border that lay somewhere below.

"Reason I'm telling you all this, Clay, is that your country needs you."

Lincoln wasn't sure anymore what his country had to do with any of it. "That's why I'm here, right?"

"Right," Franklin said. "But where you're needed isn't here." He ticked his head toward the west. "It's there."

"But that's Laos, you said."

"I did. And officially, we're not in Laos."

"Then I don't—"

"I said *officially*. Like borders, sometimes what's official isn't what's real. Laos is a neutral country. But the NVA and the VC are traveling down the Ho Chi Minh Trail, through Laos—it's their main shortcut into South Vietnam. The Chinese are there, too, and the Soviets. Officially, none of them are, but the reality on the ground is that they're all over Laos. We need to step up our presence or lose the whole country to the communist bloc. If Laos falls, Vietnam is doomed. If Vietnam goes, say good-bye to Thailand, Cambodia, the whole of Southeast Asia. After that, Japan, the Philippines, Hawaii . . . no telling where they stop."

"I'm still not sure what you're saying, Captain."

"I'm saying, you've made a mark, Corporal. People much higher up than me have noticed you. You take initiative. You don't wait to be told what to do—you figure out what needs to be done, and you do it. You're good at killing the enemy without getting killed yourself."

"That's what the job is, right?"

"That's part of it. But any army needs most of its soldiers to be followers, not leaders. They want a lot of people who'll take orders and a few who'll give them. You're not one of those people. That said, I don't know that you're officer material, either."

Lincoln didn't know how to respond to that, so he kept quiet. Franklin didn't seem to notice.

"What you are is exactly what we need in Laos. Someone who's self-sufficient. Who can determine what needs doing and figure out how best to accomplish it. Who doesn't need to be told when to eat, when to sleep, when to piss."

"But . . . Laos?"

"I can't order you there, Clay. But Colonel Giunta can. He followed your training closely, at Bragg and at Benning. You surpassed everyone's expectations, in case nobody told you. Most guys who go through the yearlong course don't catch on like you did. He wants you in Laos, and if he wants you there, so do I."

"What would I be doing there?"

Franklin grinned, like a fisherman who knows his hook is set firmly in his prey's cheek. "There's a joint Department of Defense/CIA task force going in to exfiltrate some high-value captives from a VC camp. Like I said, we're not the only ones breaking the rules about Laotian neutrality. I'm not going to tell you who the captives are, so don't ask. I'll just say that if they're transferred to North Vietnam, things are going to get ugly in a hurry. The task force is going to go in fast and hot, free the captives, and get out again."

"DoD and CIA? Really?"

"Even that's classified. Need to know, so don't go repeating it."

"When would I leave?"

Franklin looked at his watch. "You're late already."

"Guess we better get going, then."

"I guess we'd better," Franklin agreed. "The chopper's waiting."

• • •

The task force assembled at the B Team headquarters in Danang. There were eighteen men in all. A couple of them looked familiar, but Lincoln wasn't sure where he might have seen them. Maybe in Green Beret training, maybe in the bush. Most of them seemed to know one another, and he felt like the odd man out. He kept to himself, listened but didn't say much unless he was specifically addressed.

They were mostly the typical warrior types: heavy on muscle and testosterone, with big, booming laughs and fixed opinions about everything in the world, Lincoln thought. They had all been issued black uniforms with no insignia, not even Made in the USA tags on the inside. They'd had to surrender all their identification, including dog tags, and were told they'd get everything back after the mission. The gear and weapons they'd been issued had been made in other countries, including France, the Soviet Union, and Israel. While they were in Laos, an officer explained, they would carry only things that couldn't identify them as Americans.

In the crowd of men dressed in black, the only one who really stood out was one guy, who—like Lincoln—seemed to prefer his own company. He was muscular, but slender compared to the rest. His blond hair was a little longer than most of the other men's and was swept up off his forehead. Instead of a uniform, he wore a white, short-sleeved shirt with a pack of cigarettes in the breast pocket and tan pants. He could have been watching a baseball game or sitting at a soda fountain waiting for a cold drink. He looked as casual as could be, cool in the Quonset hut while everyone else had sweat rolling off in rivers, but there was something in his relaxed posture that Lincoln noticed; he was coiled and ready to strike without warning. He smoked and seemed like he was barely listening, but his eyes missed nothing.

CIA, Lincoln was sure. Maybe he was the only agent on the so-called joint task force, or maybe there were others but they just looked like the

GIs. Either way, this one man stood apart, and Lincoln thought he was a man worth keeping a close eye on.

At the front of the room, a colonel who'd lost weight in the field but hadn't had his uniform taken in stood in front of a map, holding a long wooden pointer. He was rambling on about the op. Lincoln tried to listen, but the guy had a droning voice that threatened to put him to sleep. Regardless, he would go where he was pointed and kill whoever got in his way; he didn't need to know the details for that.

He figured he would fly into Laos with these guys, they'd yank out whoever it was who'd been taken prisoner, and then he would be flown back to Lang Vei. Or at least back to Danang, and he would have to make his own way back from there.

Then the colonel was finished and the door was opened and the men filed out. Their gear had been stacked outside, and each man grabbed his own pack and weapons on the way to a pair of waiting slicks—UH-1 "Huey" helicopters used for troop transport, without weapons pods—that sat on the tarmac, propellers swirling lazily overhead. Lincoln noted the lack of any military markings on them, but he didn't question it. The less he knew, the better.

He was the next-to-last man to board. The blond guy he took for CIA got to the door before him but hung back and ushered Lincoln ahead. "After you," he said. His voice was as cool as his appearance, smooth enough for radio, Lincoln thought. He couldn't detect any accent.

"Thanks," he said, climbing aboard. He took a seat in between two burly Green Berets, and the agent sat up front, beside the pilot.

"Who is that guy?" Lincoln whispered to the man on his right, nodding toward the agent.

"No idea. All's I know is if he's here, we're about to wade into the shit. Cat like that don't show up for just any old mission."

Lincoln didn't answer, but he thought the man was probably right. Wherever they were going, whatever they were about to do, it was important to somebody at a pay grade way above his.

8

Just before sunset, the Hueys touched down on an airstrip that looked to have been slashed out of the landscape with machetes. It didn't look nearly big enough to Lincoln; as they were dropping toward it, he was sure they'd wind up tangled in the trees beyond the cleared space.

But the first one landed with room to spare. Its passengers jumped out, ducking under the propellers, almost lost in the whirlwind of dust. Then it was airborne again, and Lincoln's angled to the ground.

He'd learned the names of a few of the men on the flight—he was sandwiched between Spearman and Blair, with Kuykendall and Steinberg sitting across from them. They had all earned their berets the old-fashioned way, so Lincoln kept mum about his accelerated course. Once the chopper had settled on the strip, the door opened and the men charged out, weapons at the ready in case of attack. Finally, the blond CIA agent strolled out, hands in his hip pockets, still as cool as if he'd been taking a walk in a city park.

As soon as the men were clear, the engine roared and the propellers picked up speed and the aircraft rose off the ground, tilted, and flew off.

They were alone, somewhere in the middle of Laos.

A first lieutenant named Kirwan was nominally in charge of the mission. He huddled over a map with the CIA guy for a few minutes, consulting a compass as he did. Then he rolled up the map and stuffed it into his pack, shrugged into it, and picked up his M14. Lincoln noticed that the CIA agent had an M14 now, too, as well as a holstered Colt Commander.

Lieutenant Kirwan spoke a few words to the men and then started off into the brush. If he was following a trail, Lincoln could hardly see it, but they weren't hacking their way through, so he figured someone had come this way before.

Night fell while they hiked ever northward. Under the canopy of vegetation, moonlight penetrated only sparsely. Lincoln wasn't sure how Kirwan knew where he was going. The nameless CIA guy had fallen to the back of the pack, but whenever Lincoln looked around, he was there, often visible only as the glowing tip of a cigarette in the darkness.

Finally, they came to a halt in a small clearing near the top of a hill, and everyone gathered around Kirwan and the agent. "Okay," Kirwan began. "The camp's in the valley, at the base of this hill. We have to assume that anyone we find there is a hostile. Consider this a search-and-clear mission. We don't know exactly where the prisoners are—hell, for that matter, they could have been taken from the camp any time since we landed. So keep your eyes peeled for them."

"How will we know who's a prisoner and who's not?" Spearman asked.

The agent chuckled. "You'll know."

"We also don't know what else is in the camp. We think it's lightly guarded—we're thinking a patrol, not a company. We'll be searching for anything that might provide actionable intelligence, anything like weapons storage—you know, the usual. We believe the VC use this camp—with the full knowledge and cooperation of the Pathet Lao—as a base to run missions into South Vietnam. So anything that'll tell us what they're up to would be good to find. But our main objective is to get those prisoners out. In one piece, please."

Lincoln didn't remember seeing any mortars or other heavy armament, just automatic rifles and the like. He had a few grenades, but that was all. "We gonna soften them up with some grenades first?" he asked.

The CIA agent spun around and fixed him with a poisonous stare. "Fuck no. You want to let them know we're here? Give them time to spirit away those prisoners? No, we go in shooting and wrap this up before they know what fucking hit them."

Lincoln wasn't sure how that would work. Chances were, there were sentries around the camp who had already seen them. Even if there weren't, when they got close, there would be trip wires, and probably concertina wire they'd have to cross. He was pretty sure nobody simply walked into an enemy camp anymore, not since the invention of barbed wire. He hoped the agent's impatience didn't get them all killed.

But these men were all Green Berets or CIA-trained killers, and each one, like Lincoln, thought himself practically immortal. They moved soundlessly down the hill. Soon Lincoln could hear snatches of Vietnamese coming from the camp—a couple of guards, smoking and shooting the shit. Lieutenant Kirwan and another guy drew suppressed MK 22 Mod 0s from their holsters—semiautomatic handguns that Lincoln had thought only Navy SEALs used—and closed in on the guards. With two perfectly timed shots, both the sentries went down, almost noiselessly except that one of them raked a hand across the chain link fence as he collapsed.

Lincoln tensed, worried that that sound would alert the rest of the camp. It wasn't much, nothing that a stiff breeze might not have caused. But in close combat, relying on luck could get a man killed.

Two of the Green Berets rushed forward with wire cutters, snipping through the fence in seconds. Peeling it back made a little more noise, but the rest hustled through the gaps and were inside the wire seconds before they were seen.

Those seconds weren't enough to accomplish much. Vietcong soldiers—some in traditional black pajama–type attire, others in their underwear—burst from their huts, guns blazing. Lincoln and the others took cover and returned fire. Lincoln was on his belly behind a jeep wheel—scant protection against the rounds slamming into the vehicle's body. One tore through the tire's edge, almost hitting him and spewing rubber fragments into his face. Blinded for the moment, he blinked and rubbed at his eyes until he could see again.

The first wave of defenders was small. Lincoln picked off a couple more, and the bursts of fire from that direction became more and more sporadic. Finally, quiet returned to the camp. He and his comrades had cut through the first wave of defenders quickly, but he knew there were more to come.

"Spread out!" the CIA man ordered. "Find those goddamn prisoners."

Lincoln, Spearman, Blair, and Steinberg took off toward the east side of the camp. The place was mostly comprised of thatched huts, but Lincoln saw a few buildings that had been reinforced with corrugated steel, concrete, or both. A machine gun barrel emerged from a hole in one of those and sprayed a poorly aimed burst toward them. The rounds went high. Lincoln yanked the pin on a grenade and tossed it under the shack; then he and the other guys dropped and clapped their hands over their ears. The concussive wave rattled him and earth rained down, but the fire from inside stopped.

He got back up and kept going on his course, the other men just behind. Reaching the last hut before the fence, Lincoln slowed down, pressed himself to the wall, listened, then took a careful look around the corner. Two VC guerillas were hunkered down behind a metal frame of some kind, and they opened fire with semiautomatic rifles. Lincoln backed away from the corner as their rounds chewed through the hut. He motioned the other guys back.

Using hand signals, Steinberg and Blair indicated that they would go around a hut two back from the end. Lincoln and Spearman stayed where they were, to keep the attention of the soldiers focused on them. Lincoln edged close to the corner again, then slid his M14 past it and opened fire, blindly. Answering bursts told him the men were still in the same area. He waited until he couldn't see Steinberg and Blair anymore, then did the same thing, blind-firing toward where he thought the enemy soldiers were. This time, when their response came, it was cut short by the blast of a grenade. He peeked around the corner to confirm that both men were down.

"All clear!" he called to his comrades. "Move out!"

The four of them cleared that corner, checking each hut, then heard what sounded like a major firefight under way closer to the center of the camp. Lincoln pointed that way, and the others nodded their agreement. Before he had taken three steps, he felt a tug on his right sleeve. Thinking one of the guys was trying to get his attention, he started to turn his head that way.

Blair shouted, "Sniper!" and shoved him to the ground. The next shot whizzed past where Lincoln's head would have been, without Blair's push.

That was when his upper arm started to burn. He raised it as high as he could, angling so he could see the back of his sleeve. It was wet with blood.

"You're hit," Blair said.

Lincoln shook his head. "Just grazed me."

"Let me take a look."

"No time," Lincoln said. He clenched his teeth together, biting back the pain. It was, he feared, worse than he was letting on. But his point about the time was true. He could still move, still fight. And they weren't going to rescue those prisoners if they didn't wrap this up in a hurry. "Anybody see where the shot came from?"

"I didn't even hear it," Blair replied. "I just saw a spray of blood when it hit your arm."

Lincoln eyeballed where he'd been standing, before Blair pushed him. They were essentially at the far eastern edge of the camp, heading south-southwest. "Nobody there," he said.

"It must have come from outside the fence," Spearman said. All four men were hunched down now, blocked from the sniper's position by the same metal framework—part of an ancient automobile, Lincoln realized now—that the NVA soldiers had used for cover.

"Somebody stand up," Lincoln said.

"Are you crazy?" Steinberg asked. "That's what he's waiting for."

"Just for a second. Show him a target, then duck back down."

"Man, you're fuckin' nuts."

"One second," Lincoln said. With a tight grin, he added, "Maybe two."

"I'll do it," Spearman said. "You ready, Lincoln?"

Lincoln shook his right arm a couple of times, trying to keep it from freezing up. It was starting to really hurt now. "Ready."

Spearman nodded once and rose to his full height. He held the position for almost two full seconds, then dropped again. As soon as he started down, Lincoln shot up, M14 pointed toward the dark jungle outside the fence.

The sniper took the bait, firing a single shot at where Spearman had been a moment earlier. Lincoln pinpointed the muzzle burst and opened up on that spot, raking his fire a few feet in either direction.

There was no response, but there was no return fire, either. "I think you got him," Steinberg said.

"Got him or not, he's not shootin' at us anymore," Blair added. "Good enough for me."

The firefight was still under way in the center of the camp. "We're missing the action," Lincoln said. "Come on."

"You should really dress that arm," Blair said.

"Worry about that when there's nobody left to kill," Lincoln countered. He took off first, trusting that his companions would follow.

When they reached the site of the pitched battle, they found Kirwan and four other men pinned down fire from a tripod-mounted machine gun set up behind a wall of sandbags. Other VC troops were positioned in nearby bunkers and behind concrete walls. If Kirwan or the others so much as raised a helmet, a volley would follow.

Lincoln waved his group down before they could be seen. "We got to knock out that nest," he said. "Anyone comes up behind Kirwan and them, they're dead meat."

Steinberg pointed to a line of huts. "Same as with those other guys," he said. "If we stay behind those we can get in back of the gun, toss a grenade on it."

"They've got covering fire," Blair pointed out.

"Chance we have to take," Lincoln said. "Stay low and move fast."

They ran at a crouch, Lincoln in the lead, his gaze shifting constantly from the path ahead over to where enemy fire would come from if they were seen. Somehow, they reached a position about thirty feet to the rear of the machine gun pit without drawing any attention. A four-foot-high concrete wall offered some cover. In the east, the sky was beginning to lighten, allowing for greater visibility. Lincoln didn't mind, except it meant the bad guys would be able to see better, too.

Steinberg palmed a hand grenade. "I played center field in high school. Always had a pretty good arm."

"Go for it," Lincoln said.

Steinberg tugged the pin and hurled the grenade. It arced through the air and exploded just as it landed beside the gun.

"Good shot!" Blair said.

But the effort had turned them into targets. Instantly, fire from the VC soldiers turned their way. Steinberg, still standing tall after his dead-on throw, took three rounds to his chest and shoulder. The others ducked in time, rising above the wall only to return fire. Lincoln moved to the corner and peered around to take aim, only to see a VC pointing an RPG launcher directly at the wall.

"Grenade!" he cried, even as he heard it fire. He twisted away from the wall and covered his head with his arms, hoping the others were doing the same. At seemingly the same moment, the grenade hit with a *boom*, sending jagged shards of concrete slicing into him. Ears ringing, almost deafened, he spun around and opened fire, dropping the guy with the grenade launcher before he could follow up with a second.

Their cover was gone, and the enemy forces were taking advantage of it, sending round after round their way. Steinberg was finished—his wounds had slowed his reaction to the grenade, and the blast had ripped open his throat and chest. Blair and Spearman were dazed and bloody but alive. None of them would be for long, though, if Lincoln couldn't get them to safety.

He felt a stinging heat on the back of his thigh and looked down to see his fatigue pants torn and bloody. *Flesh wound*, he thought. But he had to get the others out in a hurry, and himself as well—the longer they stayed, the more likely they would end up like Steinberg.

He reached down with both hands and lifted Spearman, the smaller of the two, onto his left shoulder. Hoisting Blair one-handed was considerably more awkward, but he got a grip on the man. Carrying both, he half-jogged, half-limped from his spot by the collapsed wall. The impact of a round slamming into Spearman almost knocked him off balance, but it had hit only an edge of the man's boot and hadn't done any damage.

When he had a small concrete-and-steel structure between himself and the worst of the firefight, he lowered the other men as gently as he could. "You guys will be okay here," he said. "Stay put."

Blair tried to say something, but his gaze was unfocused, his words slurred. Spearman was in worse shape. They both needed a medic, but that would have to wait.

9

Lincoln left them where they were and rushed back to the action, taking a slightly different path so the enemy soldiers wouldn't see him coming. Most of the other task force soldiers had converged on that area—which made sense, he figured; the enemy's concentrated effort there probably meant there was something they didn't want found. The prisoners, most likely.

Lincoln slammed a fresh magazine into his M14 and targeted the man with the RPG launcher. He propped himself against a wall—the two wounds had weakened him more than he wanted to admit, even to himself—and stitched a line of bullets up the soldier's chest and head. Then he shifted his aim to the right, where another VC was trying to catch the launcher before it fell. As each additional soldier lunged for it, Lincoln picked them off, one by one.

Finally, the last black-pajamaed fighter fell. Lincoln took a quick tally and counted six task force members KIA, including the unfortunate Steinberg. Spearman was still woozy, but Blair was on his feet again, injured but conscious.

The blond CIA agent stepped from the darkness and started toward a concrete bunker behind the fallen Vietnamese. Lincoln was surprised to note that he was carrying an AR-30 but figured it was a souvenir from a soldier he had killed. "Lot of dead commies," he said. "Does my heart good. But those fucking VC seemed to be trying to keep us away from that," he said. "Let's see what's inside."

He walked around the bodies, kicking one or two as if checking to ensure that they weren't faking, until he reached the steel door of the bunker. It opened with a screech that seemed loud enough to wake the dead, but none of those on the ground got up to complain. Inside, he shone a right-angle flashlight for a few moments, then emerged again, a disgusted look on his face.

"What is it?" Kirwan asked.

"It's not our prisoners. Looks like they were using this shithole of a camp as an opium distribution point."

"Well, at least we shut that down," Kirwan said. "That's something."

"So's a case of the clap," the agent said. "But if it's not what you went to Saigon for, it doesn't do you any good. They're here somewhere, goddamn it. Search every bunker and hooch in this dump."

The men paired off, Lincoln with the still-shaky Blair, and moved from structure to structure. Finally, someone gave a shout, and the rest of them gathered around what looked like a thatched hut—only the thatching concealed a low-slung concrete structure with a padlocked steel door. Someone on the inside was banging on the door, but from the outside it just sounded like faint, distant thumping.

"Get 'em the fuck out of there," the agent ordered.

One of the soldiers shot the padlock until it snapped, but it took two of them to muscle open the door. As soon as it was wide enough, a white man crawled out, followed by another. They were both wearing jungle fatigues, but Lincoln could tell right away they weren't soldiers. The first one tried to gain his feet but couldn't—he had been in that tiny space for too long, and his legs wouldn't support him. When a couple of the guys helped him to his feet—and held him there, lest he fall down again—Lincoln realized that he recognized the man's face.

He couldn't come up with the name, but he didn't have to wonder about it for long. Someone else called out, "Hey, that's Stan Rivers!"

"Stan Rivers, the TV guy?" someone said.

"No shit?" another man added.

When Rivers started to answer, his words came out as a blubbering cry. Lincoln knew it was him, though. Everybody knew Stan Rivers—he was on one of the big nightly news broadcasts from New York, though Lincoln, who'd never watched a lot of TV, couldn't remember which network.

Everyone knew the man's name and face, though, and just about everybody who Lincoln knew hated him, too. He liked to call himself "America's conscience," and he had a reputation as an insufferable egotist who thought he knew what was best for everybody.

Lincoln remembered the first time he had become aware of the man. An apartment fire in the French Ward had spread to encompass most of a city block, costing dozens of lives. All the network news programs had sent their anchors to the city. While he was there, Rivers had managed to locate a mother who had lost six children and her husband in the blaze. She had clearly not wanted to talk, but he'd pressed her, unwilling to accept her reticence. His cameraman had zoomed in on her face, distraught, tears running down her cheeks and snot bubbling from her nose. Finally, Rivers had put words in her mouth, and she'd acquiesced. "She's just going along with him to shut him up," Sammy had said before turning off the TV in disgust. "That bastard will do anything for a story, no matter who gets hurt."

That phrase—*no matter who gets hurt*—seemed especially prescient now, with Steinberg and several other Americans dead in an effort to rescue Rivers from someplace he never should have been.

Finally, his face slick with tears, Rivers found his voice. "Thank you, men," he managed. "I've been in that little coffin for days. I thought for sure I'd die there." He seemed to recall that he wasn't alone and added, "This is Jimmy Turnbull, my cinematographer. You know who I am."

"What the fuck are you doing in Laos, Rivers?" the agent said. "You're supposed to be embedded with a unit in Hue."

"I heard there were American troops in Laos—which, as you know, is strictly neutral territory. So we broke away from Hue and hitched a ride into Laos. As delighted as we are to see you guys, your being here pretty much confirms the story, doesn't it?"

"Of course we're in Laos, dipshit. We came here to fucking rescue you," the agent pointed out.

"Just the same—we got footage of other Americans in Laos, before we were captured. This is going to be headline news back home. And now it'll have a human interest angle, too. I suppose our disappearance has been front-page news?"

"Not a soul in the world knows you're missing," the agent informed him. "When you vanished, we hushed it up. You're just damn lucky we got some intel pointing us here."

Rivers's face went through a series of expressions—confusion, disappointment, anger, rage—in a matter of seconds. It was obvious he'd wanted to be talked about in his absence, no doubt to make the story of his triumphant return that much bigger.

"But . . . but we—"

"I guess you're the only one who thinks you're a big deal," the agent said. "Not even your wife gave a shit when you vanished."

"I'm not married. But—"

The agent cut Rivers off again. "Even better. There are already too many grieving widows in the world. Don't worry—you'll make your precious headlines soon."

He didn't wait for Rivers to respond. Instead, he raised the AR-30 and unloaded most of magazine into the reporter, continuing even after he fell to the earth and lay still. Then he turned to the cameraman, Turnbull.

"What about you, sweet cheeks?" he asked, his tone almost polite but sinister at the same time. "You gonna be a pain in my ass?"

Sweat streamed down the young man's face, and in the glow from multiple flashlights, Lincoln saw a dark stain spread from Turnbull's crotch. "I . . . I didn't see a thing, s-sir," he said.

"What about that footage Rivers says you got?"

"Th-the VC smashed my camera and threw the film in a fire. Seriously, man, I got nothing. I won't say shit."

The agent seemed to consider this for a moment, then bore his gaze into Turnbull's eyes. "You just bought yourself a pass, kid. But if you change your mind and decide to start talking, just remember—no matter where you go I will fucking find you. And when I do, I'll make what happened to Rivers look like a goddamn mercy kill compared to what I do to you."

Tears streaked down Turnbull's face, and he nodded.

"Tell me you understand."

"I understand," Turnbull said.

"Good." The agent let his gaze slide across the surprised soldiers around him. "Anybody else got a problem?"

The whole world seemed to have slipped into a stunned silence. When nobody answered, the agent said, "Rivers got some of ours killed, all so he could air a story that would damage and humiliate the United States of America," he said. "If we have troops in Laos—and I'm not saying we do—it's because we don't want the country to fall to the fucking communists. It's a matter of national security, and that bastard would have sold us out for the sake of a goddamn headline. He'd probably have gotten a raise out of it, too."

"But . . . ," Kirwan said, ". . . he's still an American—a celebrity—and you killed him."

"No, I didn't," the agent replied. He held up the weapon, then dropped it. "He was shot with an AR-30. Clearly killed by the NVA. We'll take his worthless corpse back to Hue and 'discover' it in the bush someplace, not far from where he ran away from the American unit he was supposed to be protected by. Everyone knows the jungle's a dangerous place."

Lincoln listened with something between outrage and respect tugging at his spirits. He had no reason to like Rivers—Sammy's hatred of the man had become his own—but the TV anchor was still an American. On the other hand, as the CIA man had said, Rivers was in Laos hoping to cause trouble for the American military. Lincoln was no politician, but he had to believe that those in Washington and at the Pentagon had reasons for what they were doing. If they felt troops were needed to keep Laos free, who was he to argue? And who was Stan Rivers to try to single-handedly overturn that decision? Nobody had elected him commander in chief.

Mostly, Lincoln was impressed by the cool displayed by the agent. He had gunned down an important American TV star without breaking a sweat, a little half-smile playing about his lips as he did it. He had a rational-sounding explanation for it and a plan to cover up the crime. More than that, he had a set of accomplices—each of whom had lost brothers-in-arms—who would back up his story. The men who'd died had done so because of Rivers; nobody was likely to shed a tear for him or to publicly dispute the story that would be told about his death.

He had to hand it to the CIA man—back in New Bordeaux, he could easily become a mob boss. And to Lincoln Clay, that was high praise indeed.

10

While the men waited for the Hueys to extract them from Laos, the unit's medic patched the wounded while the others searched the rest of the valley and found more opium drop sites. Each one was blown up, along with its contents. Streamers of smoke rising into the sky must have made easy landmarks for the chopper pilots.

Lincoln's wounds had been minimal, so he had gone with the search party. Heading back to the camp from the last drop, Lincoln felt a nudge on his shoulder. He turned to see the CIA agent there, one eyebrow raised in a quizzical expression. "Take a walk with me?" the man said.

"Sure." Lincoln stepped off the path and let Spearman and Blair go on without him. When the rest of the line had passed—some tossing questioning glances at them—Lincoln and the agent brought up the rear, far enough back that their conversation wouldn't be overheard.

"Did that get your panties in a twist?" the agent asked. "What I did back there?"

"Hell yeah," Lincoln said. "When you explained, it kinda made sense. But at the moment, it sure took me by surprise."

"I figured it would," the man said. "That was the point. One of them, anyway. I had to do what I did, but if I'd told you guys beforehand what I planned, someone might have objected."

Lincoln couldn't think of anything to say to that, so he simply nodded.

"Sometimes, sacrifices have to be made for the greater good," the agent continued. "This was one of those cases. Rivers should have fucking well stayed with the unit he was assigned to and covered the war he came to Vietnam to report on. As soon as he crossed into Laos, he signed his own death warrant."

"No real loss, the way I see it," Lincoln said.

The agent chuckled. "Exactly. The guy was a scumbag, through and through. He would have handed Laos to the communists. I'm not naïve enough to think our country never makes mistakes—hell, we made a *huge* one with your people, and we're *still* trying to fix it. But I'll be damned if I'll let some rich, pampered TV star playing soldier put real fighting men at risk and endanger American interests in the bargain."

"You'll get no argument from me."

The agent stopped, so Lincoln did, too. "My name's John Donovan," the man said. "You've probably already figured out who I work for."

"That's pretty clear," Lincoln admitted.

Donovan took a cigarette pack from his breast pocket, tapped out a smoke, and offered one to Lincoln. Lincoln took it, and by the time he had it in his mouth, Donovan had flicked open a lighter. He lit Lincoln's cigarette, then his own, inhaled, and blew out a long ribbon of smoke.

"I have to say, I'm impressed with the way you handled yourself on this op, Corporal Clay. You know, I asked to have you included on the task force. And goddamn, you're everything they said, and then some."

Lincoln was astonished that he had come to this man's attention, but he tried not to show it. "That so?"

"Don't let it go to your head," Donovan said. He started walking again. Lincoln took another drag from his smoke, then hurried to catch up.

"I understand Tom Franklin talked to you about Laos," Donovan continued. "About the kind of men we need here."

Lincoln tried to remember exactly what Franklin had said. Men who were self-sufficient, he recalled, who didn't need to be told what to do but could figure out what needed to be done and do it. He wasn't sure how much of that applied to him, but he was glad Franklin thought it did.

"Yeah."

"He told me you're that kind of man. A born warrior. He said you could be counted on. And he said you could follow orders, but you're better when left to make your own decisions."

"Guess that's true," Lincoln said.

"Listen, Lincoln. You know we're not supposed to have troops in Laos. But we're not just letting the country fall to the Pathet Lao and their friends from China and the Soviet Union. That would be a goddamn shit-storm for Vietnam, Southeast Asia, and the rest of the free world. We need to protect Laos's freedom and stop the NVA from using it as a funnel into South Vietnam."

"Makes sense," Lincoln said. Left unspoken was the corollary: as much as politics ever made sense.

"We can't do it with overwhelming American force," Donovan said. "Not with the fucking Geneva Accords in place. If it was up to me, I'd just carpet-bomb the north into oblivion, but they don't let me set war policy. In Vietnam, we're going to see the burden of the war shifting much more to American shoulders than to South Vietnamese ones. Those ARVN pussies can't be counted on to defend their own country. But it would be a bigger stretch to do that in Laos, and I don't see it. Instead, we're going to have to rely on the locals. You've heard of the Montagnards, right? The people who do the real fighting back in 'Nam?"

Lincoln nodded. They were a tribe from a mountainous region of Vietnam who fought gallantly alongside the Americans—and sometimes put their ARVN counterparts to shame—against the NVA and Vietcong. Stories of their prowess in combat were already legendary. "Sure."

"Well, we don't have Montagnards in Laos, but we have something just as good. Maybe even better. They're called the Hmong. They mostly live in the mountains that rim the Plain of Jars. They're not ethnic Laos or Vietnamese but an entirely different race. And for historical reasons of their own, they hate those commie pricks almost as much as I do."

"So they're on our side?"

"The ones who know about us are. The rest will be, as soon as we can make contact. And with some help from their new American friends—mostly in the way of training and supplies—they can become a major impediment to the Pathet Lao."

They had reached the camp. Flies were swarming over the VC bodies, buzzing around in black clouds. Lincoln hoped the copters arrived soon, to take away the American dead and wounded and to get him away from these corpses.

"I still don't see what all this has to do with me," Lincoln said.

"We're obviously keeping a low profile here in Laos. Rivers said he had footage of American troops here, but I think he was full of shit. He knew the film had been destroyed, so nobody could disprove him. He probably didn't even know where the border was. Personally, I think we should have a major force here, but the desk jockeys in the Pentagon have their own ideas. Instead of a major presence, we're positioning a single man—a good man— in each of several Hmong villages. Those men will recruit the natives, win their trust, train them, and deploy them on missions against the Pathet Lao and any VC or NVA troops dumb enough to cross into Laos.

"We're looking at Special Forces soldiers particularly, because they've demonstrated the skills our guys will need. They'll remain with their current service, but they'll be on loan to the Agency. As such, they'll be paid a bonus on top of their military salary. And of course, they'll work largely without supervision, making decisions for themselves, out in the field."

Lincoln thought he understood where this was heading, but he wanted the man to say it. He kept quiet. Finally, Donovan added, "There's going to be a lot of commie ass to kick. And I want you to be the one doing the kicking. So how about it?"

"Do I have to tell you right now?"

Donovan grinned. "No. No, of course not. Take all the time you need, buddy." He sucked in one last drag of his cigarette and flipped the butt onto a bullet-riddled North Vietnamese corpse. "Just as long as you give me your answer by tomorrow morning."

11

Lincoln was barely conscious of the ride.

For one thing, he was dead tired—he'd been going nonstop since Captain Franklin had come to see him at Lang Vei. Most of the other guys, those who still drew breath, were sleeping as soundly as if they were dead. But for as exhausted as he was, Lincoln couldn't sleep. He kept turning Donovan's offer over and over in his mind, as if it were a physical thing he could pick up and examine.

He had so many questions. Could he tell anyone he was going to Laos, to live and work with the Hmong? It was surely a highly classified mission. He didn't like the idea of being out there, alone, with Sammy and Ellis not knowing where he was and what he was doing. Sammy was counting on him to come home as soon as he could, not to go native someplace he wasn't even legally supposed to be. What if something happened to him there? Would the government find his body and send him home, or would it pretend it had no idea what had happened to him? Or like Stan Rivers, would they make up a lie to explain his death? If he were captured, would he—again, like Rivers—be murdered by his own government, to avoid embarrassment?

He didn't speak Laotian, or Hmong, or whatever it was those people spoke. He barely knew any Vietnamese. Did the Hmong tribesmen know English? How could they? He just couldn't picture himself on his own in the Laotian wilderness, responsible for turning what he assumed was a bunch of primitive people—hardly advanced from the Stone Age, from the sound of it—into a fighting force capable of taking on well-trained North Vietnamese soldiers equipped with the best matériel that China and the Soviets could provide.

It was insane. He couldn't possibly do that job.

He had questions but no one to ask. Donovan was once again sitting in front, next to the pilot. Lincoln was strapped into a seat in the rear of the craft, sitting on his flak jacket to protect himself against small-arms fire from below. Donovan had made it clear that he wanted an answer, not more conversation, when they landed at Danang. And by taking him aside for the conversation, he'd demonstrated that the topic was not to be broached with the other guys.

No, Lincoln was alone on this one. He had to make the call, and he had to do it with incomplete information.

Well, it wouldn't be the first time. "Alone" was commonplace for a man who'd been abandoned by his mother as a toddler, who had never known his real father. That role had been filled for him by Father James, and then Sammy, but as hard as they tried—and they were both good men, he thought, flawed but well meaning—they both had other obligations as well. Lincoln was just one of dozens of kids at the orphanage, and by necessity, Father James and the sisters had to pay most attention to the troublemakers.

Lincoln Clay had learned early on that if he didn't want to be harassed by the orphanage staff, all he had to do was behave inside its walls and save his hell-raising for outside. If a kid gave him trouble, he didn't strike back immediately. He swallowed his anger, and then when he caught the kid away from the grounds and the staff, he made a point of reminding his opponent what transgression he'd committed—right before beating the crap out of him.

He had lost a few battles, too, early on. But it wasn't long before he grew bigger than most of the other orphans, and stronger. And the beatdowns he took taught him how to fight, showed him what he was doing wrong. More crucially, they taught him that physical pain was fleeting compared to emotional pain. Humiliation lasted a long time, but a bruise faded in a few days.

Father James had been good to him. He and the sisters had fed Lincoln, put a roof over his head, gave him clothes, and taught him. But Lincoln had always held back some of himself. How he processed those things, how he dealt with them internally, was all on him. And he had been fine with it.

After the adoption, it was years before he learned to trust his new family. Even now, although he would take difficult decisions to Sammy and Ellis for input, he ultimately made up his own mind.

He would do the same here. Instead of dwelling any further on the unknowable, he looked outside, watching Vietnam's improbably green landscape whipping past. When Donovan asked the question, he would have an answer.

• • •

The helicopters touched down at the busy air base late in the afternoon. Lincoln still hadn't slept, and the scene on the tarmac seemed to take on a surreal quality. Soldiers in olive drab or jungle fatigues rushed this way and that, everyone in a hurry but very few seeming to actually do anything. Enormous howitzers stood at one end of the airfield, like giant insects with their necks craned to catch the last rays of the sun, as wasp-like choppers circled. Airplanes landed and others took off. It was a war zone without a war. People came and went, but what was the point of all the hurly-burly motion?

Then he saw Donovan strolling toward him, the one man who didn't seem rushed or anxious. He had a lit cigarette in his mouth and had some-how come up with a light linen blazer that he carried over his shoulder, like a tourist looking for beignets in the French Ward.

He stopped in front of Lincoln and nodded over his shoulder. "There's a truck back there, on its way to Lang Vei," he said. "You can get on it, if you want. Or not. Your choice."

"If I skip the truck, then what?"

"Then you'll grab a bunk here, and in a few days you'll start your new life."

Lincoln hesitated. "New life" made it feel like a big change. He had already known it would be. When he'd been issued his Green Beret, that had seemed like a new life in itself—instead of being just one more grunt, he had become a special breed of elite soldier. Now, Donovan was offering him a different path, an elevation in status that seemed meteoric compared to his expectations when he had enlisted. The only person in Lincoln's life who wouldn't be surprised would be Sammy, who had always insisted that Lincoln was destined for greatness, one way or another.

He didn't know if he would even be able to tell his family. Again, so much he didn't know.

And Donovan stood there, tapping ash off his butt, waiting for an answer.

"You said I had until tomorrow morning."

"You believe everything you hear?"

"I'll grab a bunk," Lincoln said.

"That's what I wanted to hear. Come on, I'll make sure you get the best bunk this shithole has to offer."

• • •

Lincoln could have gone into Danang, just a short ride up a paved road from the air base. But some of the guys he met told him that it was a sleepy little *ville*, nothing compared to Saigon. He was surprised. It was a beautiful setting, on the Danang Bay with the South China Sea just beyond it, and the Marble Mountains rising behind. In the United States, it would have been a resort area packed with fancy hotels.

Instead, he sat on the beach, read a paperback book someone else had abandoned, and swam in the warm waters of the bay. He ran on the white sand and worked out in the makeshift gym set up at the base. He ate at the mess with the rest of the grunts. Even though he didn't know them, he couldn't help feeling some of the camaraderie of men in uniform, men with a common purpose. Looking around, he couldn't know which ones would be dead in a month or a year, but some would. They were all aware of it, too. That knowledge of impending danger—like the uniforms, like the training—drew them together.

The feeling was familiar to him. The Black Mob back in New Bordeaux was much the same. The city had numerous crime organizations—Sal Marcano's family first among equals—and tensions often ran high. Law enforcement was another constant thorn. Those two forces drove the men of any given gang together. And men they were; there were always women, but for the most part they were on the periphery, wives and girlfriends who took care of the home front. Having been raised in that environment, the sense of soldiers at war was a kind of homecoming.

But that camaraderie was short-term, for him. He had agreed to leave this all behind—the Army, Vietnam, the forced bonding of men under fire—and instead would be alone in a different country, with foreigners of a kind he had never met. He couldn't quite picture what it would entail, what conditions would be like, how he would live and work with those strangers. And once again, there was no one to ask. Before he'd left, Donovan had made clear that Lincoln was to talk to no one about his new assignment. If men wondered why he was just hanging around the air base, he was to make something up or put them off.

As it was, nobody asked. There were whole companies hanging around Danang, not sure of where they were headed or what it would be like when they got there. One man in that boat didn't raise any eyebrows.

Still, he was getting impatient. Sitting still wasn't his style. When Donovan showed up again, four days later, Lincoln was more than ready.

12

"We shall organize, we shall organize
We shall organize today
Deep in my heart I do believe
We shall overcome someday."

Ellis belted out the words to the old spiritual alongside Vanessa, his voice a surprisingly rich counterpoint to her dulcet tones. They were marching on a picket line outside city hall, where many promises regarding segregation had been made but precious few kept. Ellis remembered reading about Native American treaties in school; he thought he had a pretty good idea what the Indians must have felt like every time a new oath was sworn in Washington. Fool me once, shame on you. Fool me twice, shame on me. Fool me three times—I'm gettin' my gun.

Of course, Vanessa didn't hold with that viewpoint, and he could see where folks like Dr. King were having a more profound effect on public opinion than the Malcolm Xs of the world had ever had, so he was willing to do it her way. For now.

They'd been at it for only about a half hour and were just starting the fifth and final verse when red-and-blues lit up the street and distorted voices over megaphones started ordering them to disperse.

Vanessa looked over at him.

"You don't have to stay for this part," she said. Other people were already ditching their signs and running. Vanessa looked scared but determined. Ellis knew for a fact she'd never been arrested before. He also knew her parents would freak when they got the call to come bail her out, though they'd post the money without question. But her being willing to face their

73

wrath—which terrified her more than the thought of being in police custody—because she believed so strongly in what she was doing just made him admire her that much more. And she was already about as far up on a pedestal as any woman besides Perla could get.

"You stay, I stay," he said, and the look of gratitude she gave him almost made him feel guilty. He wasn't afraid of being booked. It wasn't like the inside of a jail cell was new territory for someone who'd grown up the way he had. Sure, Sammy would be pissed about having to bail him out, especially for something as dumb as protesting, but the old man would do it just the same. And once he knew there was a girl involved, he'd probably congratulate Ellis for having the gumption to go all out to impress her. Any punishment would be forgotten. Hell, he'd probably buy Ellis a drink.

But Vanessa didn't know any of that. She had no idea about Ellis's family—about Sammy, or Perla, or Lincoln, or the family business. Ellis was afraid if she did know about it, she wouldn't want to see him anymore. And while their "seeing" each other thus far had consisted only of a handful of movement-related events, he'd been angling for more, and he thought she was receptive to the idea. He was pretty sure if they got arrested together, that would seal the deal.

Maybe then, after she got to know him better, he could introduce her to Sammy.

Or maybe he'd just wait until Lincoln got back.

Or maybe he'd just keep her away from all of them for as long as he could and hope for the best. He wasn't used to feeling embarrassed by who he was and what he did, but being around Vanessa made him want to be someone different, someone more . . . worthy of her, he guessed.

Just thinking that ought to make him angry. He was Sammy Robinson's *son*, for God's sake! He was worthy of *any* woman.

But . . . this was Vanessa Dautrieve. Upper middle-class family, college student at SUNB, father a banker, mother a socialite. She didn't just run in different circles, she ran in a different world, breathed a more rarified air.

She was too good for a mob boss's son.

Hell, she was probably too good for *anyone's* son. But damned if he wasn't going to try for her anyway, do whatever it took to land her. He ignored the little voice that asked what would happen if what it took was making a choice between her or Sammy and Lincoln.

It hadn't come to that. Not yet, anyway. Not today.

Today all it was going to take was getting roughed up, cuffed, and booked. *Fastoche.*

"You're a real hero, you know that?" Vanessa said, her dark eyes wide with admiration. "A knight in shining armor." And then she leaned over and kissed him with those lush, full lips, and Ellis prayed she wouldn't ask him to do anything in the next few seconds, because there would be nothing on the face of the Earth he could deny her.

And then there was a uniform pulling them roughly apart, and all Ellis could see was the stark fear on Vanessa's face as she looked to him for guidance, all her earlier confidence forgotten as her arms were twisted behind her back and metal bracelets were snapped onto her wrists by a burly white officer whose face was half mustache.

"Ellis!"

"Ellis?" the cop who had a hold of his collar repeated, spinning him around to get a better look at his face. "Ellis Robinson? Shit." Ellis recognized him as one of the good ole boys in the department who wasn't too good to take black money to look the other way.

The cop looked over at his partner.

"Let her go."

"The hell I will!"

The first cop shrugged, slipping his own cuffs back into his belt.

"Your funeral, man. I ain't arresting Sammy Robinson's boy, *or* his girlfriend. I need trouble with the Black Mob like I need a hole in the head. You got a death wish, you go right on ahead. I ain't stoppin' ya."

"Fuck."

"Exactly."

The mustachioed cop uncuffed Vanessa and shoved her none too gently toward Ellis, who caught her in his arms and pulled her close.

"You two get out of here before I change my mind or someone who doesn't know—or care—who your daddy is gets hold of you." When neither of them moved, he frowned. *"Now!"*

They didn't need any further prompting. They ran.

• • •

They'd taken Lincoln's Drifter to the demonstration, so when they got back to it, they just got in and drove until it got dark. Ellis wasn't even sure where they were headed; he just followed traffic, stopping at red lights, going when they turned green, waiting for Vanessa to say something. Anything.

Finally, she did.

"Turn right up here."

Ellis did as he was told. She gave him a few more directions and soon he was in a part of New Bordeaux he wasn't particularly familiar with. Southdowns—Vanessa's part.

They came to a small wooded area nestled in between big manor houses with sprawling yards and long driveways. There was a playground with swings, a slide, and a seesaw, where flower-lined walkways abounded. A sign warned that the starlit park was closed after 9:00 p.m., which would explain why theirs was the only vehicle in the lot.

Vanessa got out of the car and Ellis had no choice but to follow; he certainly wasn't leaving her here alone, at night, even if one of these big houses turned out to be hers, which would probably be the case. He'd see her to her front door like the gentleman he desperately wanted her to believe he was. Whether she wanted him to or not.

She led him over to the swings and sat down in one. He took a seat in another.

"So, you're part of the . . . mob?"

She didn't look at him as she said it, instead staring off into the darkness of the humid New Bordeaux night. He didn't want to be having this conversation. Ever, if he could have helped it, but especially not now. It was too soon. She barely knew him.

"My family is, yeah," he hedged. He tried to laugh it off. "Some people run diners and dry cleaners; we run nightclubs and numbers."

She didn't even crack a smile.

"And the cops are *afraid* of you?"

Ellis chewed on his lip. She didn't sound disgusted or condemning, just curious. Maybe being a mobster wasn't the black mark against him he'd imagined it would be. He decided to answer her questions as honestly as he could, without giving away any family secrets.

"Some are, I suppose—they know what we do to people who get in our way. Some we pay off to look the other direction. Some get a harsher treatment."

She nodded at that, still not looking at him.

"And you—what do you do to people who get in your way?"

He had to tread carefully here, he knew. But he couldn't just lie to her.

"People don't tend to get in my way, because of who I am."

"And who is that, exactly? Just who *is* Ellis Robinson, besides a smart, handsome young man interested in the civil rights movement?"

His heart may have skipped a beat or two when he heard the word "handsome," but he tried to focus on her question.

"You heard the cop. I'm Sammy Robinson's son, and Sammy's the head of the Black Mob in New Bordeaux. People mess with me, they know they're messing with Sammy, and most of them don't want to do that. So mostly I don't get messed with."

And that was true as far as it went. It didn't include people like Lincoln and Sammy himself, of course.

"So why is the son of a mob boss—a man who lives and breathes violence—hanging around with a woman who preaches nonviolence as a way of life? We're like day and night."

Ellis surprised himself by having an answer.

"Because Sammy's way of life can only get me so far. It'll never get me the respect of the people in these big houses." He stopped, took a deep breath, rushed on. "It'll never get me someone like you."

She looked up at that, and her eyes were pools of diamond in the starlight.

"Don't be too sure about that," she said, and leaned over to kiss him for the second time that day. Only this time there was no one to pull them apart, and the kiss soon turned into something more. Vanessa led him in among the trees, and there was some fumbling with jeans and skirt and underwear. Then she was drawing him down to the leaf-carpeted ground, into her embrace, into *her*.

I would do anything for her, Ellis thought, right before all thought was blown away on a wave of pleasure and passion.

"Vanessa," he whispered into her hair, and then neither one of them was able—or wanted—to say anything coherent again for a very long time.

13

"What I miss most is pie," Corbett said. "In Saigon and Vientiane they have these tiny little French tarts, but they're not really pie. I mean, like a full-size apple pie, or blueberry, or cherry, with a good crust and all that delicious filling. These people, the Vietnamese and the Laotians, all they learned from the French is those stupid little tarts. Maybe if we're over here for a hundred years or so, they'll learn about pie."

Brad Corbett was a pilot for Air America, which was a not-very-secret CIA front company, and he was flying Lincoln and Donovan into Laos in a U-10 Super Courier airplane. Donovan, as usual, was in the copilot's chair, but even with the engine noise and the wind battering at the plane, Corbett's nonstop monologue was loud enough for Lincoln to hear in back. Corbett was a big man with long, wavy brown hair and a five-day growth of beard, wearing a Hawaiian shirt with pictures of those plastic hula dancer figurines people put in their cars, with springs in their waists so they swayed with the motion of travel. He was supposed to wear a survival vest, Lincoln knew, equipped with a radio, flares, and other gear, but he'd explained that he found it too constricting, so he kept it behind his seat, easy to reach in an emergency.

"Maybe not, though. It could just be something in the Oriental makeup that they just don't get pie, you know what I mean? Here's what I do know about them—they just don't care if you live or die. I mean, unless you're related to 'em or something. If you're just some guy, some round-eye especially, they wouldn't piss on you if you were on fire. Not that I'm prejudiced or anything. I'm not a, what do you call it, a bigot. I just know what's true. Like your colored folks"—here he stopped and nodded his head toward

Lincoln, in the back—"not *you*, if Donovan says you're good people, then you're good people, and anyone who puts on the uniform of the good old US of A is okay in my book—I'm talking about the ones that march around on street corners and complain all the time that the white folks are picking on 'em."

He paused for a moment, scanning the ground ahead for landmarks, Lincoln supposed. Or maybe he was just trying to remember what it was he didn't like about "colored folks." Either way, when he started up again, he had shifted gears. "Anyway, whenever I get home, I'm having a nice big slice of apple pie. Maybe I'll have the whole pie. With a glass of milk. We got the best milk in Wisconsin, I'm telling you. You've never had Wisconsin milk, you got to try some. Also the best beer. And blond girls—we got the best blondes anywhere. I know you colored guys like blondes. I don't know why people like these Oriental chicks over here. They're so tiny; I always feel like I'm gonna break 'em. Tell you what, you give me a blond girl I have to climb a ladder to kiss, a glass of Wisconsin milk, and an apple pie, and I'm a happy man."

"I'll make a note of it," Lincoln said.

"Hah!" Corbett's laugh reminded Lincoln of a mule's bray. "Hah! He'll make a note of it. That's a good one. You got a ripe one here, John, a real ripe one."

Donovan half-turned in his seat and met Lincoln's gaze, raising one eyebrow. He had said before the flight that Corbett was an acquired taste, and Lincoln was learning what he meant. Growing up black in the American South meant he was used to casual racism, and even in the Army, where the uniform was supposed to be the great equalizer, it never really went away. All the kids at the orphanage had been black, and they weren't allowed to use the public swimming pool during the prime hours, when it was reserved for whites.

Things were changing, but people like Corbett were a reminder that there was a long way to go. What was that line that Dr. King had quoted? "The arc of the moral universe is long, but it bends toward justice." Maybe that was true, but there was still a lot of bending that needed doing.

Before they'd left, Donovan had explained that Lincoln was officially on detached service to the CIA and confirmed his supplemental pay. Donovan would be his handler. He had filled in Lincoln more on what his duties with the Hmong would be—helping to develop the village, bringing it into the twentieth century, along with supplying and training the men for combat against the VC, NVA, and Pathet Lao.

And he'd explained that despite his rough edges, Brad Corbett could be trusted. "Corbett's kind of a madman," Donovan had said. "But he's earned the right."

"Earned it how?" Lincoln had asked.

"Do you know what JACK was?"

"I don't know jack shit," Lincoln said with a low chuckle.

Donovan ignored the joke. "Joint Advisory Commission, Korea. It was a CIA-sponsored Special Forces op during the Korean War. Those guys went through hell, but they got the job done. Brad Corbett is a big part of the reason why. Now he's under exclusive contract to Air America, and they keep him around because he can fly anything. Slap some wings on a Ford Mustang and he'll get that bastard to twenty thousand feet in five minutes."

The Super Courier was a small single-engine aircraft with overhead wings sporting what seemed like an unusual profusion of flaps. Corbett sometimes referred to it as a helioplane, but Lincoln hadn't bothered to ask what he meant by that. Although it could seat five, at the moment Lincoln was surrounded by crates of gear intended for the Hmong in a place Donovan called Vang Khom.

Corbett's apparel was far from regulation, but Air America was its own kind of beast—allegedly, a private corporation, but everyone seemed to know it was really CIA. Lincoln couldn't complain, because he was out of uniform, too. He and Donovan were both wearing black uniforms like the one Lincoln had worn on the task force mission, with no identifying marks. It was just one more indication that this trip would be far outside the usual Army procedure.

Lincoln wasn't sure when they had crossed into Laos. As usual, the landscape they passed over was a spectacular, almost crazy-making blend of green on green. Lincoln supposed the occasional river or groomed plantation could serve as landmarks for someone who flew it often enough. They were flying lower than Lincoln had expected, which Corbett had said was to avoid radar. Lincoln wasn't sure the enemy had radar, but he wasn't going to argue. He just wanted to get where they were going before someone shot them out of the sky, because he knew the enemy had guns that could reach their present altitude.

As if reading Lincoln's mind, Corbett glanced over his shoulder. "Another thirty minutes, tops, and we'll be on the ground at Vang Khom. Their 'air strip' isn't much to brag about—it's basically a slash of land on top of a hill where they cut away the trees and maybe graded, to use the word loosely, with shovels—but that's the beauty of the Super Courier. This baby is STOL—short takeoff and landing—and she can touch down just about anywhere."

Donovan pointed out the windshield. "See those mountain ranges ahead?"

They were approaching a series of them, each one seeming from here to be a little higher than the one in front. Lincoln nodded.

"That's where the Hmong live. They like the highlands. Past that last one is the Plain of Jars."

"Plain of what?" Lincoln asked.

"You'll understand why when you see them. They're not really jars," Donovan explained. "More like big fucking urns. They're in clusters, scattered all over the place on the plain. Some people think they were funerary jars, or crematories, or something. It's strategically important, though—the juncture of Routes 7 and 13, at the western entrance, is critical, and right now it's in Pathet Lao hands. We need to boot their asses out of there and take it, so we can control traffic through this sector. That's going to be up to you and your men. The goddamn Laotian army is as useless as the South Vietnamese—like tits on a boar—so they won't be any help, but the Hmong are tough bastards, and they'll be glad to kill some commies."

My men, Lincoln thought, wondering what his men would be like and how they would take to their new American chief.

He looked out the windshield again. They were rapidly approaching the first of the mountain ranges, and Corbett hadn't seemed to notice. A jungle-clad wall loomed ahead of them. At nearly the last possible moment, Corbett put the craft into a steep climb, and they skimmed just above the treetops. At the summit, updrafts and downdrafts buffeted the plane, but Corbett jockeyed through them, and soon they were dropping into the valley on the other side.

"Loaded down like this, she doesn't always like making the climbs," Corbett said. "But she'll do it—I just have to nudge her a little bit."

"Long as you know what you're doing, it's okay with me," Lincoln said.

"Oh, he does," Donovan assured him. "He may be a racist son of a bitch, but he can fly a plane."

"Don't get me wrong," Corbett added. "I've lost a couple. Well, four."

"'Lost,' how?" Lincoln wondered.

"Crashed three," Corbett replied casually. "Shot down once. A few broken bones, but no fatalities."

"Well, that's something, I guess."

"I told you, Lincoln, if you're flying into some heavy shit, there's no one you're better off with than that man right there."

"Hah!" Corbett released another of his braying laughs and half-turned in his seat to address Lincoln. "That's because the others are all dead! I outlived the bastards."

Another mountain range was filling the windshield. "Uhh, you might want to keep an eye out front if you're going to keep outliving them."

Corbett adjusted the controls, and the plane launched into another climb. Lincoln thought he could make out individual branches on the trees outside his window, and at one point, he thought he saw a figure in the woods, half-dressed, holding a spear. It could have been a trick of the light, though, and when he looked back, they were too far beyond the spot.

If the man had been real, though, Lincoln was taking an airplane ride into prehistory.

This range was taller than the previous one, and the winds at the summit were even more ferocious. Corbett actually looked tense as he fought to control the craft, but once they were headed down the far side, he relaxed again. "Two more to go," he said. "We'll go over this next one, and then land on the one after that."

"You sure you can put this down on top of a mountain?" Lincoln asked.

"Mister, I could land this baby on top of an Oldsmobile driving down Route 66."

"I think the bastard really could," Donovan affirmed. "But I don't think it'll be necessary. Like he said, Vang Khom has an airstrip. Or they did. I haven't been out there in a couple of years—hopefully they haven't let it get too overgrown. They're good warriors, but not such great groundskeepers."

"Hopefully," Lincoln echoed. This mission was sounding more seat-of-the-pants every minute. They were flying into a neutral country where the American military was strictly forbidden from operating, so Lincoln could turn people who spoke another language and hunted with spears into a military force capable of wrenching a plain full of dead bodies in jars away from well-organized and supplied communist forces. *Nothing to it.*

He looked out the windshield again, as they plowed toward yet another mountain range. Lincoln didn't know why they had to fly so low—the craft was clearly able to withstand higher altitudes, so they could have flown at a steady height above the mountain ranges, instead of making the ups and downs. For all he knew, Corbett thrived on the challenge or got his kicks from danger. Given that Lincoln was strapped into a rear seat and surrounded by wooden crates, he didn't think he wanted to know which it was. He just wanted to get on the ground in one piece.

"This one's the highest," Corbett said. "She's gonna groan a little going up and over, but don't let that worry you."

Lincoln didn't answer. Corbett angled the nose up and they climbed past the steep walls of rock and brush. Near the top, the airplane did indeed start to groan, and Lincoln wondered if the effort of making the extreme climb weighted down with cargo was too much for it. But Donovan said Corbett knew his stuff, and he'd been flying around Asia for years.

Anyway, they'd made it over the other summits, and this was the last. Soon they'd be on the ground. Lincoln tried to relax—worrying wouldn't help Corbett fly the plane.

But then they were passing over the peaks and the winds were furious, updrafts and downdrafts hitting the tiny craft seemingly at once. Corbett looked worried as he struggled for control. The airplane buzzed mere feet above the treetops, then started to climb away from them—but just as suddenly the nose plunged down, and Corbett shouted, "Hang onto your ball sacks, gents! We're goin' down!"

14

All was chaos.

The Super Courier dropped to treetop height. Corbett fought to regain control, but Lincoln could hear—and feel—the impact of the trees against the landing gear and the bottom of the fuselage. Then they seemed to be snagged on something, and the plane's forward progress came to an abrupt halt. Crates broke loose from their straps and slammed into Lincoln. He thought they would just come to rest there, but instead, the airplane flipped over, nose first, and then branches were crashing in through the windows and crates were splitting open, spewing out rifles and ammunition and foodstuffs and more, and they skidded along that way, upside-down.

Something struck Lincoln in the head and he must have lost consciousness for a few seconds, because when his mind swam back to awareness, he was dangling, held in by his seatbelt, and the plane was still. When he looked up—no, down—all he could see were the trees they'd become tangled in, and flashes of the ground below.

But he smelled something that wasn't jungle foliage. It took a few seconds for the odor to sink in. Fuel. That meant the tank had ruptured. A single spark in the wrong place could kill them all.

"Donovan?" he said. "Corbett?"

No answer. He looked toward the front of the plane but couldn't see either man. Tree branches filled the windshield area. Had they fallen out? Or become impaled on the branches?

He didn't have time to sit and wonder about it. He unbuckled his seat belt, bracing for the crash he knew would result. The fall to the aircraft's ceiling wasn't that far, but he was going headfirst. He thrust out his hands and managed to lower himself, relatively gently, to the ceiling.

His door was jammed shut, wedged into the trees so tightly that he couldn't budge it. He could scramble across the upended crates and spilled weaponry to the other door, but it looked about the same. His best escape route was out the back—the tail had mostly snapped off in the crash, so behind his seat was an opening wide enough to crawl through.

As he did, the plane shifted, cramming itself lower in the trees. Again, the fear of a spark struck him—metal scraping against metal could set off a fire that would engulf him, the airplane, and the trees in an instant.

He managed to free himself from the wreckage. He worked his way into a tree, coming to rest on a thick, sturdy branch that disappeared into the Super Courier's interior a few feet away. Every inch of him was sore, and he knew he would hurt more later, but for the moment, he appeared to be intact, with none of the broken bones Corbett was so proud of.

He still couldn't see the pilot, though, or Donovan.

If they were in front of the airplane, or near the front, he couldn't reach them from here. The bulk of the aircraft's cabin was in the way, and he couldn't risk going through or over that, not the way it had slid and shifted when he had simply tried to crawl out. Instead, he turned his sights downward, picking out a seemingly safe route of descent, and climbed down from the tree.

On the ground, the underbrush was dense and almost waist-high, with plenty of smaller trees growing up between the big ones. He could have hacked his way through with a machete, but if there were any among the plane's cargo, they were still twenty-some feet up, in the canopy. Instead, he worked through it as best he could, shoving smaller trunks aside, wading through brush, hoping there were no snakes or other venomous creatures lying in wait.

Above him, the plane creaked and settled. The smell of fuel was stronger here, and he saw where the trickle rained down to the jungle floor. He didn't dare travel directly below the airplane, in case its weight suddenly became too much for the trees to bear, or something set off the explosion he dreaded. He pushed and tugged his way around it, until he was in front of it, looking up at its battered, upside-down cockpit.

There was Donovan, apparently unconscious, wedged in the crook of a limb. One foot might have been stuck inside the airplane, but Lincoln couldn't quite tell from where he stood.

He spotted Corbett a few moments later, awake but dazed. He was somehow mostly above the airplane and starting to shift around in the branches. With each movement he made, he was pushing on the plane, rocking it ever so slightly. Every nudge, Lincoln feared, increased the risk of that stray spark.

"Hold still, Corbett!" Lincoln cried. "I'm coming!"

Corbett answered with a wordless moan and a motion that rocked the plane even harder.

He didn't want the pilot to blow up his own plane. But his first priority had to be Donovan. If the airplane went up in flames, the CIA agent was toast.

Fortunately, the foliage was thick enough that it was easy to gain elevation, and Lincoln climbed up to a reasonably substantial branch that angled out toward Donovan's position.

The agent still hadn't moved. Lincoln saw blood and wondered if he was too late. Was Donovan already dead? He edged closer. No, the man's chest rose and fell. He'd been cut, by tree limbs and probably windshield glass, and he was going to be in a world of pain, but he would live. At least, if Lincoln could get him down in time.

"Take it easy, Donovan," he said as he reached the agent. "I'm just gonna get you loose from these branches."

Donovan's only response was a louder exhalation. Maybe he heard Lincoln, and maybe not. Lincoln hoped he hadn't suffered any major injuries—a perforated lung, a broken neck, brain damage. He couldn't tell from here. He'd had some medical training in his abbreviated Special Forces school, and he knew that accident victims shouldn't be moved until the extent of their injuries could be determined and they could be properly braced, if necessary. But he didn't think that applied to people dangling in the upper canopies of trees, in which the remnants of an airplane might crash down around them and/or explode into flames at any moment.

He got a good grip on Donovan's shoulders and tugged, trying to extricate him from the branches. Donovan moaned. Lincoln pulled harder, and the agent's body seemed to stretch toward him—but only so far—before stopping short. Lincoln tugged with even more force. Same result. Something was holding Donovan fast.

Lincoln looked below the agent's position and above. He was resting on tree limbs and was possibly impaled on some, but it didn't look like there were any sunk so deep in him that they wouldn't let go. Certainly nothing had come out the other side.

Then he saw Donovan's left foot, the one still partially inside the cabin. It was trapped between the upper edge of the windshield frame and a thick branch. The branch Lincoln sat on pressed against that one, about seven feet away. He got a better grasp on Donovan's shoulders and shifted his weight to rock the branch, hoping he could free the man's foot without sending the whole airplane crashing through the trees. Nothing was happening, though—he was moving the other branch only slightly, and in such a way that it might have been increasing the pressure on Donovan's ankle rather than releasing it. In his mind, he saw a flash of himself trying to explain to Donovan how his foot had become amputated and decided a change of plan was called for.

His new plan might have been more dangerous still, though. He would have to get closer to the plane—practically right on top of it—to lift the branch off Donovan's ankle. At first, his additional weight would force the branch down even more, running the risk of crushing the bone. But after a few steps, he would be able to climb off onto another branch, relieving the pressure on Donovan. Then the biggest risk was that his weight on that other branch—one that had thrust through a side window into the cockpit—would upset the plane's precarious balance. Lincoln was torn—he didn't want to set off any sparks, but the longer Donovan hung there in the trees, the more danger he was in if a spark happened incidentally.

Lincoln had to try for it. He raised his feet to the branch and stood, reaching out to other limbs for balance. In that way, he walked up to the branch pinning Donovan in place. From here, he could barely reach Donovan at all, but he was able to get a hand on one shoulder. That would have to do. Awkwardly, reaching at the farthest extent of his arm to pull on Donovan, he used his other hand to try to lift the branch.

It wasn't going to work. He didn't have a good angle. The branch was wedged tightly into the cockpit, probably weighted down in there by the cargo crates. And even if he could budge it, how could he get Donovan free without being able to pull him by both shoulders?

He gave it one last try, almost bouncing on his branch as he yanked upward on the other and tugged at the CIA agent. The airplane squeaked and groaned, Donovan gave a low, unintelligible moan, and the foliage rustled. Then the plane slipped and dropped, almost a full foot. Lincoln held his breath, waiting for the blast.

It didn't happen, but the shift had released Donovan's foot. Lincoln looped an arm under Donovan's right armpit and across his chest, and pulled. Donovan slid toward him. Lincoln got a firmer hold, clutching Donovan to his chest, and climbed down from the trees. Finally on the ground, he carried the agent over his shoulder to a clearing well away from the spilled fuel and the precarious airplane overhead, then went back for Corbett.

By the time Lincoln got there, Corbett was mostly conscious. "What the fuck?" he muttered.

"Number five," Lincoln said. "Come on, man, we got to get out of here. Plane's dumping all its fuel onto the ground. If that ignites—"

"Boom!" Corbett said. He spread his hands, shaping an explosion. The action shifted the branches holding him up and he dropped down several inches. If he fell much farther he would land on top of the Super Courier, and that impact might well be enough to jostle it loose. Donovan was the only one who would be safe, if that happened.

"Easy," Lincoln said. "Don't move around too much. The plane's right under you. If you fall—"

"Boom!" Corbett said again. He started to make the same motion with his hands but thought better of it. Instead, he anxiously grabbed hold of some of the sturdy branches supporting his weight.

"Right. Just work your way toward me. Carefully. We don't want to shake the plane too much."

"My vest is in there. Behind my seat."

"Right where we can't get to it," Lincoln said. "Good plan. Just come on."

Corbett nodded—gently—and obeyed. He weighed more than Lincoln and was older, both factors that made tree-climbing a less-than-ideal practice. And he still seemed partially dazed from the crash. Lincoln was afraid he would slip or lose consciousness.

"Come on, man," Lincoln said. "Just a few more feet."

Corbett shook his right leg. His pant leg was snagged on a limb. The more furiously he tried to shake it free, the more Lincoln worried about the effect his thrashing would have on the airplane a few feet below him.

"Slow down," he urged. "Your pants are stuck, is all. I can get them."

"Get 'em fast, then," Corbett said. "I don't want to be here when that thing goes."

"Don't do the boom."

"No boom. Just get me the fuck offa here."

"Just think about pie," Lincoln said. "And tall blondes and glasses of milk."

A dreamy grin spread over Corbett's face. Maybe he had a concussion, Lincoln thought. If he couldn't keep his wits about him, they could still both die up here.

He moved onto another limb—one that shifted disturbingly under his weight but held—and found the branch that had snagged Corbett's pants. He worked it loose, then hurried back to his earlier perch. "Okay, there you go, Corbett. Keep coming toward me."

Corbett pulled himself from branch to branch, half-swimming through the trees, swaying with each step he took. Finally, though, he reached the big tree that Lincoln had climbed up.

"Doing good, man," Lincoln said. "It's easy from here. Straight down, just like a ladder. Plenty of places to put your feet, you dig?"

"I dig," Corbett said. He was still wearing a half-smile, and Lincoln wasn't reassured about his mental state. This was not, as far as he was concerned, some kind of fun adventure. He didn't want to be killed by wind and trees and fire before he had even met his Hmong counterparts.

"Just watch where I go," Lincoln said. "Do what I do. You can do that, right?"

"I can do that."

"Cool. That's cool. Here we go."

He descended, branch by branch. After a few steps, he stopped and watched Corbett. The pilot managed to make most of the same steps and avoided plummeting down from the heights. Soon they were both on solid ground, and Lincoln was leading him toward Donovan's position.

Just as Lincoln got Donovan in sight—sitting up with his back against a tree, watching for Lincoln's return—Corbett startled Lincoln with another braying laugh.

"What the hell, man?" Lincoln snapped. "We don't know who's around here."

"I just got the joke," Corbett said. "Number five. Plane crash number five, right?"

"That's right. Now keep quiet. Sit over here by Donovan. I'm going back to see if I can salvage any of those guns."

Some rifles had spilled from the airplane. He wasn't sure what condition they were in or if he would be able to find any ammunition for them, but he had to try. His sidearm had come out of its holster at some point, and he didn't want to be here, defenseless, when the Pathet Lao came to investigate the crash.

But he was too late. He had taken only two steps toward the plane when it shifted again, its weight finally too much for the canopy holding it up. He threw himself to the ground as it crashed and squealed toward the earth, and he stayed there, hugging dirt, as the world went bright and a wave of incredible heat passed over him, curling leaves.

15

The fireball, Lincoln was sure, could be seen for miles. Wherever the Pathet Lao were, they'd spot it and hurry to check it out. He hustled Donovan and Corbett away from the flames before they could spread too far. "We've got to get off this mountain," he said. "Double-time."

Both men were conscious now, able to walk on their own, though Donovan remained a little unsteady on his feet. He still had a holstered .45-caliber Colt, but that was the only firearm between the three of them. Lincoln had a survival knife strapped to his ankle, with jagged teeth across the top of the blade, in a leather sheath with a sharpening stone in the pouch. Corbett, in his tattered Hawaiian shirt, was unarmed. They wouldn't be much good if a Pathet Lao division found them.

They knew the direction in which Vang Khom lay, and their best hope—their only hope, as far as Lincoln was concerned—was reaching it before the bad guys found them. No problem—it was just down from this mountaintop, across a valley that was probably heavily traveled by Pathet Lao and VC, and up the next mountain. At 150 miles per hour, it would have taken no time at all. On foot, badly banged up, through dense jungle, it would be a marathon.

Lincoln thought about the airplane's radio, doubtless burned beyond recognition. He thought about the guns, some of them possibly still usable, but at the bottom of a superheated bonfire. They didn't have a map or a compass or a canteen or any food.

Their situation wasn't hopeless, but it lived right next door to that. It was, in the immortal language of American soldiers, FUBAR—fucked up beyond all repair.

Progress was slow without a blade adequate to chop their way through the brush. In a half hour, they had gone less than a mile. Probably less than a kilometer, Lincoln thought. He could still see the smoke behind them, the flames licking at treetops. The smell of burning was everywhere, as if it were traveling with them. "On the bright side," Corbett said after a while, "the racket probably scared away all the tigers for miles around."

"Tigers, shit," Lincoln said. "Thanks a lot. I've been over here worried about the enemy and completely forgot to worry about tigers."

"And don't forget the snakes," Donovan added. "Malayan pit vipers. Banded kraits. Laos is full of the bastards."

"That's a big help."

"I'm just looking out for you, buddy. It's what I do."

"You were lookin' out for me, you coulda found me a pilot who didn't crash into mountains."

"Hey, man, that wasn't my fault!" Corbett protested. "We were too heavy for those downdrafts."

"You couldn't fly a little higher over the mountains?"

"And be a target for Chinese radar? We'd be fighting off MiGs right now."

"Really?" Lincoln asked. "The Pathet Lao can scramble Russian fighters at the drop of a hat?"

"You don't want to know," Donovan said. "Both of you guys, knock it the fuck off. We're alive. We're on our way to get help."

"We were supposed to show up at Vang Khom looking like their saviors, with an airplane full of arms," Lincoln said. "Not crawling in, starving and injured, with one gun between us. That's not exactly gonna be awe-inspiring."

"They know me," Donovan said. "I'll explain, don't worry."

"I'm tired of being told not to worry. At this point, I think some worrying is called for."

"You worry all you want," Corbett said. "I'm saving my breath. Man, I hate walking."

"Can't fly everywhere," Lincoln said.

"Why not?"

"Man, you can't fly *any*where! You sure you only crashed five planes? I think it's probably more like fifty."

"Lincoln!" Donovan snapped. "Give it a goddamn rest."

Lincoln shut up. Donovan was right. Arguing with them wasn't going to do anybody any good. They would have to rely on one another to survive this little excursion after all.

"Sorry," he said. Then he was silent, focused on pushing through the brush, watching for snakes and listening for tigers.

It wasn't a tiger he heard, though.

It was a man.

He stopped suddenly, raising one fist. Donovan caught it and froze, but Corbett stumbled into him. Lincoln shushed him.

He had distinctly heard the rustle of foliage and the snap of a branch or twig on the ground. A tiger wouldn't be so careless. A communist might be, though.

He motioned toward the ground, and all three men lowered themselves into crouches. Donovan drew his Colt, and Lincoln silently unsnapped his knife.

More rustling ahead. It didn't sound like a group of soldiers, though. It sounded like one man—or one careless man, walking at the head of a patrol comprising more careful ones.

Lincoln waited. A shape appeared, just a shadow on the brush. *Shoot him*, Lincoln thought. Donovan's gun was aimed at him, his other hand steadying his gun hand, but he didn't pull the trigger.

The shape came closer. *Shoot him!* Lincoln thought. He was almost ready to scream it when the man finally broke into view.

He probably wasn't really more than a hundred years old, but he looked like he was close. Ninety, anyway. He wore a robe belted at the waist with a length of rope and tied at his left shoulder. Lincoln couldn't see his feet but assumed he had on sandals of some kind. In one hand, he carried a staff, which he used to delicately part the jungle ahead of him. He was completely hairless, with furrowed skin the color of the knotty pine paneling in the dining room of the orphanage Lincoln had grown up in. When he saw the three Americans, his ancient face broke into a gap-toothed grin. He babbled something that sounded like gibberish to Lincoln, but Donovan answered in the same tongue. Soon, they were conversing back and forth like old friends.

"He's the chief of a village somewhere nearby," Donovan said after the exchange. "He wants us to go with him."

"He's Laotian?" Lincoln asked.

"He's Hmong."

"From Vang Khom?"

"No, we're still too far from there. But he's Hmong. And considering he's not exactly a fan of the Pathet Lao, he likes us."

"How do we know he's not going to lead us into a trap?"

"Why would he do that? He's on our side."

"I'm with Clay," Corbett said. "For all we know, he's some kind of cannibal. Maybe he's got a nice big cook pot simmering, just waiting for us."

"The Hmong aren't cannibals," Donovan said. "He hates the fucking commies. And he says he has a radio."

"A radio?"

"Yes!" Donovan said something else in Hmong, and the old man laughed, then made a cranking motion with one hand and held his other up to his head, as if speaking into a radio headset.

"I'll be damned," Corbett said. "Maybe he really does have a radio."

"If he does, it's left over from the French," Donovan said. "God knows if the fucking thing works. But we have to go with him. At the very least, we can get some food. And maybe we can get help."

Donovan and the old man exchanged a few more sentences, and then the man gestured for them to follow. Donovan holstered his gun, and Lincoln slipped his knife back into its sheath.

• • •

The village was picturesque, in its way. Carved from the jungle in a saddle just below the highest peak, it sat on the bank of a narrow river. Water buffalo cooled themselves in the river—Lincoln thought they were boulders, until one lifted its massive, horned head to shake off water—and some of the women knelt by the banks, washing clothes. Good-size huts were raised off the ground on stilts, which meant that during the wet season, the river probably overran its banks. The roofs of most overhung the walls enough to form shaded areas for cooking and other chores. Some huts had smaller, secondary ones standing nearby, which Donovan said were basically pantries or larders, for storing goods and foodstuffs.

At the sight of the old man, accompanied by the three Americans, the village's children went berserk. Naked or nearly so, they ran in circles, around and around the newcomers, many of them holding out their hands, almost all of them jabbering something Lincoln couldn't begin to understand.

"They're hoping for treats or coins," Donovan said. "They've heard stories of French troops coming through with their pockets full of candies and coins for the children."

"Tell them our pockets are empty," Lincoln said. "And if we had any coins, they'd be American money and useless here."

Donovan tried to wave the kids away, but he kept a smile on his face and a lightness in his tone. Finally, the furor died down. Now Lincoln realized the village's men were lined up, watching them carefully. Many carried spears, some bows and arrows. There were only a couple of rifles in evidence, and they were ancient. The women, likewise, watched from their doorways or their shaded work areas. They weren't smiling, but they weren't attacking, either, so that was something.

The old man spoke to a few of the younger ones. Once they had gone back and forth a couple of times, two of the younger ones ran to a hut near the edge of the village. They dashed inside and came out quickly, bearing a radio. It looked older than the rifles. Lincoln doubted that even Nilsson, the radio genius from Lang Vei, could have raised anyone on it.

The men set it down in the dirt, connected a hand-cranked, tripod-mounted generator to it, and the old man sat down beside it. One of the younger ones started to crank the generator, and as he did, the old man keyed it, trying to raise someone. Eventually, most of the other villagers wandered off to do whatever it was they did, and Lincoln, Donovan, and Corbett sat down in the shade to wait.

Finally, someone responded. Lincoln hoped it wasn't the VC. The old man spoke in rapid-fire Hmong as he keyed the message, and Donovan translated what he could catch. "He's in touch with someone in Vientiane, apparently. They'll let the government know that we're out here, and they'll inform the American embassy."

"So, what, we'll be here two weeks? Three?" Lincoln asked.

Donovan shrugged. "Best we can do is the best we can do."

"We could start walkin' again, head for Vang Khom."

"Makes sense to me," Corbett added.

"Look at it this way," Donovan said. "If he really was talking to someone in Vientiane and that person really does go to the government, and whoever he talks to goes to the embassy, then at least someone will know where we are. When Corbett doesn't get back, they'll know we're missing—that'll light a fire under their asses. They might already be looking for us. This way, just maybe they'll find us quicker. If we take off by ourselves and try to walk to goddamn Vang Khom, the chances of running into a fucking Pathet Lao division are greater than the chances that Americans doing a flyover search will spot us. And even if we do make it to Vang Khom, we're in the same boat as we are here, except they don't have a fifty-year-old French radio."

"Well, when you put it like that," Lincoln said, "I guess we could stick around for a little while."

"That's what I thought you'd say."

"Did I mention I hate walking?" Corbett asked.

"Three or four hundred times is all," Lincoln said.

"Well, it's true." He considered for a moment, then added, "You suppose any of these people know how to make a pie?"

16

The sun was balanced on the lip of a mountain range to the west when they heard the buzz of a distant airplane. The three men rose from the dirt but stayed in the shade, each of them shielding their eyes with one hand and scanning the sky. Lincoln saw it first. "There!" he said. It was a dot in the distance but growing progressively larger.

It was a twin-engine propeller job. As it came closer, Corbett gave a shout. "It's a Beech Baron!" he cried. "It's our guys!"

"Our guys?" Lincoln asked.

"Air America," Donovan explained.

"Can it land here?"

"There's nowhere to put down," Corbett said. "Even my U-10 couldn't land here." He stepped out of the shade, waving his hands over his head. Donovan followed suit, so Lincoln joined them.

The airplane came closer, dipped down, and circled over the village three times. The third time, it wagged its wings in response.

"He saw us!" Corbett said. "My guess, that's Tommy Pinchot in the cockpit. He loves his Baron."

Lincoln watched the plane flying away, back in the direction from which it had come. "It's leaving."

"He can't land," Corbett said again. "Best he can do is send back a chopper."

"How long is that going to take?"

"I think we can look forward to enjoying the hospitality of these fine folks overnight," Donovan said. "Could be worse."

"Damn straight," Corbett agreed. "They could be cannibals."

"I told you, the Hmong aren't goddamn cannibals."

"That you know of."

"I'd know."

"That's what they always say about cannibals, until they find tooth-marks on human bone. Then the story changes."

"Jesus fucking Christ, Brad—" Donovan began.

Corbett cut him off. "I'm just giving you a hard time, Donovan. Nobody's been looking at me like they're hungry, and I'm definitely the most appetizing one of us." He glanced over at Lincoln, then added, "Unless they like the dark meat."

• • •

After a dinner of roast pig, chased down by the tribespeople with plenty of the local liquor, the chieftain let his distinguished guests use his long-house for the night. The thatched bamboo structure contained a functional bamboo table and a couple of chairs, a shelf jutting out from one wall containing his entire wardrobe, and a framed-in bed of fresh grasses and leaves. Donovan claimed the bed, so Lincoln and Corbett stretched out on the woven floor. It was more comfortable than Lincoln had expected, and he fell asleep quickly.

The sun had not yet cleared the horizon when he was awakened by hor-rific, anguished screams. He snatched up the knife that he'd kept close all night and dashed out the door, closely followed by Donovan and Corbett. The screams continued, from down by the river. "What the hell?" Corbett asked as they hurried toward the scene. "Sounds like someone's being slaughtered."

This high up on the mountain, once the sun broke above the eastern horizon, full light came on almost at once. When it did, Lincoln saw six of the tribeswomen, naked or nearly so, standing in the shallows at the edge of the water. Each held a machete, and they were all drenched in blood. Then he saw a water buffalo, down on its knees in the slow current, bleed-ing from a dozen spots. It was no longer screaming, but it let out pained bleats that grew weaker with every passing moment.

The old chieftain stood nearby, just far enough away to avoid being spattered with blood or river water. He said something to Donovan, who translated for the others.

"Apparently we're to be the guests at a feast this morning. That buffalo gave its goddamn life for us."

"They let the women do the killing?" Lincoln asked.

"Men do the hunting, but this is food preparation," Donovan replied. "Women's work, in their culture."

Lincoln had never seen a woman acting so savage. He had known men—hardened gangsters—who would shy away from chopping up an animal that way, much less a human being. He didn't have much patience for that. If you were going to live the life, with all the benefits that came along with it, you had to take the dirty jobs along with the clean ones. Sometimes you wanted a body to disappear forever, which meant a deep grave or incineration or maybe a long bath of lye. Other times you wanted to make a certain kind of statement, one that could best be made with the judicious placement of somebody's head, or the timely delivery of a finger or a hand or some other recognizable body part. He didn't enjoy that kind of work—though he'd met a couple of people who did—but he didn't avoid it when it had to be done.

They stood and watched as the buffalo's lifeblood drained away into the river, a long pinkish stream that caught the morning sunlight as it vanished around a bend. The women kept hacking at it, cutting it into manageable chunks and tossing them onto the shore. Others, clad in more traditional Hmong dresses and wraps, collected those pieces and carried them to the open space at the village center. A huge fire had been lit there, with flames licking eight to ten feet tall. Lincoln was reminded of the U-10's fate.

Which reminded him of their own. A feast in their honor was nice enough, but all things considered, he would rather be rescued before he had to spend another night on the old man's floor.

By nine o'clock, the sun was high and Lincoln was famished. The smell of buffalo roasting over open flame filled the village, and his mouth was watering. Most of the villagers had put on their best, brightest attire; the women wore sparkling silver jewelry adorned with gemstones, along with fine, colorful pantaloons and blouses or dresses. Many of the men wore loincloths, but others had put on fancy, bright shirts and some wore jewelry that outshone the women's. Jugs of the tribe's liquor—foul-tasting but strong—had been set out, along with drinking goblets. People chattered amiably, not seeming to mind that of the three Americans, only Donovan could understand a word they said, and then less than half of it.

Then the buffalo was ready. Big slabs of it were handed to the guests and the tribal elders, including the chieftain. He said something over his that Lincoln took to be some kind of blessing, then ripped into it with teeth that seemed plenty strong despite his age. Donovan shrugged and followed suit. When the crowd roared in appreciation, Lincoln and Corbett did the same. It tasted even better than it smelled.

An hour later, pleasantly full and more than a little drunk, Lincoln was sitting with Donovan, Corbett, and a group of young village men. They wanted to know what was going on with the war across the border and with the communist forces within Laos. Donovan was doing his best to translate between the two groups and had told them right off the bat that he couldn't discuss the American presence in their country. It was dangerous enough to be there, in a village where he'd had no previous contact, where there might be communist sympathizers who would be happy to inform the Pathet Lao that Americans had visited. But thanks to the plane crash, it couldn't be helped. Now they waited for a helicopter that would further confirm the American presence.

"After you've worked with the folks in Vang Khom for a while, see if they've got friendly relations with these people," Donovan said to Lincoln. "They seem amenable to the cause. Maybe you could put together some volunteers."

"Hold up," Lincoln said. "I thought I was supposed to focus on the men in Vang Khom. Am I also supposed to be recruiting from other villages?"

"Can't hurt. If you catch a break in Vang Khom, those people might have friends or relatives in other villages who want to join up. The bigger the force you can muster, the harder you can take it to those red bastards."

Lincoln nodded. So far, Donovan had been fairly vague on just what he expected. He seemed to think Lincoln would understand what needed to be done and would just know how to do it. That, Lincoln remembered, had been part of what Captain Franklin had stressed—saying that Lincoln had an aptitude for it. But he was a mob kid from New Bordeaux, not a hardened intelligence agent.

"Sometimes it sounds like what you want is a Peace Corps volunteer who has also worked as a drill sergeant," Lincoln said.

Donovan laughed. "That's a pretty good summary, Lincoln. Except you forgot one thing."

"What's that?"

"I need a man who knows how to kill. If you're not afraid to die, that's even better."

"I'd rather not die," Lincoln said. "I want to get back to New Bordeaux after this is all over."

"You'll be home before this fucking war is over. You'll probably be an old man before it's over, the way those Pentagon assholes are running it. If they'd let us turn northern Laos and North Vietnam into another Dresden—or Hiroshima—it'd be over in a goddamn blink. And if we still had Kennedy in Washington . . ." He paused, shaking his head sadly. "No point in going down that path, though."

One of the younger men, barely out of his teens, interrupted to ask Donovan another question. The agent made him repeat it, slowly, until he understood what was being asked.

"He says he wants to kill communists. He says he doesn't care if it's with his bare hands, knives, arrows, or guns; he just wants to soak the earth with communist blood."

"He's enthusiastic, I'll say that for him," Corbett said with a chuckle.

"Remember this kid, Lincoln," Donovan said. "When the time comes, this is a motherfucker you want on your team."

Lincoln couldn't quite imagine himself ever speaking the Hmong language well enough to recruit people from other villages. And this one was several days from Vang Khom on foot, across a valley that was reportedly a Pathet Lao hotbed.

Still, he didn't want to sound like he wasn't fully on board with this mission, whatever it would turn out to be. "I will," he said. He studied the young man's face, trying to commit it to memory.

He hadn't even started yet, but he already felt like he was in over his head.

17

The slick came while the feast was winding down. The big fire was still going, and since the three Americans didn't have a smoke grenade between them, they corralled as many villagers as they could into soaking leaves at the river and throwing them into the flames. The smoke cloud from that was sufficient to guide in the unmarked chopper. On the other side of the river, livestock had grazed a clearing big enough for it to land. Lincoln and his companions bade quick good-byes to their hosts, charged into the river, then, soaking wet and laughing like madmen, scrambled aboard.

Corbett recognized the pilot. "Tommy, it's you! Was that you in the Baron last night, too?"

"You think I'd let someone else fly my bird?" the pilot asked. He was rail-thin, with a blond crew cut and aviator shades. He wore an olive drab jumpsuit with the requisite survival vest that Corbett had refused. "Somebody else might wreck it. Not that I'm pointing any fingers."

"Hey, that wasn't my fault," Corbett replied. "Man, some people never let you live anything down."

"One of the five, I'm guessing?" Lincoln asked.

"Five?" Tommy echoed. "I knew it! You dumped another one. Did you lose all the cargo, too?"

"Oh, shut up," Corbett said.

Tommy got the helicopter airborne. Flying over the valley, they drew some small-arms fire from below, though none of the rounds came close enough to worry about. The flight from mountaintop to mountaintop was a relatively short one, but Lincoln was glad they hadn't had to make the trip over land. Tommy had brought AR-30s, grenades, ammunition, and survival vests for all of them, so Lincoln felt a little more equipped to face the Laotian countryside.

After about twenty minutes in the air, they dropped down toward a village much like the one they'd just left. This one looked like it had been there for longer. The houses were more substantial and bore the signs of having survived the elements for years. Again, they were raised up on stilts, and a creek trickled right through the village, bisecting it. Cleared areas outside the main collection of huts looked like cultivated fields, but they didn't appear to be very productive. Beyond those was a rice paddy that looked like it had completely dried up.

Tommy Pinchot put down on one of those fields. Prop wash flattened the vegetation and fluttered the loose clothing of the villagers who had gathered to watch. They wore somber expressions, as if unsure of who would arrive in such a craft, or why.

But some of their faces brightened when Donovan climbed down and headed their way. Villagers started toward him, arms out in welcome.

Corbett moved from a rear seat up toward the copilot's position. Lincoln eyed him with surprise. "You're not coming?"

"You're on your own, man," Corbett said. "Well, you and Donovan. I'll be back in a few days, to pick him up and bring you supplies."

"Okay, cool," Lincoln said. "Try not to crash this time."

Corbett didn't smile at the jab. Instead, he offered his hand. "You watch your back, Lincoln. You're gonna be alone out here, and it could get hairy. If I can do anything to help, let me know. Donovan will tell you how to contact us. I mean, you know—soon as I bring you a radio. Until then, you're on your own."

Lincoln clasped the pilot's hand, thanked him, and let him go. The chopper lifted off the ground before he was even out from under the propellers. Then it was gone, and he and Donovan were alone in Laos.

At the edge of the field, Lincoln met up with Donovan, who was standing with a lean but sturdy Hmong man who was wearing only a loincloth and a band around his left biceps. He had a thick shock of black hair and an open, friendly expression on his face. "This is Koob Muas," Donovan said.

"He's an old pal. Speaks pretty good English, too, and some French. I call him Koob. Koob, this is my friend Lincoln Clay."

Koob gave a short bow and clasped Lincoln's hand. "Lincoln," Koob said. "Welcome to Vang Khom."

"Glad to be here," Lincoln said. "Especially after all we went through to make it."

"Koob's father, Kaus, is the chief around here. He's a great man. But Koob is the next generation, and he'll be your main man."

Koob beamed at the compliments; at least, what he could understand of them. "I look forward to working with you," Lincoln said.

"I with you, also," Koob said.

"It's been a while since he's had English speakers around," Donovan said. "So you might want to take it slow at first. He's spent time with American units in Vietnam, and he's had some training with ARVN forces, for whatever *that's* worth. But he wanted to come home, and we thought he'd be more useful here." He turned to the Hmong man. "Koob, Lincoln is going to be with you for a long time. He'll work with you, train your men to fight the Pathet Lao and VC, and he'll bring guns and supplies."

"We kill the Pathet?" Koob asked.

"Many Pathet," Donovan said.

Koob clapped his hands together once. "We love killing those Pathet fucks!"

Lincoln grinned. Apparently Koob had spent a lot of time with Donovan. "Koob," Lincoln said, "I think we're gonna get along just fine."

• • •

Donovan turned out to be well-known in Vang Khom; he had been to the village several times, and most of the people greeted him warmly. Lincoln's reception was more muted. "You're a stranger," Donovan said after several cool responses to his introduction. "It takes them a while to get accustomed to anyone new, especially anyone who's not Hmong. Plus that last woman said your skin's a 'funny' color. Most of them have never seen a black man before. They'll get used to you, but it'll take some time."

"How much time?" Lincoln wondered. "You're only here for a few days;

then I'll be alone with them. I don't want to have to be watchin' my own people for assassins the whole time, on top of watchin' for the VC and Pathet Lao."

"Trust me," Donovan said. He shook a cigarette loose and lit it, without offering Lincoln one. "We'll work with them for a few days. Once they see you're genuinely interested in helping them out, they'll come around."

"Helping them out, how?"

Cigarette between his fingers, Donovan indicated the village with a sweep of his hand. "Look around. What do you see as the biggest problem these people have? Besides the obvious fact that they're living in the Stone Age."

Lincoln wasn't sure how to answer that. He was used to New Bordeaux. Even the poorest person there owned more than the richest in Vang Khom. This place didn't have paved streets or buildings made of materials that could stand up to fire or flood. No fixed addresses meant no mail service. For that matter, he doubted that they had any government services at all. As far as they were concerned, Vientiane was like a place from a fantasy story, something they'd heard of but that didn't really exist in their world.

They had no electricity, much less TVs and radios and refrigerators. They had some water buffalos and a handful of bicycles, but no farm equipment or motorized vehicles. The stream threading through the village had scant flow, but a man was pissing into it, and a little farther down, an old woman squatted over it. *Toilets*, he thought. *They need toilets*.

But before he spoke, he considered the broader implications of that. "They need a real water supply," he said. "They can't have plumbing if they can't control their water, and that little creek doesn't cut it."

"That little creek will get a hell of a lot bigger in a few weeks, when the monsoon season hits," Donovan said. "But you're right: Even when that happens, it's still untamed water. After a heavy rain, the creek might swell to the point that it's fucking deadly. The village will flood, and some of the floodwater will reach the fields, and the crops will grow. But they still don't have water on demand, at their houses. They don't have irrigated fields. They need wells and an irrigation system. What else?"

"Money," Lincoln said. "So they can buy stuff."

"There's not much to buy up here on the mountain," Donovan replied. "But yeah, wealth would help. They don't need much, but if they had some, they could build some infrastructure. They could buy goods so they didn't have to spend every minute of every day fetching water or food or making the things they need for bare subsistence."

"Right," Lincoln said.

"On the other hand, there's virtually no crime here. They die of natural causes, disease and so on, most of which we would treat in five minutes at a doctor's office. Sometimes there's a fight. Sometimes the Pathet Lao soldiers come in and kidnap their young women, or they get into a feud with another Hmong tribe, but among the villagers, things are generally peaceful. They have to work for their daily bread, but they don't starve to death. They're a little low on provisions at the moment, but when the rains come, their rice will come back, and they'll be flush for a while. Ideally, they'll set aside enough to get through the next dry season."

"So you're saying they don't really have it that bad."

Donovan sucked in smoke and blew it out in a long stream. "I'm saying they don't have it good or bad. It is what it is. If I had to pick between being a Hmong or being Laotian or South Vietnamese, I'd pick Hmong in a heartbeat. At least these guys are warriors. They're free, and they'll fight anybody who tries to take that freedom away. But a few small improvements could make a world of difference to the village. Some wells, some pipes, and lessons in basic hygiene. The Hmong believe that bathing washes away a soul. And that they each have thirty-two souls, so losing even one is a problem. If they could get past that and just fucking bathe more, half of their medical issues would vanish. If they had any clue about how to care for their teeth, that would help, too. And if they could establish steady supply of food and clean water, that would fix most of what's left, maybe more."

"So I'm, what? Supposed to be their social worker or their drill sergeant?"

"What's wrong with being both?" Donovan asked.

"I thought I was here to fight communists," Lincoln said.

"Don't get me wrong. I hate this social work, myself. But it's what the Agency bureaucrats want. Hearts and minds and all that happy horseshit. Trust me, you'll get to kill plenty of commies. But during the downtimes, you're going to get bored out of your fucking mind. You'll be glad for some projects."

Before being sent to Vietnam, Lincoln had thought that serving in the Army might involve a lot of digging ditches and filling them up again, but that hadn't been the case. Now it looked as if he might be digging ditches for real. Every day, the temperature seemed to grow hotter, the humidity more intense. It sapped a man's energy and left him dying for cold water.

But in Vang Khom, there would be no cold water. No air conditioning, or even the omnipresent ceiling fans of Saigon and Danang. And he would not only have to turn villagers into warriors, he would have to function as a handyman. Probably confessor and cop, too, if Donovan had his way.

He had agreed to the mission, though. He could claim ignorance of its true nature, but he doubted that Donovan would let him off the hook. They were here now, and they'd almost died trying to make it.

The whole task seemed suddenly hopeless. Impossible. These people wouldn't be dragged into the twentieth century; for the most part, they hadn't even reached the nineteenth. Even if they could be, how could he do it alone?

It was a little late for second thoughts, he decided. He was here. He was stuck.

He was all they had.

18

"So, I wanted to ask you something."

It was Saturday night, a week after Ellis had finally slept with the woman of his dreams, and they were sitting in the front seat of Lincoln's car at the park where it had happened, him wondering if a repeat was in the cards, her looking pensive. They'd just come from another rally, this one not interrupted by the boys in blue, which had seemed to disappoint Vanessa.

"Anything," he said, and thought he meant it.

"You said before that some of the cops were afraid of your family, and some worked for you?"

"More or less."

"So . . . what if you started bringing some of your people to the rallies?" She looked over at him, her eyes wide and brown and endlessly captivating. "Then we wouldn't have to worry about the cops breaking things up. You'd be like . . . I don't know . . . bodyguards or something. We'd be able to demonstrate in peace."

Ellis held up a hand.

"Whoa! Slow down there, beautiful. Only some cops—mostly in the Hollow. I told you, we got lucky at city hall. It's not like that's going to happen most of the places we demonstrate at."

The crestfallen look on her face made him feel like a piece of shit. He had to do something to erase it, but what? He grasped at the first straw that came to mind.

"Listen, I can try to get some of my friends to come along next time. Giorgi Marcano is an even bigger name with the cops than I am. They see him, they'll turn their cars around in a hurry, believe me."

If that was an exaggeration, it wasn't much of one. Sure, Giorgi was Sal Marcano's son and held all the privileges one would expect of the heir apparent to the city's Mafia. And Sal owned the NBPD, lock, stock, and barrel.

But Vanessa didn't need to know that. And Giorgi probably wouldn't agree to it, anyway. Social justice wasn't his scene. It was just something to say to wipe that disappointed expression off Vanessa's features and get her thinking more along the lines of kisses and caresses and other intimate things.

It seemed to work. Vanessa smiled gratefully at him and he opened his arms. She slid into them and rested her head on his shoulder and all was right with the world, at least for the moment.

• • •

Ellis wasn't even going to bring it up to his friends, but he knew he wouldn't be able to face Vanessa with a clean conscience if he didn't, so when he saw them the next evening, he casually broached the subject. They were drinking at Sammy's while the old man was out. Just beer, not 'shine—it was too early for that. Much to his surprise, both Giorgi and Danny Burke agreed. Nicki was all in until she found out there was a girl involved; then she accused Ellis of using the movement as a way to get laid and refused to have anything further to do with it. The others laughed as she stormed out, then went back to their bottles.

"Hell, if Ellis can find some girl at one of these rallies, anyone can, amiright, Danny?" Giorgi said, elbowing Ellis in the side as he clinked his beer bottle against Danny's and the two of them yukked it up.

"Look who's talking," Ellis countered. "Your face could make a brother wish he was at a Klan rally so it would be under a hood. Anyway, Vanessa's not just 'some girl.' She's more high-class than any chick either one of *you* could bag, that's for sure. Anyway, she just wants to keep the rally peaceful, so I told her I'd ask some of my friends to come and make sure the cops kept their distance."

"Jesus, Ellis, that's a tall order, even for me." Giorgi wasn't laughing anymore.

"I know. I tried to tell her that. So I figure you guys show up, I introduce you, you make a show of looking like peacekeepers or whatever.

Then if the cops do come and break things up, at least I can say we tried. I'll still come off looking like the good guy."

"And wind up getting laid, huh?" Danny added with a good-natured smirk, earning another laugh from Giorgi. "Looks like Nicki had the right idea."

"Nicki's just upset that Ellis's chick isn't looking in *her* direction," Giorgi scoffed dismissively, then looked back at Ellis. "When's the next rally? We'll be there, with a few of our closest buddies." He patted his waistline and the gun he had hidden underneath his vest for emphasis.

"*Merde*, Giorgi, you can't bring guns. Vanessa would freak! And you'll get everyone killed, besides."

Giorgi gave him a smug smile. Having decided to do it, Ellis knew, he was already plotting out how it would all go down. Giorgi liked to be seen as the mastermind, ready to take over from Sal whenever that became necessary. "What's the phrase they use these days—'peace through superior firepower'? You want to keep things running like clockwork, you gotta make sure the gears are greased. You can spread around some cash, but if we don't know who's gonna be assigned to work any given demonstration, we gotta go with the next best thing—cold, hard steel."

Ellis didn't have enough cash of his own to pay off a bunch of New Bordeaux cops. Giorgi knew that better than anyone, since Sammy kicked back a portion of his take from the lotteries to Sal. He wasn't sure whether Giorgi would kick in any of his own, but probably not. They were friends, but friendship had its limits, too.

And if the wrong cops saw them carrying, it was going to cause problems for more than just Ellis—it could undermine everything Vanessa and CORE were working so hard to achieve.

Maybe he should just forget the whole thing. Tell her his friends had said no. Risk that look of disappointment—surely it was better than the look he'd get if Giorgi and Danny showed up with guns tucked into their waistbands? Or, worse, wound up drawing them? He could see the headlines now: "Mob Boss's Son in Firefight at Civil Rights Rally." Sammy would kill them both. If Sal didn't get to them first. And even that paled in comparison to what Vanessa might do.

"You know, guys, maybe this isn't such a good idea. Maybe—"

"It's a *great* idea!" Danny interrupted, clapping him on the back. "It sounds like this girl's a keeper. What kind of friends would we be if we didn't do whatever we could to make sure you hold on to her? We'll be there—*sans* guns, right, Giorgi?"

Giorgi shrugged, held up both hands, palms out.

"Okay, okay. I know when I'm outnumbered. No guns. Doesn't mean I'm not bringing a knife or two, though . . ."

"*Giorgi . . .*"

"Kidding!"

The three of them laughed—Ellis, mostly in relief—and finished off their beers before arranging to meet at the next rally, in three weeks, back in Heritage Square. Giorgi promised to bring a little extra muscle along to make up for the lack of firepower, and Ellis gratefully accepted his offer. What had started out looking like a potential disaster might actually work out in his favor. He saw his friends to the door, then headed upstairs for the night, smiling and whistling the tune to "We Shall Overcome."

19

The next day, Lincoln got his first closeup look at the Plain of Jars.

The plain couldn't be seen from Vang Khom, which was situated on the southern slope of a mountainside, just below the crest. He and Donovan, accompanied by Koob and four of the other young men from the village, had to climb up that side, over the top, and then follow well-trod but often precarious footpaths down.

Lincoln figured he would learn everybody's name, eventually. So far, they mostly sounded like random combinations of letters; things that might have been formed by taking a child's ABC blocks and throwing them up in the air. Sometimes even when he thought he had one down, he couldn't manage to say it the way the Hmong did. Then again, they had a hard time with "Lincoln," though most could get "Clay" right.

Emerging from the jungle-choked slopes into the plain was like walking into a different world. "Plain" might have been a misnomer, since it implied flatlands, and this plain was a vast, hilly expanse. But instead of the lush palms and bamboo stands and other trees that seemed to carpet most of the country, here what trees existed were stunted. Mostly, as they headed into the plain itself, they walked through spiky elephant grass.

"Watch your step," Donovan warned Lincoln. "We've been bombing in here since '64. You'll see plenty of craters from the 250s that went off, but there are a lot that didn't. Every now and then, some random water buffalo or dog gets itself blown to bits. Sometimes people, too."

"Thanks for the tip," Lincoln said. "When do we see those jars?"

"Patience," Donovan said. "Once you do see 'em, you'll never forget 'em." He turned to Koob, who carried a bow, with a quiver of arrows strapped to his back. Only one of the Hmong had a gun, and it was a French bolt action from somewhere around the turn of the century. It was remarkably well preserved, and Lincoln guessed it could kill somebody, if it had to. He was almost disappointed that it didn't have the bayonet, because that would have been an impressive sight.

"Koob," Donovan said. "Have you seen VC around here? Or Pathet?"

"No Pathet here," Koob answered. "VC, yes. Some."

"Do they have a camp around here?"

"No camp. They just pass by."

"Okay. Everybody stay sharp."

He resumed his conversation with Lincoln. "It's worse in the bush, but even here, it's dangerous. The VC are so good at camouflage, even if you're looking for the fuckers—even if you know they're there—you can be standing two goddamn feet from them, looking right at them, and not even see them. They blend in, and they can stand so still they're just part of the scenery. Like I said, it's harder here, where there aren't as many trees and the grass is shorter. But even so, they could be down in a hole or trench, and unless you fell in, you wouldn't even see it."

"Or unless they shot you," Lincoln suggested.

"Or that. Still, I'd rather go up against a hundred VC than thirty NVA. Those guys are real soldiers. They've got fire discipline. They know their tactics. They follow orders. And they don't mind dying if they have to, but you can be damn sure they'll take some folks to hell with 'em when they go. I wouldn't count out the Pathet Lao, either—they've got some tough motherfuckers in that army."

Lincoln didn't really understand what the agent was driving at. He'd been exposed to NVA tactics before he even left the States, and again after he'd arrived in Vietnam. He'd seen plenty of combat. At Special Warfare School, he'd been trained in guerilla tactics, which included comprehensive analysis of North Vietnamese and VC combat styles.

"I've been in-country for a while now," Lincoln reminded him. "I've seen my share of action."

"I'm just saying, it'll be different here. You won't have a squad with you, much less a platoon. It'll be you and some half-naked tribesmen, and they're going to be looking to you for leadership."

There it is, Lincoln thought. *That's the difference.* In Vietnam, he had been a grunt, a soldier taking orders from officers—some of whom had more experience—or NCOs, all of whom did. He'd had to make decisions under fire, and some of those decisions had paid off. He hadn't been killed yet, so that was something.

But he hadn't had the responsibility for large numbers of men. And he certainly hadn't been responsible for taking and holding huge swaths of territory. The Agency didn't expect him and the men of Vang Khom to secure the entire Plain of Jars, but they did want this sector of it, including a crucial crossroads, to be won.

"You wouldn't have put me here if you didn't think I could do it," he said.

Donovan tossed him a quick grin. "That's right. I'm just reminding you that it's not gonna be a goddamn picnic. You'll earn your keep, Lincoln. And then some."

Cautiously, they climbed up a hill. Nearing the top, they crouched, then flattened themselves at the summit to look out over the territory below without being silhouetted against the sky.

And there were the jars.

Lincoln hadn't been sure what to expect, but the sight exceeded any expectations he could have had. There were hundreds of them, it seemed. It was hard to get a sense of scale from here, but they looked huge. He had thought they would be knee-high, maybe, but these clearly dwarfed that. They were thick-walled, formed from some dark stone. Most were open at the top, but some had discs over them that could only be lids.

"Fuckin' A," he said.

"I know," Donovan said. "I've seen them half a dozen times. It never fails to blow my mind."

"All clear," Koob announced. "No Pathet, no VC."

"You want a closer look?" Donovan asked.

"Hell yes. I'm not even sure what I'm lookin' at."

Donovan stood and motioned the others up. The agent lit another cigarette as he started down the slope toward the jars. "Nobody is," he said. "Scholars aren't certain who made them. They're estimated to be a couple thousand years old, maybe made by some indigenous people who lived here for a while, then moved on. I've poked around in a few, found bones and teeth—"

"Human ones?" Lincoln asked.

"Yeah. Some nonhuman, too. A rat falls inside one, it might have a hard time getting out. Sometimes birds fall in and die. Mostly there's rank water and spider webs, but every now and then you'll find most of a human skeleton. Others have human figurines inside, mostly shattered now, but some are whole."

As they drew closer, the ground dipped, then rose again, so they were walking up a gentle incline toward the first of the jars. Some were as tall as Lincoln, others shorter, but still four or five feet tall. Stone discs had fallen off many and lay crumbling on the ground, returning to the earth.

"So they'd toss someone in and cover them up?" he asked.

"Basically," Donovan replied. "Some people in Southeast Asia believe that after death, the soul moves through stages on its way to the afterlife. If those people were related to the ones who did this, it's thought that they might have put a body in one jar, let it decompose a bit, then moved it to another one for the next stage, and so on."

"That would mean a lot of lifting those lids off and putting them back on."

"Yeah. And they weigh a couple hundred pounds each. Whoever did this—and however they pulled it off—it wasn't something they did on the spur of the moment. It took hundreds of years, probably, and a lot of effort. Not something your present-day Laotian pansies could pull off."

Lincoln walked among the massive urns, speechless. He couldn't imagine the thinking that had gone into building them. And then, having done all that work, just walking away from it.

"There are other patches around the plain just like this," Donovan said. "Some have a few more jars, others less, but basically the same."

Koob said something in Hmong, and the other men broke into laughter. "What was that, Koob?" Donovan asked.

"These were not for the dead," Koob replied. "These were made to brew rice wine, for giants. Some people got drunk and fell inside."

"That's another theory," Donovan admitted. "I'm not so sure I buy that one."

Lincoln pressed his palms against the rough upper edge of one jar and hoisted himself up. In the late-morning sun, he could see nearly all the way to the bottom. Mostly it looked carpeted with wet leaves and the spider webs Donovan had mentioned.

But underneath that layer of leaves? Who knew? He could go in, dig around, but it would take years to check every jar, so why start?

The world was full of mysteries that would never be explained. New Bordeaux had its share, with its heritage of voodoo and piracy, its depthless swamps, its narrow alleys and old buildings.

This place, though, was unworldly on a whole different level. In New Bordeaux, at least, the history was mostly known, even if the bodies were never found. The Plain of Jars, with its origins lost in the mists of time, was something else entirely.

He was creeped out and fascinated at the same time.

As he lowered himself from the jar, he heard one of the Hmong men make a clicking sound with his tongue. An instant later, Donovan said, "Lincoln! Pathet!"

Lincoln dropped to the ground and scooped up his AR-30.

Donovan scrambled to his side. Crouching behind the jar, he jerked a thumb toward the northeast. "There's a road over there. Not much of one, but it stays drier than the main road during the rainy season. Sometimes it gets used when people want to avoid the Ho Chi Minh Trail."

Lincoln moved around the jar until he could see the road Donovan described. Sure enough, a couple dozen men in khaki uniforms and soft Mao hats walked up the road in a loose line, keeping enough distance from one another to make them hard targets. Most of them wore rubber sandals on their feet; Lincoln had heard that they made them from old tires.

He scooted back to Donovan. "Should we engage?"

"And get our asses handed to us?" Donovan asked. "We've got seven guys, four of whom have bows and arrows or spears. Two guns—"

"Three," Lincoln corrected. "Thong has his Enfield or whatever that is."

"His name's Thoj," Donovan said. "And it's a Lebel, from 1890 or some damn time. Ten-round magazine, but we'd be lucky if he has five rounds in it. It's not useless, but it's damn close. Look, Lincoln, you'll get your chance to take these guys on, but today's not that day. Unless they see us, we're not engaging."

"So we just hide up here and hope they pass us by?"

"We could hide inside the jars, but they'd see us getting in. You've heard about shooting fish in a barrel?"

Lincoln could see that the agent was right. He took another peek and determined that the Pathet men were much better armed, in addition to outnumbering them by more than four to one.

He was heartened, though, that they were just walking down the road, in plain sight, instead of somehow melting into the background. They were alert, and their column was tactically sound, but they could be easily seen. That meant they considered this area safe territory.

"Not safe for long," Lincoln promised in a whisper. "Not for too damn long."

20

The trek back to Vang Khom, uphill in the afternoon heat, was much more wearying than the downhill morning stroll. As they hiked, Lincoln tried to talk to Koob, to get his take on the villagers, their needs, and their capabilities.

"How many of you speak English?" Lincoln asked.

"Six, maybe seven," Koob replied. "More speak French. Eleven or twelve." He laughed and added, "We are not all barbarians, you know."

"I didn't think you were," Lincoln lied. From everything Donovan had told him, he had expected to find a tribe not far removed from the days of the cavemen. His first impressions hadn't done much to change that expectation. "Donovan said the village's most important need was plumbing, to control the water supply for health reasons, and to provide irrigation for your crops. Maybe he's right, but the way I see it, you're the ones who live here. What do you think you need the most?"

Koob was silent for a while, but Lincoln could see that his lips were pressed together, his brow wrinkled. Either he was thinking it over, or he was trying to understand what the hell Lincoln was saying. He wasn't used to speaking English to non–English speakers, and he wasn't sure how clear he had been.

For that matter, he wasn't used to thinking like a social worker. For most of his life, he would have been trying to figure out a score, a way he could make some money off these people. But they didn't have any of that, so racking his brain in that direction was pointless.

"A school," Koob said after a while.

Lincoln wasn't sure he'd heard him right. "School?"

"Yes, school. Teach the young ones about the world. We are not barbarians, but we are not educated."

"Look, I might not know much about plumbing, but I can put a couple of pipes together. I don't know the first thing about runnin' a school. My best subject was playin' hooky."

Koob gave him a blank face. That one had gone completely over the man's head, and it wasn't worth trying to explain, so Lincoln let it go.

Then Donovan ambled up beside them. "Did I hear something about a school?"

"Koob thinks the village needs one," Lincoln said.

"Yes," Koob agreed. "We need a school."

"That's a *great* idea," Donovan said.

Lincoln shot him a glare. He was trying to think of ways to talk Koob out of it, and now the agent was encouraging the man. "Like I was saying, I don't know anything about how to start a school, how to run one. We got no buildings, no bells, no hot lunches—"

"You're talking about a school *system*," Donovan said, cutting him off midstream. "They don't need any of that shit. They can meet anywhere. What they need is a teacher."

"Oh, great," Lincoln said, guessing Donovan would try to volunteer him for that role.

Donovan ignored him. "Koob, who's the smartest person in the village? The most educated?"

"My father is smart," Koob said. "But not educated."

"And he's a grumpy old fart," Donovan said. "Someone the kids would listen to, not be scared away by."

"Ahh," Koob said. "Shoua Na!"

"What's that mean?" Lincoln asked.

"Shoua Na is a person?" Donovan said. "I don't think I know him."

"She is a girl," Koob replied. "Her mother worked at a French plantation. Shoua Na was born there, went to school with French children."

"A girl?" Lincoln repeated. "How old is she?"

"Maybe eighteen, maybe twenty years."

"That sounds perfect," Donovan said. "How long has she been back in the village?"

"Two years. No, three. Three monsoons."

"Does she speak English?" Lincoln asked.

"English and French," Koob said.

"I guess we'll have to talk to her when we get back." Lincoln looked up the mountain. They'd made it only halfway to the top, and the day was getting hotter as they climbed. "*If* we get back."

• • •

Shoua Na was stunning.

They found her at the creek, skinning a feral pig. She had one hand inside the thing with a knife, slashing the tendons that held the skin to muscle. Both slender arms were slicked with blood up to the elbows, and there were splashes on her forehead, cheeks, and chest. She wore a short, pleated skirt and a wraparound bodice on top.

Somehow, none of that mattered to Lincoln.

There was something about her that separated her from the other village girls. He had noticed her earlier, but she'd been just one of the crowd, and he had been too busy trying to figure out who was who, and what his place in all this would be, to do more than that. Now, looking down at her working, he realized what the differences were.

Her skin tone was a little lighter than the average Hmong's and her hair maybe a shade lighter, with reddish highlights accentuated by the sun. Her cheekbones were higher and more pronounced; her figure more voluptuous; and her eyes were brown like theirs, but just the tiniest bit rounder. He guessed her mother had done more than work at a French plantation. If not through her mother, then there was some non-Hmong influence elsewhere in her lineage.

At a glance, she looked like the other young women of the tribe. Up close, though, she was just unique enough to stand out. Lincoln realized he was staring and quickly shifted his gaze to the pig.

As he usually did, Donovan took the conversational lead. "You're Shoua Na?" he asked in English.

She glanced down at the animal, then back at him, a little shyly. "Yes."

"And you speak English and French?"

"A little," she said.

"You've been to school? At a plantation, Koob said?"

"Yes."

"Can you read and write?"

"A little, in French. Not so much English. As Hmong we write our stories on fabric, with"—she paused as she grasped for the word, then brightened when she remembered it—"with embroidery."

"Shoua Na is a lovely name. What does it mean?"

She scrunched up her forehead and considered. "In English, it is 'sound of rain.'"

"I'm John Donovan. In English, that means 'sound of gunfire.' And this is Lincoln Clay."

"I know," she said. She flashed a smile then, and it changed her whole face. Lincoln thought she actually sparkled a little. "Everyone talks about you."

"I guess it is noteworthy for us to be here. You know Kaus invited us, right?"

"Yes." She finished what she was doing under the pig's skin and brought out her bloody hand and knife, then started to peel the flesh away. "You will help us fight the Pathet Lao."

"And the VC."

"And after, you will go away? Like most French did?"

"They fucking abandoned you," Donovan said. "Americans don't do that. When someone helps us, we help them."

"Good."

"Shoua Na, Koob said the village needs a school. We can help with that—I can get books sent here, pencils and paper to teach writing, whatever you need. But a school needs a teacher, and that's something we can't provide. Koob said you were the best choice for that."

She looked down at her work again, and Lincoln saw a flush around her neck and collarbone. "No, I cannot," she said.

"Why not?"

"I am just a girl."

"You're a lovely, intelligent, educated woman," Donovan countered. "You have more education than most of the people in the village, especially the children. Surely you could share what you've learned."

"Well . . . ," she began, then trailed off.

"Say you'll do it," Lincoln urged. "I'll do whatever I can to help you."

"You will?"

"I'm only here for a few days," Donovan told her. "But Lincoln's here to stay."

"For a while," Lincoln amended.

"Until the job is done," Donovan said.

"If you will help, Lincoln, then I will be the teacher."

"That would be great, Shoua Na." Lincoln garbled her name, and it came out sounding more like "Sho Nuff." With a chuckle, he said, "Maybe I can just call you Sho?"

"Sho," she repeated slowly, as if trying it on for size. "Sho. Yes, I like that. I will be Sho, the teacher."

Lincoln put a hand on the CIA agent's shoulder. "Okay, I got that part done, John," he said. "Now it's your turn. You better get busy diggin' some wells."

21

The next few days passed quicker than Lincoln had expected.

He and some of the men—under Donovan's supervision, if not with much of his participation—dug a well at the northern end of the village. They had to go deeper than either of them guessed, but Donovan insisted that because there was a spring feeding the little creek, there must be a water table somewhere. Eventually, they found it. They would need a pump to raise it to the surface and a network of pipes to bring it into the village and to the fields outside it, but it was progress just the same. Donovan radioed in a requisition for the necessary parts but could get no confirmation of when they might arrive.

When they weren't working on the well, they focused on the village's security. There was a good chance that once they started actively interfering with the communist presence on the Plain of Jars, they would make targets of themselves. With that in mind, Donovan directed some of the men to build a weapons shed to store guns and ammunition in. He wanted something stronger than the typical thatched bamboo, and he wanted a lock on the door, but that would have to wait; for now, they improvised a latch from scrap metal. He also set the women to making and filling sandbags, which the men positioned in strategic spots as bunkers. It wasn't much, but it was a start.

During the afternoons, the heat and ever-rising humidity conspired to bring most manual labor to a halt. Lincoln sat with Sho at those times, in the shade of the longhouse he had been given, and helped her plan out lessons for the school. Mostly, she planned and he tried to encourage her efforts, but once in a while he was able to reach back into his own childhood and suggest things the kids should learn. Already, most villagers were excited by the prospect, even if some of the children viewed it with trepidation.

Lincoln and Donovan held planning sessions in the evenings. Koob and the other English-speaking men translated, and all the able-bodied men and older boys of the village attended, at the insistence of Koob's father, Kaus. Donovan took a back seat at most of these, offering ideas as needed, but Lincoln took the lead. He told the villagers what they were up against, described communist battle tactics, and explained what their role in the fight would be. Some of the men had their own ideas, and some of those were more realistic than "Charge down from Vang Khom and crush them all like babies under our feet!" Lincoln kind of liked that one, but he wasn't sure how to implement it.

On Donovan's last night, he and Lincoln went for a walk, up toward the mountain's summit. There, looking out at the moonlit expanse of the Plain, the agent lit a smoke and gave one to Lincoln.

"I know you're nervous about tomorrow," he said.

"It ain't tomorrow got me worried," Lincoln said. "It's all the days after that."

"You'll be fine, Lincoln. You're a natural leader. You know what you're doing, and you know how to share it. These guys don't look like much now, but when you have the weapons and you can start drilling, they'll surprise you. They're dedicated. They want the communists dead as much as you and I do. If the dumb fucks at the Pentagon had any brains, they'd stop sending over green kids from Akron and Memphis and just enlist every Hmong and Montagnard and Bru they could find. Pay and equip them like American soldiers, turn them loose on the enemy. The war would be won inside of a year."

"You think so?"

"I know it. The trouble with the goddamn bureaucrats is they've never been in the shit. They don't know what war's really like. Especially this kind of war. The Pentagon brass are afraid to treat it like World War Two or Korea. There you had an army on this side of a line and an army on that side, with their tanks and howitzers and air support, and they fought until somebody lost. But they're not giving this war that kind of support.

"In this war, the North Vietnamese consider human life another replaceable asset, like bullets. They'll keep throwing men at us until they wear us down. When they're not amassing huge forces, they'll snipe at us from the goddamn jungles. If it were up to me, I'd just rain down bombs and blow the whole country to kingdom come. Trying to fight them on their own terms is insanity. It's never going to work here. But what you're doing—that can make a difference. A big difference."

Lincoln thought Donovan meant what he was saying. He wouldn't have brought Lincoln here just on a whim. He believed this kind of mission could have an important impact on the struggle to keep Laos—and by extension, the rest of the world—free. "I'll do what I can," he said.

"That's all anyone can ask, brother. Just do what you can."

• • •

As they all did these days, the morning dawned all at once. The evening before, the village had been abuzz with excitement over the coming weapons shipment, even if the enthusiasm had been tempered somewhat by the knowledge that Donovan was leaving. Lincoln was better known than he had been, but Donovan was still the one who had some history with Vang Khom—and the only one of the two who could get the Hmong names right, much less speak a word of their language.

Lincoln wasn't sure what to expect when he left the longhouse, but the village was noisier than usual. When he stepped outside, he saw why—just about everyone in the village was gathered in the central open space, and most wore their finest outfits. The women were in black skirts with colorful aprons, with bands of silver coins at their waists. They had elaborate headpieces and silver jewelry, and the embroidery Sho had mentioned was everywhere. Most of the men had on fancy black harem-style pants with shirts and vests, not quite as colorful as the women but impressive nonetheless.

Lincoln found Sho in the crowd, dressed in her own traditional finery. "You look great!" he said. "Is there a holiday today?"

She giggled. "Today the guns come, silly."

"You're all dressed up because an airplane's bringing some guns here?"

"We are Hmong, Lincoln. We like to dress up, to celebrate. Any reason will do. But also, because your guns will let us kill the Pathet." She took his arm in her hands, and the unexpected contact thrilled him more than the easier girls he'd had back home ever had. "And you will teach us to use them," she added. "Lincoln, you will be a great Hmong warrior."

"I don't know that I'll ever be Hmong," he said. "But I'll try to be a warrior."

The landing strip was a slash near the top of the mountain. It ran up a slope that must have been twenty degrees and was flat only at the end, making Lincoln wonder what kind of plane could possibly land there. Corbett had claimed his U-10 could touch down almost anywhere, but so far Lincoln had seen only one catch in the treetops and crash.

By eight in the morning, the crowd had gathered around the strip. Ordinarily, Lincoln would have expected to set out a flare or a smoke bomb to direct the pilot in, but in this case, he was pretty sure the morning sunlight reflecting off all that silver could be seen by satellites in orbit.

Donovan had his duffel packed, and he waited with the others, standing in the shade of some palms flanking the strip. "You'll be fine, Lincoln," he said. "You've got Koob to help you communicate. And Sho—she seems to like you."

"She's way too special for someone like me," Lincoln said.

"Don't sell yourself short, man."

"I just mean—I'm from the streets, right? An orphan and all."

"And she's the daughter of a Hmong village woman and who the fuck knows who? What's your goddamn point?"

"I don't know, she just seems like royalty to me."

"She's just a girl, Lincoln. You're a man. Whatever happens, happens. The Hmong have their own traditions, but they're not hung up on our western morality. Not when it comes to sex. Just, you know, be careful. You don't want to leave any little Lincolns running around."

Lincoln had not expected to have a sex life at all in Laos, unless it was with B-girls in Vientiane while on R&R. That had been one of the drawbacks of accepting this assignment. He had finally decided that serving in

Vietnam wasn't going to be any better in that respect—the A-team camp at Lang Vei wasn't exactly crawling with women.

"I'm not planning to," he assured the agent.

Before he could say any more, a cheer went up from the assembled villagers. In the distance, a silvery speck in the sky grew larger, transforming into an airplane with wings above the fuselage. Having been inside one, Lincoln recognized a U-10 Super Courier.

"It's Corbett!" he said.

"That'd be my guess," Donovan agreed. "He's not the only Air America pilot who flies those, but he did promise to come back."

The crowd parted as the U-10 rumbled in for its landing. It hit the slope and started up. For a moment, it seemed to pause, and Lincoln worried that it would roll down the mountain and into the trees below. But the pilot gunned the engines and muscled it to the flat stretch of runway on top.

There was another cheer from the assembled multitude, and as soon as the pilot killed the engine, the people rushed the airplane. They opened up the rear doors and started hauling out crates. Lincoln was surprised by how much the plane could carry with no passengers.

Corbett emerged with a huge grin on his face. He was wearing a different Hawaiian shirt and still had no survival vest on. "You're both still alive!" he said as he greeted Lincoln and Donovan.

"I was more worried about you," Lincoln said. "I've been on solid ground, but you've been in the air. Crashed number six yet?"

Corbett shot him a punch, stopping it well short of landing. "I don't know you well enough yet to let you insult my aeronautical skills like that," he said in mock anger. "Not till we've crashed together twice."

"Shouldn't take long, then," Donovan said.

"It will if I keep my feet planted," Lincoln said. "Which I intend to do."

"Hey, you went through jump school, right?" Corbett asked. "You should be used to jumping out of airplanes."

"I did, and it was the worst week of my life."

Donovan nodded toward the aircraft, where the Hmong men were mobbed around open crates, pulling out carbines and boxes of ammunition.

"Don't let them start shooting until we give the okay. They're not exactly in formation; someone's liable to get hurt."

"What else did you bring, Corbett?" Lincoln asked.

"I got a pump and parts for a windmill," the pilot answered. "Some piping. Grenades, a few mortars and rounds. Handguns and knives. Oh, and mail for you."

"For me?"

"There another Lincoln Clay on this hill?"

"I highly doubt it."

"You know anybody in New Bordeaux?"

"As a matter of fact, just about everybody I know's in New Bordeaux."

"Then I guess it's for you. I'll grab it."

While Corbett went back to the cockpit, Donovan took Lincoln's hand in his. "This mission is gonna be a giant pain in your ass, Lincoln," he said. "But I have no doubt you're the right man for it."

"When are you coming back?" Lincoln asked.

"I don't know. When I can. Mostly you'll see Corbett, though. You know how to radio for supplies. Keep your code pad handy. Oh, and don't forget to burn your mail after you've read it."

"I know. Nothing to ID me as an American."

"That's right. I wish I could send you some James Brown records, but they'd be a dead giveaway."

"Plus, no electricity."

"Well, you'll have a windmill, so that's a start. Stay frosty, big guy."

"You know it," Lincoln said to Donovan's back. The agent walked toward the U-10 and climbed into the passenger seat without looking back.

About the time he got there, Corbett returned with a courier envelope containing several letters. "I wish there was more," he said as he handed it to Lincoln.

"It's cool. Not many people gonna write to me anyway."

Corbett leaned in closer and pulled Lincoln to the side. "Listen, I didn't know you were from New Bordeaux. Lot of action there, huh?"

"What kind of action you mean?" Lincoln asked.

"You know. The kind where a guy can make a few bucks. Do I have to spell it out?"

"Look, man, if you got something you want to say, just say it. Just you and me here." He grinned; they were surrounded by almost three hundred other people. "I mean, that speak English."

"It's just, you know. Working for the government is great and all, but it doesn't pay that well."

"You're tellin' me," Lincoln said.

"So if there's a way to make a little something on the side, well, I'm always on the lookout, right?"

"You're gonna have to be more specific."

"Okay, here it is. You've got this village, and there are some poppies already growing over there." He pointed to a patch of dried-out vegetation at the edge of a field. "They're not much right now, but I just brought you irrigation equipment, right? Get some water going on those, and they'll take off. Soon as the rains come, they'll grow even faster. A few other villages are doing it. I sell their product for them, and they make good money off it. I get a little piece, too, so it's win-win."

"I bet you do."

"Well, I have the plane and I'm taking all the risks. But still, most of it goes back to the villages, so they can buy things they need."

"You're a real humanitarian, Corbett."

"I'm a businessman. I keep my suppliers happy, and I can keep my customers happy."

"Makes sense," Lincoln said. He was trying to think through the ramifications of what Corbett was saying. He was talking about growing opium poppies, which meant heroin. There was good money in it, but Sammy had always been strictly opposed to it. "That stuff would kill our own, if we let it in New Bordeaux," Sammy had told him once when he'd mentioned it. "I won't have anything to do with it. Not now, not ever."

"So what do you say?" Corbett asked. "You seem like a guy with a good head for business."

Lincoln interpreted that to mean, "You're black, so you're probably a criminal." But the fact was that he was a criminal, although that didn't necessarily follow from his skin color. If he had been adopted by a law-abiding family, he might be in some other line of work.

"I can see if I can get something going here," he said after considering the question. "But under one condition: None of it goes to New Bordeaux. You got to understand that. If any of your product goes into New Bordeaux, you and me will have a big problem."

"Hey, I dig it, man," Corbett said. "I just thought you might have a connection there who needed some product. But if you don't want it there, I'm with you. There's no shortage of markets for it. I can move it in Chicago, New York, Philly . . . lots of places. I'm not out to make enemies, right? I just want to make a few bucks and help my friends make a little, too."

"Long as that's understood," Lincoln said.

"Absolutely, man."

"Okay, then. I'll see what I can do, and I'll let you know next time you come this way."

"Works for me, man," Corbett said. "Time for me to get airborne. I'll see you on the next go-round, okay?"

"Fly straight," Lincoln said. He stood at the edge of the airstrip while Corbett had some of the Hmong men turn his U-10 around, then watched it taxi down the slope and launch into the air.

He guessed Corbett had recognized some outlaw spirit in him that the pilot shared. It was easier than thinking that Corbett assumed any black man was an automatic drug dealer. Then again, the worst bigots were usually the ones who swore up and down that they weren't prejudiced, and that description fit Corbett like a glove.

But he had worked with worse people back home. There was money in the drug trade, and no better place to grow opium. What the man said made financial sense. And considering the paucity of his corporal's paychecks— even with the CIA's bump—he was glad to get a little something going.

• • •

Later that day, after the men had put away their finery and donned their regular daily garb, Lincoln took them back out to the fields. He carried a carbine and an AR-30, with ammunition for each. Koob carried a grenade, which Lincoln had warned him to be very careful with.

At the edge of the field, a young palm grew. It had reached a height of about seven feet. After the demonstration Lincoln had in mind, it wouldn't grow any taller.

First, Lincoln held up the carbine, an Italian-made copy of an American M2, and slapped home a thirty-round banana clip. "This is a .30-caliber carbine," he said, then waited for Koob to translate. "This magazine holds thirty rounds, and the gun's an automatic rifle that fires at a rate of about 750 rounds per minute. It's a good defensive weapon, with a practical range of about two hundred yards."

He aimed at the palm tree and emptied about half of the magazine. The rounds shredded some of the leaves on the trees. As the echoes of the shots died off, Lincoln said, "If you want to be issued one of these, raise your hand." Unsure whether they knew the concept, Lincoln raised his to demonstrate.

Out of the sixty-some men gathered around, about thirty raised their hands in the air—some both hands, some waving them around enthusiastically. The carbine was shorter than a standard rifle and lighter, making them popular with the ARVN soldiers to whom they'd been issued.

"Okay," he said, setting down that weapon and raising the other gun, an Israeli version of Russia's AR-30. "This is an AR-30, also with a thirty-round magazine," he said. "And a similar rate of fire. It's a little heavier, though. Here's how it works." He set the weapon on full auto, aimed it at the same tree, and squeezed the trigger.

The rounds utterly denuded the tree, leaving only what remained of the trunk standing up like a half-sharpened pencil—or, he thought, a middle finger.

"Who wants one of these?" he asked.

Instantly, every hand in the crowd shot up.

"That's what I thought," he said. "You're lucky—we have enough for all of you. As we add more men, some will have to take the carbines. They're still good guns and will serve you well, but they're not quite as scary as the AR."

Koob translated, then turned to Lincoln to translate the responses. "They want guns that will kill the most Pathet the fastest."

"I've got one more thing to show them," Lincoln said. "Hand me that grenade."

Koob gingerly passed it over. Lincoln checked to make sure everyone was still well away from the palm, then said, "This is a hand grenade. Here's how it works."

He yanked the pin and tossed it at the tree. His aim was true; it hit the lower trunk and dropped to the base. Moments later, with a deafening blast and a roar of flame, the trunk was splintered, leaving only a smoldering, uprooted stub leaning at the edge of a crater.

Lincoln didn't even have to ask. Every hand in the crowd flew up again.

"You'll all learn how to use these," Lincoln promised. "You need to be careful—all these weapons can be dangerous if they're used incorrectly. If you're not careful you can accidentally kill your own people. But once you've been trained—and demonstrated to me that you can use them well—then we can go out together and use them against the Pathet Lao and the VC."

Koob translated, and a cheer went up from the throng. Lincoln looked at their faces—eager, enthusiastic, ready to go out and wreak havoc against their ancient enemies.

Many of them had no clue what war was really like. Raised up here in the highlands, they had largely been protected from the conflicts that had raged across Southeast Asia. They would find out soon enough. But first they had to learn which end of the guns to hold and which to point, how to aim them, how to control the weapons when they tried to kick out of their hands. They had to learn how long to hold a grenade before throwing it and how far to throw to keep themselves and their comrades safe.

It would be up to him to train them. And he had to do it fast, because the war wasn't getting any shorter. The children of Vang Khom would get their school, but for the men and older boys, Lincoln was the only teacher they'd get.

22

In the mornings, they worked on the windmill and laid the pipe. In the early afternoons, they drilled, practicing the combat techniques Lincoln taught them. After the day's worst heat, they had target practice.

After dinner, on the day the windmill first operated the pump and brought water from the well into the village and beyond, to the fields, Sho came to Lincoln's longhouse. He was sitting at a bamboo table the villagers had built for him, perusing aerial photos Donovan had sent, via Corbett, showing the location of a Pathet Lao base on the Plain. When she entered, he turned the photographs over on the table and rose.

"I want to thank you for everything you do for us," she said. "The school, the well. Teaching the men how to make war. You are like a . . . I do not know. Like a big man in our village. Like a hero."

Lincoln shook off the praise. "I'm just doin' my job, Sho."

"I think you do more than your job, Lincoln. Those poppies we grow—you said they will bring riches to Vang Khom. Is that also your job?"

Now that the irrigation system was up and running, the villagers could start cultivating the poppies. They would bring wealth, though Lincoln wasn't sure he wanted to explain to Sho what the end product would be.

"In a way," he said. "I'm supposed to help the village. Not just to fight the communists but to thrive, to be self-supporting after the war. So I'm doing what I can."

She crossed the space between them and put her hands on his arms. "Well, you are an . . . impressive man."

"Sho," he said, feeling like a fool before he even launched into his sentence. He'd had a feeling this moment would come, and he had gone back and forth on how to handle it. She was mixed race, like him. Like him, she had never known her own father. She was undeniably smart, and in their conversations she had come across as utterly genuine. "You're a beautiful woman. One of the most beautiful I've ever known. You're brilliant, and I think you're a great teacher for those kids, and . . . ah, goddammit, I don't even know what to say. I want you like I've never wanted anyone. But if you're gonna offer yourself to me, I want you to do it because you want me, not because you feel like it's your duty, or because you have to thank me on behalf of the village."

"You like me?" she asked, a smile forming on her lips. "You want me?"

"Hell yes, I like you. And yes, I want you."

"I want you, too," she said, running her hands up his biceps to his shoulders, then over his broad chest. "Not for the village, Lincoln. For me."

"You sure?"

"I am . . ." She struggled for the words, then continued. "I am more sure than I have ever been."

Pressing her hands flat against his chest, she leaned into him, tilting her face up toward his. Even on tiptoe, she couldn't reach his mouth, so he lowered his neck, wrapped his strong arms around her, and held her close. Her body was warm, supple, her curves as firm and comfortable against him as he had hoped they would be. He brought his lips to hers, tentatively at first, then, when she responded, hungrily. He felt her tongue slip between his teeth, and he thought, *She did learn some things from the French*. Then her hands were all over him, and his ran down her back to her taut behind, drawing her even closer, and he forgot to think at all; he only felt.

• • •

He didn't wake until the morning, when he realized she had slept in his arms all night, her head against his chest. The first thing he thought was that he wanted some more of what they'd shared the night before. The second thing—delayed considerably by the urgency of the first—was of the photographs he'd been studying before she had come to his door.

The Pathet Lao had built a base near the intersection he was supposed to be working to clear, and according to the pictures Donovan had sent, they were busy expanding it. Corbett had delivered the photos on the same trip that he brought the seeds, and with them, he'd had a message from Donovan.

"The head gook at the camp is this Laotian warlord named Colonel Phan Phasouk, Donovan says. He's trying to become a major player on the Pathet side, and he claims he's gonna secure the crossroads and hold it, no matter what. Donovan says you've gotta take out that camp, man. If you hit it hard before he can build it up more and bring in more men, maybe you can give old Phan second thoughts."

"My guys aren't combat-ready," Lincoln had protested.

"This ain't me talkin', brother. I'm just tellin' you what the man said. Donovan was pretty clear. He said the brass wants you to mount an op ASAP. The longer you wait, the stronger they'll get."

"Tell him—"

"You got a radio, man. You want to get crosswise with that cat, tell him yourself. I wouldn't want to be on Donovan's wrong side."

He had given Lincoln the photographs and pointed out what Donovan said looked like the weakest points in Phan's defenses. The trouble was, none of Phan's theoretical weaknesses were as meaningful as Lincoln's biggest weakness—a sixty-man platoon that had never seen combat. Most of the guys were getting pretty accurate with their weapons, on a shooting range. That was different than going up against people who were more experienced and trying to kill them. Lincoln had considered live-fire exercises, making the men crawl on their bellies while he fired over their heads, but had decided they weren't even ready for that yet. The last thing he wanted was for one of them to panic and get killed before they ever saw combat.

Now he was being told to rush them into harm's way. He had been studying the maps, trying to formulate a plan with some modicum of chance for success and the lowest likelihood of casualties. Then he had spent the night with the most exotic, fascinating woman he'd ever met, and it had all flown out of his head.

Sho got up and started putting her clothes back on. "I am late for school," she said. "The children will be wondering where I am." With a mischievous grin, she added, "The ones who don't already know."

"You think they know?"

"Nothing remains secret in a village this size, Lincoln. By now, all the adults know. Probably the children, too."

"They gonna be upset?"

"They will wonder why you waited so long. If they knew what I know about you now, they will be happy for me."

"What you know . . . ?"

"I already told you," she said. "You are a big man in village." She stepped close, gave his crotch a firm squeeze, kissed him, and headed out the door.

• • •

He returned to the photographs and the dilemma they represented: How to take out Phan's camp with the very limited, untested resources he had? He didn't even know how many soldiers Phan had. At this point, he was hesitant to go up against the handful they had seen by the jars that day, before Donovan's departure, and he had to assume that was only a small part of the Pathet force.

First things first. He knew some of the men were skilled hunters. That implied the traits of patience and stealth, two attributes useful in scouts. He went to find Koob, first looking at the man's house, then at the village center. Everywhere he went, people snickered or openly laughed, and a few made remarks he could only assume were obscene. Finally, one grabbed his right arm with his left hand, bent the right at the elbow, made a fist with that and held it up straight. That needed no translation; Sho had been right about word traveling fast.

He found Koob at the well, explaining windmill maintenance to a couple of the other men. When he saw Lincoln, a wicked grin crossed Koob's face. "You like her?" he asked.

"Who, Sho? Of course I do."

"Good. She is much liked here," Koob said. "Be good to her."

"I intend to, but I didn't come for romantic advice. I need a few scouts to go into the Plain of Jars with me. Who's the best hunter in the village?"

"My father is the best," Koob said.

"I mean of the young men. Ones who can make it down the mountain, spy on a Pathet camp, and come back up. Preferably at least one who can speak some English."

Koob pondered the question for a moment. "Burlee," he said. "And Pos. Burlee is the best hunter, but Pos knows English."

Lincoln knew the names and thought he knew which villagers they belonged to, but he wasn't sure enough to seek them out by himself. "Bring them to me," he said. "We have to leave this afternoon."

"Is it dangerous?" Koob asked.

"Very dangerous. We need to look at the camp so we can decide how to mount an attack. So this mission is dangerous, and after it's over, then it gets more dangerous."

"Good," Koob said. "The men have been waiting for danger. That means it's closer to time for killing some Pathet."

"Oh, we're close," Lincoln said. "We're so damn close I can just about taste it."

23

Burlee didn't live up to his name, or what it would have implied in English. He was one of the smallest men in the camp, barely five feet tall and likely could have held on to two ten-pound dumbbells and still weighed in at less than a hundred pounds. If not for the lines etched deeply in his face, Lincoln would have taken him for one of the teenagers. Pos was bigger, broad-shouldered and deep-chested for a Hmong.

They met Lincoln at his longhouse in the late afternoon. Pos brought a spear along, but Lincoln took it from his hand. "You won't need that," he said. He handed each man an AR-30 and a few magazines, then, realizing their loincloths and loose shirts didn't give them any way to carry those, found web belts and canteen covers for them in the supply stash he was building. He gave each man two canteens as well, for water, but the spare covers were for carrying magazines. Each would hold seven or eight, as opposed to the two or three that fit into a regulation ammo pouch. He helped Pos strap on a knife, but on Burlee it had to go around his calf because the strap wouldn't cinch tight enough to stay on the man's pencil-thin ankle.

Lincoln wore his usual black uniform, with two canteens of his own, a couple of spare covers for ammunition, and a few grenades. At his hip he had a .45, and his survival knife was strapped to his ankle. His pack held some containers of rice and a medical kit that he devoutly hoped he wouldn't need to use.

"We're going down into the Plain of Jars," he explained. "And we're going to go to a Pathet camp down there. Not to go in, just to watch. We'll try to count how many men they have and see what their defenses are like. Do you understand that?"

Burlee looked at him, stone-faced, but Pos nodded. "Yes. I will tell him." He spoke a quick sentence in Hmong that didn't sound like it could have conveyed half of what Lincoln had said. At the end of it, Burlee nodded. "He understands," Pos said.

"You sure you told him all that?"

"I told him everything."

"Okay. We're not going down to fight them, just to have a look. The main thing is not to let them see us. Got that?"

"We understand," Pos said.

Lincoln regarded Burlee, whose face remained blank. He wasn't sure the man had the slightest idea what was going on. He could have been a department store mannequin—the kind they used in the boys' section.

"All right," Lincoln said. "Let's go."

• • •

By the time they reached the Plain, the sun had set. The moon was just a sliver of fingernail overhead, with wispy clouds drifting across it now and again. Soon, clouds would be the norm and the monsoon rains would drench the land. Lincoln was glad that hadn't started yet. Coming down those switchback trails in the dark was bad enough; contending with them when they were slick with mud would be a nightmare.

He had studied the aerial photographs until he'd memorized every detail that could be discerned from them, and he had drawn his own rough sketch of the Plain and the junction of the two main roads that cut through it. The camp was a few kilometers beyond where the first set of jars stood. It had been carved from a thickly forested area, and the vegetation around it had been scalped to the dirt to provide clear lines of sight and fire from inside the fence. Lincoln had been able to discern bunkers at regular intervals along the wire and square objects that might have been guard towers at the northwest and southeast corners.

They cut through the field of jars, which looked even more strange and forbidding in the scant moonlight. He supposed New Bordeaux's traditions surrounding death, including funeral parades with brass bands and burial in aboveground sarcophagi, would seem just as odd to the people who had built these as the jars did to him.

A couple of clicks north of the jars, they descended a gentle slope into a scattering of bamboo and trees that quickly turned into full-blown jungle. Game trails cut through it, so machetes weren't required—which was good, because they hadn't brought any. Hacking one's way through jungle brush pretty much destroyed any hopes of a silent approach, and secrecy had to be the watchword on this mission.

He was beginning to wonder if he had misjudged the distance to the camp when he spotted lights twinkling through the screen of trees. For a few minutes, he was afraid they were just stars, but as they got closer, they resolved into the lights of the camp. Once he was certain about that, he stopped the others.

"There it is," he said. "We have to be really careful here. They probably don't have sentries outside the wire, but they might. And the clear space around the outside is probably mined, so we stay off it. We won't leave the cover of the forest."

"Okay," Pos said.

"Tell Burlee."

"He knows."

"How does he know? I just told you. Tell him."

Pos shrugged and said something to Burlee, who nodded once. Lincoln realized Pos might have just said, "Clay is one freaky-ass motherfucker," and Burlee's response would have been the same. He resolved to work harder to learn some Hmong, so he could know that his words were being appropriately translated or he could deliver instructions directly.

Not really satisfied but unsure what other options he had, Lincoln started toward the lights. He moved silently down the narrow game trail. Every dozen feet or so, he checked his six, because the Hmong men were so quiet he wasn't sure they were still back there. They were, though, and in that manner, they made their way to the tree line.

The camp looked much as he had pictured it from the photos. Two tall fences surrounded it, the outer one chain link topped with barbed wire and the inner one ten strands of closely spaced barbed wire. Concertina wire was stretched along the ground in between. Wooden watchtowers rose just above the eight-foot fence at the corners he had identified, and machine gun emplacements protected by sandbag walls were where he'd expected them. Maybe fifty yards of cleared ground separated the trees from the first fence.

He saw the glow of cigarettes in various places—in the towers, moving slowly between darkened buildings—but except for a few soldiers standing in the occasional pools of light, he couldn't see many actual people. Six long, one-story wooden buildings were probably barracks, which he judged could have held up to thirty people each, but from their position there was no way to know if they were even occupied, much less how sparsely or jam-packed.

Lincoln checked his watch. A little after three in the morning. If they waited for a couple of hours, the sun would rise and the camp would come to life. At that time, he could get a better idea of the force size.

Of course, the people in the camp would also have a much better chance of spotting them. That was a risk they'd have to take, he decided.

"We're gonna stay here until it's light," he told Pos. "So we can get a look at them when they wake up. Tell Burlee."

"I will tell him." Again, Pos said something unintelligible, and Burlee nodded once. He seemed to have no opinions of his own about anything. Lincoln could have told him—through Pos—that his legs were on fire, and he would have nodded once and stood there, stone-faced.

"Let's get off the trail," Lincoln said. "Into the trees. I don't want to be in the way if a tiger or something comes through, and I don't want to take the chance that the Pathet will look this way and see us in the open."

He waded into the brush, not moving far from the trail but looking for a place where he could sit or crouch and remain hidden from the camp. Pos jerked his head at Burlee, and both men did the same. Within moments, they were almost invisible, even though Lincoln had watched them go to positions almost right beside him. Asking for skilled hunters had been a good idea, he decided. He'd rather have had skilled soldiers, but none of the men really fit that description yet.

And yet, whoever was running this from the Pentagon wanted him to attack this heavily fortified camp with the resources he had. From here, that looked like a suicide mission.

Thirty minutes passed. The sky had not lightened even a smidgen. Lincoln rose, stretched his muscles. The other men stayed put, seemingly content to squat in the brush as long as necessary. As he sat down again, he brushed against a broad leaf, making a rustling noise.

In the same instant, a strange voice barked out a question. *Shit*, Lincoln thought, *there's a sentry after all*. He could glimpse the man now, his green fatigues largely camouflaging him, just feet away but illuminated by the light spilling from a window.

"Lao!" Pos whispered. "He ask who is there."

Two options—stay silent and risk the sentry raising an alarm, or take him out.

"Tell him ain't nobody here but us chickens."

"Hmnh?" Pos said.

"Just say it."

In English, Pos said, "Nobody here, only chickens."

Not exactly what Lincoln had been hoping for. He'd wanted a joking answer, in Lao, that might have made the sentry think he had just stumbled upon a fellow soldier.

Instead, at the sound of English, the man made a startled sound and started to swing his gun into position.

That wouldn't do. Lincoln burst from the brush, yanking his knife at the same time. He hit the sentry hard, before the man had a chance to fire, and drove him to the ground. There he slammed a knee into the sentry's gun hand, knocking the weapon from his grip. In the same instant, he slashed his knife across the man's throat. Blood spilled from the sudden gap, and bubbled up through lips that moved in soundless agony. Lincoln stayed on top of him until the light vanished from his eyes and his struggling stopped.

He climbed off the dead man and found Pos and Burlee right behind him. "Sentry," he said. "I couldn't let him alert the camp."

"A chicken is a bird, no?" Pos asked.

Lincoln chuckled. "Yes, a chicken is a bird. It was a joke. Not a very good one, I guess."

He watched the camp for a few minutes, to make sure that the commotion hadn't been observed. Still dark and quiet. But where there was one sentry, there might be more. And it was possible that he would be expected to report in at any time. They couldn't stay until daylight now. He started to say that, but then he had another idea.

He turned back to the dead man. Pos and Burlee had both crouched down beside him, huddled around his head. *Checking for life?* he wondered. "He's dead," he said. "Trust me."

Pos shifted position to show Lincoln what he was doing. His knife was out, and he held on to the sentry's ear with one hand and sawed at it with the other. "We know," he said.

"What the fuck are you doing?" Lincoln asked. He didn't need an answer. They were taking souvenirs. "Stop that!"

He was afraid his order might have been heard at the camp, so he lowered his voice and said it again. "We don't take parts off bodies," he said. "We're better than that."

Pos looked disappointed, but he told Burlee to stop and shoved his knife—still dripping blood and tissue—into its sheath.

He knew soldiers often took mementos of their dead. It happened back home, too. He remembered a job he had done with a couple of Sammy's men. It had been a vengeance killing of a very personal sort. Two men—unaffiliated with any of the city's mobs—had assaulted a parishioner at Saint Jerome's Catholic Church. Father James had mentioned the attack to Sammy, and Sammy had instructed Lincoln to find the culprits and punish them appropriately.

Lincoln had gone to question the victim, a woman he knew from church. She told him she had recognized one of the men, because he worked at a butcher shop she occasionally patronized. She had been there two days before the attack and wondered if she had been targeted because the man had seen her that day.

With the description she gave him, Lincoln easily identified the man as a redneck named Toussaint. He and the other men from the mob took turns watching the butcher shop and trailing Toussaint after he left work, until they were able to determine who his accomplice was. One night, three weeks after the attack, the two were drinking in Toussaint's ground-floor apartment. Lincoln and his friends knocked on the door, and when Toussaint opened it, beer in hand, they had barged in.

Lincoln had known from the moment Sammy gave the order that they were going to kill the men. It wasn't what Father James would have wanted, and Lincoln didn't know how the victim would feel about it. But while Lincoln had no compunctions about killing a couple of rapists and hadn't minded getting covered with blood in the process, he had drawn the line when one of the other men pulled down Toussaint's pants and started to slice off his dick.

"What the hell are you doing?" Lincoln had asked.

"I'm puttin' it in the other guy's mouth," the man answered. "It's kind of a lesson."

"Ain't nobody comin' in here but the police, and they don't need that lesson," Lincoln said. "We don't desecrate the bodies. Shit is wrong."

The man looked chagrined and left the body alone.

Now, Lincoln shook his head. "Shit is wrong," he said, knowing Pos wouldn't understand. He indicated the sentry. "Pick him up. We're taking him with us."

"We take?" Pos asked.

"That's right. You two carry him. Let's get out of here. Double-time."

The men did as they were told. Pos took the man's arms and Burlee his legs. His head lolled back, barely connected to his shoulders, and blood spilled onto the brush. There was no way the Pathet wouldn't find this spot, but Lincoln hoped the blood trail would peter out before too long. He started quickly back up the way they'd come, with the Hmong men and their grisly burden close behind.

He knew the communists would figure out that their sentry was dead. The blood and disturbed brush would paint a clear picture. What he hoped was that they wouldn't know whether what had killed him was human or animal, and the disappearance of his body would disturb them.

Lincoln was furious with himself. He had screwed up this simple mission, big time. He'd lost the opportunity to gauge the size of their force, and he might have inadvertently tipped them off that an enemy knew where their camp was. But maybe the nature of that enemy could be disguised. If he could unsettle the men in the camp, make them anxious, maybe lose sleep, that would work to his advantage. He knew from being inside American camps that when the enemy was out there in the bush and you never knew when the next mortar round might come in or the next sniper's bullet—or, worst of all, a sapper on a suicide mission inside the wire—then it messed with morale. Men suffering from nerves were less prepared and more apt to make fatal mistakes.

He couldn't outnumber the Pathet Lao, and his men were far less experienced at war. But if he could wage psychological warfare on his enemy, he might still have an advantage.

The sky was growing lighter by the time they reached the jars. He had been checking their back trail now and again, and the sentry's blood had indeed stopped marking the way. He found a jar that was taller than him, its walls almost seven feet high. "Toss him in there," he told Pos.

The man looked at the high walls of the jar, then at the body in his hands, then back at the high walls. "Give him to me," Lincoln said. Without waiting for an answer, he stepped forward and took the dead sentry from the others. Fortunately, although the man was dead weight, he was slight, and Lincoln was able to throw him up to the wall, then push him the rest of the way in.

The Pathet Lao soldiers might find him in there, but probably not soon or easily.

And even if they did, what would they think had left him there?

24

Without lugging the corpse, they moved faster, and they were back at Vang Khom by late morning. Sho was in the village center, surrounded by the children she was teaching. She shot him a smile as he passed by, and he heard some of the kids making what he assumed were smart-aleck cracks. He didn't stop, though. He was filthy, and one of the things he'd built with the materials Corbett had brought was a crude shower right behind his longhouse. It had no showerhead, but opening a valve released a cascade of water from a few inches above his head. He used it to rinse off, then shut it off to soap up, turning it on again to rinse that away. He had no privacy and often saw women—and sometimes men—staring at his naked body, but nudity wasn't a big deal to these people, so he got over any concerns about it quickly. They stared only out of curiosity, because a big, muscular black man was something different. If a moose wandered into their village, they would stare at that, too.

Feeling sufficiently clean, he lay down, still naked, on the framework of leaves that passed for his bed, for a quick nap. It still smelled like Sho there. He wanted her again. He knew if he called, she would come to him. But he had stressed the importance of the school having regular hours—he didn't know why schools were that way, but he assumed there was a good reason—so he didn't want to interrupt her lessons. Instead, he closed his eyes and tried to come up with a plan to attack the Pathet Lao camp that might have a ghost of a chance of succeeding.

$$\cdots$$

When he woke, she was there, sitting cross-legged beside the bed. He hadn't heard her come in. "How long you been there?" he asked.

"Little while," Sho said. "I wanted to touch you. But I did not want to wake you."

"It'd be okay," he said. "I never mind waking up when you're here."

He pushed himself upright and reached out to her, drawing her near. His lips found hers. He pulled her onto the bed, kissing her, running his hands through her thick, dark hair. Her weight on him was pleasant, right. After a few minutes she started kissing down his neck, down his chest, taking his nipples in her mouth and tonguing them. Then she continued, across the flat plane of his stomach, and lower. She took him into her mouth, and he lay back, enjoying her ministrations until he was spent.

After that, she wiped her mouth and peeled off her clothes, snuggling next to him. "When I saw you, you were covered in blood," she said. "I had to make sure it was not your blood."

"Not mine," he assured her. "I took a quick shower."

"I can wash your uniform for you."

"You don't need to do that."

"I don't need to. I want to. In a Hmong family, the woman does the wash."

Family? he thought. *Is that what we are now?*

It had taken him by surprise, but he found that he didn't mind the idea. "Well, it sure as hell needs washing."

"I will do it."

"Thank you, Sho."

"No need to thank me," she said. "I am your woman now. I do things for you."

"You don't have to—"

She pressed a finger against his lips. "I am your woman. I do these things. And other things. Better things."

"Better is right." He let his hands roam across her body, feeling her smooth flesh, cupping her full, heavy breasts, penetrating the moistness at her center. "Looks like it's my turn to do for you," he said.

"You do not have to—"

He silenced her by pressing his lips to hers, then said, "Not have to. Want to."

• • •

Later, he adjusted his map and drew a more detailed sketch of the camp as he remembered it. Using that he again studied the aerial shots, filling in the blurred and unclear parts in his mind's eye. Now he had a pretty good idea of how the camp was laid out. He thought he knew which building—a smallish, square one, facing onto an open space that probably served as a sort of parade ground—was the headquarters of Colonel Phan, the man Corbett had called a "warlord." He had seen that security was fairly lax, although that might change when the sentry's death was discovered. He still didn't know if the open area around the camp was mined, though. If he'd been running the camp, it would be. He would mine the perimeter of Vang Khom if he didn't think it would mostly blow up unsuspecting water buffalo and the occasional villager.

As he formulated a plan, he drilled the men with it in mind. They practiced advancing under fire, one man running forward while another man covered him, then switching off roles. He worked them on their bellies, and after a couple of days, he added live fire to those exercises to teach them to keep their heads down. He made them practice with mortars, RPGs, and hand grenades. He set up targets of varying sizes and had them shoot from different distances, until they had internalized how changing conditions could affect their accuracy.

Using bamboo and brush, he mocked up a model of the fence line they were going to attack and had them practice going through it. The model didn't much resemble real chain link fences and barbed wire, but he didn't have those materials to work with. He explained what it would look like, drew pictures of it for the men, and told them how to deal with it.

He also worked with them on the art of retreat. Green Berets were generally opposed to the whole concept of retreat, but he believed they would be vastly outnumbered and outgunned, and he didn't want his men running blindly into the jungle in that event. He noted spots along the trail down the mountain where they could rendezvous and stressed the necessity of breaking up into smaller units and spreading out if retreat was necessary, rather than everyone running the same way.

He still didn't think they were ready to go up against a force of that size—whatever the size of the camp's force might be—but then he got a coded message from Donovan. "Time to go," it said, and Lincoln knew what it meant.

As before, they left the village in late afternoon and reached the Plain under the cover of night. This time he had sixty-four men, not two. He didn't have uniforms for them, so they wore their own clothes, but each one had weapons and a pack and a belt for supplies. They were all being paid with Laotian currency Corbett brought with him on each trip, so even if they weren't combat-hardened, they were by definition professional soldiers. He had even made Koob a captain, recognizing that the rank carried no weight at the Pentagon.

They threaded their way between the jars. Lincoln's eyes were drawn to the one in which he'd deposited the sentry, but he wasn't about to climb up to see if the corpse was still there. Lincoln didn't want to see what condition it was in now, anyway.

He made them walk in single file down the game trail that led toward the camp. It had been less than two weeks since the scouting trip, and he knew the Pathet might have taken new precautions—stationing more sentries, even booby-trapping or mining the path. He doubted the latter, since if it was genuinely used by large mammals, as it appeared, they would be more likely than attacking soldiers to trigger the mines. But he knew it was possible, anyway, and he wanted to do everything he could to minimize the danger to his men.

As they neared the camp, Lincoln took the lead, watching the trail closely for trip wires or other defenses, and for signs of ambush. He saw none. Maybe the sentry's death had been ruled accidental or been ascribed to animals. There were plenty in the Laotian jungles that could carry off a grown man, after all.

Then again, maybe the camp's warlord felt the place was secure against an attack by poorly trained, untested troops. In that, he might be right.

They made it to the spot from which Lincoln, Pos, and Burlee had watched the other night. The camp was in clear view from here and looked much as it had on that occasion. Lights burned in some places, and cigarettes glowed in others. There were men in the towers and the bunkers, ready to fight.

From here, Lincoln's plan—such as it was—grew more complicated and relied heavily on the stealth of his Hmong soldiers. Moving unheard through the jungle was an almost impossible task. Instead, they would have to flank out at the jungle's edge—in full view of the men inside the wire, if they had spotlights to train across the open space. Lincoln was counting on the cover of darkness and the ability of the soldiers to move quickly and silently. He didn't want to attack from the south—the direction of the village—but from the east and west. The men on the east would engage first, with the rising sun at their backs. Once the camp's focus had shifted that way, then the main force would come in from the west. They would throw woven mats over the barbed wire to neutralize it, climb over the fence, and take the Pathet Lao by surprise.

Captain Koob was in charge of the squad coming in from the east, and Lincoln would command the western flank.

Using hand signals and as few words as possible, he communicated to Koob that they had arrived. Koob understood his job, and he led a group of ten men toward the camp's eastern end, traveling just at the fringe of the tree line. They ran quickly, at a crouch, and by the time they were twelve feet away, Lincoln couldn't hear them anymore, or see them through the pitch-dark night.

"Come on," he whispered to Pos, his second-in-command. He started toward the west, and the other thirty-plus men followed. Lincoln thought he sounded like a lumbering elephant, in his boots and fatigues, compared to the Hmong. Still, no alarm was raised in the camp.

A few minutes later, they were in position and ready. Nothing to do now except wait for the sun and hope for the best.

Instead, they would face the worst.

<u>25</u>

When the brilliant ball of the sun cleared the eastern horizon, Lincoln heard the first thump of a mortar, followed by a blast as the round landed inside the camp. Shouts came from the Pathet soldiers, and almost instantly, machine guns on the camp's eastern edge started to spray into the trees on that side.

Next came an RPG. Lincoln swelled with pride as it struck the watchtower at the southeast corner and exploded. Etched against the rising sun, he could see people inside it thrown out and falling to the ground. The drop wasn't far enough to be fatal, but the blast might have been, and it would make the men dizzy and disoriented, at any rate.

More mortar rounds landed inside the wire, including one that came very close to Colonel Phan's headquarters. By that time, the barracks had emptied out, and the vast majority of the soldiers were rushing to defend the eastern flank.

"Here we go," Lincoln said. There was still the watchtower at the northwest corner to contend with, and soldiers had spread out all around the camp, to defend against just this sort of attack. But he was sure those soldiers would be busy counting their blessings that they weren't under direct fire and, at the same time, looking over their shoulders to see what was happening behind them.

He gave the signal, and two soldiers with RPG launchers at the ready fired. The first grenade just missed the guard tower, sailing to a harmless landing outside the fence. The second also missed its target, a machine gun bunker at the center of the western flank, but landed close enough to spray the soldiers manning the gun with dirt and shrapnel.

With those as a cue, the soldiers who had carried a mortar into the woods behind Lincoln's team opened fire. One round hit a barracks, starting a fire. The next landed on the empty space in front of the colonel's headquarters. A third barely missed a bunker Lincoln had identified as a possible ammo dump.

Lincoln grabbed Pos and held his palms together, then, keeping them connected at the base, spread his fingertips about half an inch apart. "Get back to that mortar, fast," he said. "Have them shift their aim that much to the right of that last shot. No more, no less."

Pos scurried off to do his bidding. The men with the RPGs had reloaded and fired again. This time, one hit the roof of the watchtower and the second fell just in front of the machine gun.

There was no more time to waste. On the eastern side, the men were already advancing, as Lincoln had shown them, alternating running forward at a crouch and covering one another. His men had to get closer, too, because the big machine guns had more killing power at this range than his ARs did.

"Go!" he cried. He'd rehearsed this with the men enough that they understood the English word. "Go, go, go!" He charged with them, his AR-30 blasting toward the defenders amassing on the western line. After running for a stretch, he dropped to one knee and provided covering fire for the next man.

On his third sprint, Lincoln heard the mortar from behind him and watched the round arc into the camp. The angle looked good, the trajectory seemed right. He winced before it hit, because he knew what was coming. Then it dropped right into the bunker he had identified, and the ensuing explosion told him he'd judged correctly. A cheer went up from his men as the ammo dump blew.

He was pleased with that result, but he could already tell the battle was lost. The machine guns facing this way were still operable, and when his men tried to cross the open space, it became a killing field. He couldn't tell for sure what was happening to the east, but they had started with far fewer men. It seemed like more of the Pathet soldiers were shifting toward the west, to face the main attack force.

Desperate, he threw a grenade at the central machine gun. It landed a few feet short, rolled, and blew. It bought a moment's respite, but not enough. He had lost six men—no, seven—that he could count so far.

"Fall back!" he cried. He gave the hand signal he had taught them for retreat and shouted again, "Fall back!"

The men did, gladly. The machine guns at the camp didn't stop firing, and more of Lincoln's men fell before they were out of range in the woods. It looked like the men on the eastern flank had retreated at the same time, but he couldn't see them anymore.

He knew the Pathet would send out a force to mop up the retreating Hmong, so there was no time to lick their wounds and—as much as he hated to abandon them—no way to collect their dead. For that matter, some of those who had fallen might still be alive, just badly hurt. By retreating, he was leaving them to become prisoners of the Pathet Lao. Who knew what they might tell their captors, including the information that the attack had been led by an American?

He had no other option, though. His men weren't ready for that kind of assault. He'd tried to convey that, to Corbett and via coded message to Donovan. He had been ordered to make the attack anyway, and he had obeyed that order.

It had been a tragic mistake.

One he wouldn't make again.

From now on, he was in charge of this op, top to bottom. If Donovan didn't like it, he could replace Lincoln. But as long as Lincoln was in charge of the men of Vang Khom, he wouldn't risk their lives for nothing.

• • •

They rendezvoused at the far side of the jars, just below the path back up the mountain. The Pathet had given chase for a while, but their hearts weren't in it and it hadn't been long before they had given up.

Fourteen men were missing from the rendezvous. Lincoln was furious. Sixty men weren't an army. American soldiers had more experience and training coming out of boot camp than his Hmong had. And Lincoln was no drill sergeant. What had the brass been thinking when they'd ordered this? Donovan was right; the deskbound fuckers at the Pentagon had no idea what was what over here.

And why had he even agreed to the mission? He had known he was unqualified for this task and that his lack of qualification would get people killed. Now he would have to go back into Vang Khom and explain to wives and mothers and children and sisters that some of their men weren't coming back, and it was his fault.

The creed of the Special Forces said you never left your dead behind on the battlefield. Did it matter if the dead weren't Americans? He didn't see why it should—the Hmong men were fighting for the same cause—but trying to retrieve them would just have resulted in more dead.

He had been stupid, stupid, stupid. For the men who had willingly, bravely followed him to death's doorway, his stupidity had cost them their lives. He would never be able to lay down that burden.

Back in the village, only one woman—Burlee's mother—actually struck him. Two others spat on him. The rest wept in his arms, or turned their backs on him, or simply refused to react in his presence, though he later heard wailing from houses throughout the village. Kaus made the trip to Lincoln's longhouse to tell him what a mistake he had made in agreeing to let an American stay with them and lead them against the Pathet. Lincoln agreed with him, which only seemed to piss off the old chief even more.

Later, Sho held him and stroked his forehead and tried to tell him that it was all right, that the men had known they might die and had gone anyway, that ridding Laos of communists was worth any sacrifice. She had told him the Hmong were used to sacrifice. Her people had been driven from China, had migrated into Laos and Vietnam and Cambodia and Thailand in search of someplace they could live in peace, but always they found more strife, more conflict. They were not afraid of it. Their souls would be reincarnated.

None of it helped. Not one little bit.

26

As promised, Giorgi and Danny were at the Heritage Square rally three weeks later with a couple of their "closest buddies"—the flesh-and-blood kind, not the sort manufactured by Alfredsson, Ellis was relieved to see.

"Vanessa," he said, "these are the friends I was telling you about. This is Giorgi."

Giorgi took her outstretched hand and brought it up to his lips with a flourish.

"*Enchanté, mademoiselle,*" he said, bowing to her gallantly. Ellis had never wanted to punch him more than he did at that precise moment. Right in that smarmy Italian kisser.

"Yeah," Danny added, sticking out his own hand to shake hers. "What Giorgi said. Ellis said you were a knockout, but—no offense—I mean, it's *Ellis*, so . . . well, we didn't really believe him."

Danny he *did* punch, in the shoulder. Hard.

"Ow! Sorry, man, but it's the truth. You're not exactly Sidney Poitier."

"You're no Burt Reynolds, either," Ellis shot back.

"Well, *I* happen to think Ellis is *very* handsome," Vanessa interjected, obviously trying to head off the exchange of more blows, good-natured or not. "I really appreciate your coming today. I hope your presence won't be necessary, but it makes me feel that much safer knowing you're here."

"Anything for Handsome Ellis," Giorgi quipped, earning him a laugh from Danny and chuckles from the two other guys he'd brought along— Ellis thought their names were Mickey and Tonio; they'd pulled a job together a year or so back. Competent enough, if not too bright. Generally how Giorgi liked his muscle.

His women, too, now that Ellis thought about it. He supposed he shouldn't have bothered getting jealous when Giorgi started sweet-talking Vanessa. He didn't have anything to worry about—she was way too much woman for the likes of Giorgi Marcano.

Vanessa excused herself for a moment to go talk with some of the other rally organizers, and Ellis took the opportunity to reiterate the rules of the road.

"This is a strictly nonviolent event, got it? Cops show up and aren't immediately persuaded by your good looks and charm to turn tail and run, then you fade into the woodwork. *Comprend?*"

"Yeah, yeah, we got it, Saint Ellis. No guns, no knives, no fisticuffs. We're just here to look appropriately menacing. Jesus, you're gonna owe me about a case of beer for this. And maybe a hooker or two."

"I'm easy," Danny said. "Just let me borrow Lincoln's Drifter tonight. I got a hot date with Nicki's friend Wanda. You know, the one with the boobs?" Danny cupped his hands in front of his chest for emphasis.

"After the mess you left last time? *Hell* no. Lincoln would fucking kill me if he knew what you did in his back seat."

"But that's the beauty of it, Ellis," Danny said, coming over to him and slinging a brotherly arm over his shoulder. "He's in 'Nam, man. He never has to know."

"*I'll* know, so forget it," Ellis muttered, wrinkling his nose in disgust. Then Vanessa returned, and he and Danny had to shelve their discussion on the etiquette of getting laid in the back seat of a borrowed car for another time.

Ellis shrugged off Danny's arm and walked over to Vanessa, Giorgi trailing behind like an annoying younger sibling.

"Everything okay?" he asked, noting the frown lines marring her usually smooth forehead.

"Everything's fine. It's just . . . we have donors, people who give money to the cause privately, who don't want to be publicly associated with the movement because it would hurt their business or whatever. We don't necessarily like it—it's the worst kind of hypocrisy, if you think about it—but we're not really in a position to turn down their donations."

"Right . . . ," Ellis said, not really following her. Except that he kind of thought accepting the money made her group hypocrites, too.

"Well, sometimes the donors like to show up at rallies—usually in disguise, so if someone's snapping pictures for the local newspaper, they won't be recognized. They want to see how we're spending their money. And Oretha just told me we're going to have one here today. So it's more important than ever that your friends keep the police at bay if they show up. Because this guy donates a lot of money—not just to us but to a lot of civil rights organizations—and if this is anything other than a peaceful rally, he could up and pull his support. I don't know what we'd do then."

"Don't you worry your pretty little head about a thing," Giorgi interjected. "We'll make sure everything runs smooth as silk."

Ellis looked at him askance. There was something in the other man's tone he didn't like, some oily, car salesman bravado that he usually reserved for marks in a con. What the hell was he up to?

"I sure hope so. Because we're about to start."

• • •

". . . and so I say to you, my fellow citizens of New Bordeaux—do not go gentle into that good night! Rage, rage, against the dying of the light! It's not old age we're fighting against here—well, not most of y'all, anyway," the last speaker, a pastor from Vanessa's side of town, quipped, to much laughter. "It's stagnation. If we don't fight against the way things are, the way things have always been, then that's the way they will always continue to be. But just because something's always been done a certain way, that doesn't mean it's the best way, does it? We used to light our homes with candles and lanterns before we harnessed electricity. We used to travel by horse before Mr. Ford and his Model T. We found a better way to do things. It's called progress and enlightenment, and it makes the world better—for everyone."

Ellis had time to wonder if the candlemakers thought so, but then the pastor was talking again.

"It's the same thing with segregation. Just because it's always been done that way, here in the South, that doesn't mean it's the right way to do things.

Denying a man his basic rights is not the mark of an enlightened society, but of one still in the darkness. We need to shine the light on inequality and not let it die out until inequality itself has died. We need to rage against anything that would threaten to snuff out that light.

"And before y'all get excited about that word, 'rage'—I'm not advocating violence. That's not what we're about. We're about *action*!" The crowd erupted into cheers at that. As Ellis applauded along with everyone else, he scanned LaValle Street for any sign of cop cars. If the pastor would just hurry up his rhetoric, they might get out of this without any unpleasant encounters.

As the pastor droned on, Ellis became increasingly more nervous. He was the last speaker. The longer he talked, the more likely it was that their luck would run out.

And then it did.

Three black and whites pulled up to the curb, and a pair of cops climbed out of each one. One of them had a megaphone, and they all wore helmets and carried billy clubs. As they made their way to the sidewalk, Ellis saw Giorgi, Danny, and the others move to intercept them.

Damn it, what was he going to do? Fight them? It was four to six, so good odds, even with the cops being armed, but still—not exactly what Vanessa had wanted when she had asked them to keep the police at bay. Ellis started moving through the crowd toward them, not sure what he could do but knowing he'd better intervene before things got ugly.

But Giorgi and the others were closer, and Ellis could only watch as they approached the cops and Giorgi reached inside his white vest.

Shit! Had he brought a gun after all?

Ellis started to run.

But before he'd made it more than a few steps, he saw that it was a thick envelope Giorgi held, not a weapon, and the cop with the megaphone took it and stuffed it into his shirt after a few moments of conversation. Then he turned and motioned to the other cops and they all got back into their cars and drove away.

Ellis reached Giorgi and the others a few moments later, out of breath. "What did you just do?" he asked when he could talk.

"Got rid of the cops. Just like you and your little honey mama asked me to do."

"Jesus, Giorgi, I didn't think you'd have to bribe them. I thought your dad already owned them."

"He does, but that doesn't mean they wouldn't expect a little bonus at a time like this. Anyway, you wanted them gone, and they're gone. All copacetic, right?"

Ellis started to relax. His worst fear had been violence, some show of force, and that had not been realized. "Right," he said. "And thanks. I owe you one."

"You definitely do, buddy boy," Giorgi said with a grin, "and I'm here to tell you exactly how you can pay me back."

Ellis felt a chill at the words.

"And how is that?"

"Easy. I found out who their donor is. And you and Danny here are going to help me rob him."

• • •

They were back at Sammy's after the rally, sitting at the bar, talking about Giorgi's proposed heist.

". . . if you rob him, he won't have money to give to CORE or any of the other civil rights organizations. It's like you're taking money from them. From Vanessa!" Ellis protested, slamming his beer bottle down on the table.

"When *we* rob him, you mean," Giorgi replied. "And that's a real shame. But you should have thought about that before you asked me and Danny to play security at your little rally. I did you a solid—the Marcano family did, really—and now you owe us—"

"What's this?" Sammy's voice came from behind them. "Ellis owes Sal money? How did that come to be?"

Ellis heard the fury in his father's tone and winced before turning slowly to face him. "Not money," he said quickly. "A favor."

The frown didn't leave Sammy's face. "How?" he asked again.

"You know I've been seeing that girl with the civil rights group,

Vanessa? Well, Giorgi and Danny and some guys were protection at this latest rally. They wound up paying the cops off the keep them off our backs. It's not about the money, it's just that they did me a favor, and now I owe them one. It's no big deal. I'll handle it."

"You'll handle it?" Sammy scoffed. "You know in our business, owing a debt—even a favor—can *always* become a big deal. And for some girl? You don't have the sense God gave a goose!"

"I'll make this right, don't worry."

"You had better."

Sammy turned as if to go, then looked back at Ellis.

"You haven't even brought her around to meet me. Whatever happened to good manners? To respect?"

Then he walked back into the kitchen without another word.

Ellis stared after him. He'd pissed off the old man plenty of times, but he never wanted his father to think he didn't respect him. Disappointing him was almost worse than making him angry.

"You'll have your chance," he said softly, though he had no idea how he was going to make that happen, or if he even should. But that was a worry for another time. He turned and looked at Giorgi. "What did you have in mind?"

27

The only thing that would help was revenge.

Father James had always taught that vengeance belonged to the Lord, but Sammy Robinson hadn't seen it that way. "His vengeance takes too long," Sammy would say. "Time He gets around to it, the guy might not even remember what it was he'd done wrong. I say take your revenge now, while it's fresh, and let the Lord have His turn later on."

Colonel Phan ran that Pathet Lao camp, and he was the reason the Pentagon brass had wanted it attacked. If Lincoln could take out Phan, the whole thing would collapse. The rest of the men would probably go back north, where they belonged, and leave this end of the Plain of Jars to the Hmong.

Even if they didn't, it would be worth it. Killing Phan would avenge his men. It wouldn't bring them back, but it would enable Lincoln to live with their loss.

Maybe he wasn't officer material. Not cut out to lead an army. But if there was one thing Lincoln Clay was good at, it was killing people.

He would kill the warlord, and he would do it soon. While it was fresh.

• • •

Sho tried to talk him out of it. "It is too dangerous," she pleaded. "Lincoln, I love you. I cannot lose you. You will be killed!"

"What about the other men who were killed?" he asked. "Don't their women feel the same way about them?"

"I do not love them," she said. "I do not care about them, only you. If you die, too, how would that help them?"

He couldn't answer that one. There was no answer. His death would do nothing to make theirs more worthwhile.

But Phan's would. Without their leader, what would the Pathet soldiers do? Lincoln didn't think they had the unit integrity to hold together. They were followers. Killing Phan would not only be sweet revenge, it would bring about the outcome he had been hoping for in the first place.

"I have to do this, Sho," he said. "It's why I'm here.

She threw her arms around him and buried her face against his chest, sobbing. "You will not come back."

"I will," he assured her. "Don't worry about me. I'm good at this kind of thing."

Lincoln hoped he would come back, anyway. If he didn't, then killing Phan might not count for much after all. The men of Vang Khom weren't much of a fighting force yet with his help, but without him they were even less useful. He needed more time to work with them, to train them. And he needed to bring in men from other villages to forge a large enough unit to do the enemy real harm. That wouldn't happen until he could point to some successes with what he had.

The success of this mission required two elements—Colonel Phan's death and his own survival.

He wondered if he could pull it off.

• • •

Every day, the afternoons grew hotter and more humid, sapping Lincoln's energy. He kept working with the men—those who had survived and who still wanted anything to do with him—and his relationship with Sho deepened. But his focus was on his next self-assigned mission, and he spent hour after hour planning it out. The rainy season was coming, and cloudy nights would mean dark skies. Rain would also discourage the Pathet Lao soldiers from being outside, which would make it easier to reach Phan's quarters. He would wait until the first week of the monsoon—any longer and the soldiers would be accustomed to it, would know they had to make their rounds regardless, but during that first week, he hoped, they would resist.

Besides, Corbett was coming in a few days, and although Donovan had given him free rein to take action, Lincoln wanted an American to know where he was going and what he planned to do there.

On the morning Corbett flew in, Lincoln took him for a walk while the villagers unloaded the supplies he had brought and loaded up the poppies they had cultivated since his last visit. Lincoln didn't know where he had them processed, or really what was involved. He didn't ask, either—the less he knew about the heroin trade, the happier he was. Sammy would be pissed that he was even this involved. But a man had to have something going on, and Lincoln had decided to keep 10 percent of what the village made for himself. He didn't plan to go home from the war without something to show for it.

Usually, Corbett did most of the talking. He liked telling Lincoln stories of his Korean War days and offered combat and survival tips he'd learned over the years, which Lincoln enjoyed hearing. This time, however, Lincoln had an agenda in mind, and he got right to it.

"That plan to attack the Pathet base was a disaster," he said as they strolled into the village. "I told him they weren't ready, and I was right. I lost fourteen men."

"I heard," Corbett replied. "Sorry, man. I was hoping you were just underestimating their preparedness. I should've known better."

"It's cool," Lincoln said. "You weren't the one who ordered us in there; you were just passing on orders."

"I know, man, but I hate to see anyone fighting for our side die. There's already been too much of that, and it's not going to end any time soon."

"Well, my next trip down there won't wind up with any Hmong casualties."

Corbett raised an eyebrow. "How's that?"

"I'm going in solo. On a moonless night, in the first week of the rains. I'm going to take out Colonel Phan."

"That's a suicide mission," Corbett said, stopping in his tracks. "You can't do that."

"I can, and I will. I've got it all figured out. I just wanted to make sure someone knew where I was going and when. Just in case."

"Brother, Donovan's going to be pissed."

"He'll understand."

"He might understand. Don't mean he won't be pissed."

"When the unit falls apart without their leader, he'll come around."

"We'll see," Corbett said. "Why don't you let me say something to him first? He could order a bombing run, take the camp out that way."

"Why hasn't that already been done?" Lincoln asked. "Because we're still trying to pretend we're not in Laos? Anyway, they'd just rebuild, right? Human life doesn't mean shit to them—there are always more soldiers to throw at the problem. They need to be scared off. They need to know that it's never going to work, that no matter who's stationed there, or how many people, they'll never be allowed to control the Plain. That's what I'm going to do."

"Yeah, okay," Corbett said. He stood there, seemingly thinking over Lincoln's words. After a few moments, Lincoln realized he was looking at something. When he followed Corbett's gaze, he saw what it was.

"That's Mai," Lincoln said. "Sho's best friend. You want to meet her?"

"She's a beauty," Corbett said. He hadn't taken his eyes off the young lady. Lincoln understood why. She was, in his opinion, second only to Sho in looks among the villagers, a beautiful woman with a model's face and a pinup girl's physique. She was sitting in the shade of a hut, grinding flour, and her hands and the tip of her nose were dusted with it.

"She is," Lincoln agreed. "She's no seven-foot-tall blonde, but she's single. I can introduce you if you want."

"I'd like that."

Mai hadn't lost anyone in the attack on the camp, and because she was close to Sho, Lincoln had spent a lot of time with her. She knew some English, which would make it even easier, though Corbett's mastery of Hmong was pretty advanced. "Come on," he said.

As they approached, Mai put down the pestle she had been using and rose to her feet. "Hello, Clay," she said.

"Mai, I'd like you to meet Brad Corbett. Brad, this is Mai."

"I know who you are," Mai said. "You are the pilot."

"That's right," Corbett said. He offered his hand, and she dusted flour off hers and took it. "It's great to meet you."

"I'm gonna go check on Sho," Lincoln said. "I'll leave you two alone to get acquainted."

"Works for me," Corbett said. Mai was silent, which Lincoln took to be tacit approval of the idea.

Back in his longhouse, he told Sho what had happened.

"Corbett?" she asked, bursting into laughter. "With Mai?"

"I don't know if she'll go for it. He saw her and it was like he was in a trance."

"She's very pretty."

"Not as pretty as you," Lincoln said. "But yes, she is."

"More pretty than me," Sho said. "She's more Hmong."

Lincoln shook his head. "No. Nobody in the village is prettier than you. Nobody I've ever seen."

"Even in America?"

"Even there. There's nobody like you. And being more Hmong doesn't matter. My mother was black, but nobody really knows what my father was."

"Like me," she said.

"Like you. We are what we are, and that's cool with me."

"Sometimes it is lonely here," Sho said. "Everyone else has big families, but not me."

Lincoln took her in his arms. "You have me."

Suddenly sad, she dropped her gaze to the floor. "I wish you would never go away, Lincoln."

He knew what she meant. He had always told her that his time in Vang Khom was limited, that one day he would be rotated back to the world. He didn't intend to spend the rest of his life on a Laotian mountaintop. Some American soldiers would, he expected, take Vietnamese women home to marry, but he doubted that he could do the same, given the secret nature of his assignment here.

So his romance with Sho was always going to be short-term. He had made sure she knew that going in, and she had agreed to it. Now she was having regrets about it. So was he. But it couldn't be helped, so he pretended to misunderstand her concern.

"It's okay," he said. "I'll only be gone for a few hours. Overnight. I promise I'll come back to you, Sho. I will."

"That not what I—"

He cut her off. "Shh. Let's not talk about it, okay? Let's go see how Mai and Corbett are gettin' along."

She shook her head and lowered herself to her knees. "I have a better idea," she said. "Let's give them more time together . . ."

28

The rains came two days after Corbett's visit.

The first one was light. Refreshing, because it broke the humidity and freshened the air. Children played in it, laughing and splashing in newly formed pools. But the next day's rain was a heavier downpour, drenching everything, turning dirt paths into muddy bogs. Most of the villagers stayed inside, fighting leaky roofs and trying to stay out of it. The temperature plummeted, lightning split the skies, and the thunder seemed to rock the very foundations of the mountain itself.

Lincoln decided he would go the next night, unless the weather took a sudden turn.

By midafternoon on the third day, it was obvious that conditions were only getting worse. A ferocious wind blew through the village, tearing at bamboo walls and threatening to dislodge roofs. Ominous clouds piled on top of one another, forming thunderheads that looked tens of thousands of feet high. Major storms, including hurricanes, were regular visitors to New Bordeaux, and Lincoln had survived plenty, but this one looked sinister even to him. The rain started to patter against his walls and roof before he had even left.

All the better for his plan. He'd already loaded his pack with the things he thought he would need and set aside the equipment he wanted to take. Getting down the mountain would take longer than usual under these conditions, so he kissed Sho good-bye, ignoring her tears and her pleas for him to stay, and set off into the storm.

The route was treacherous. Trails that were easily passable in the dry season had turned to slippery muck. Water roared down the slopes, forcing Lincoln to struggle against powerful currents in formerly dry creek beds.

Visibility was down to feet, not miles. Within minutes of leaving the long-house, he was soaked to the skin, which made walking more difficult.

Several times he thought about turning around, going back to Sho's loving arms and a warm fire. To keep himself focused, he pictured the dead men of Vang Khom and pushed himself onward.

Night fell before he reached the jars, though the day had turned so dark it hardly seemed to matter. Lincoln was curious about the jars—had the past three days filled them to their brims? The sheer tonnage of falling water seemed adequate to the task. But he had someplace to be, and the dark was his ally; he had to get there in time to make use of it.

The jungle between the jars and the camp seemed louder than usual. Rain drummed against the canopy overhead, and every drop seemed to hit a thousand leaves as it trickled through and fell to the earth. The usual animal sounds were missing; either they had all taken cover, or they were just drowned out by the downpour.

He left the game trail before he reached the tree line, not trusting that the Pathet hadn't finally booby-trapped his path. From here, he would cut through the forest. The way would be harder and slower, but the storm's racket would dwarf any noise he might make.

Finally, scratched and bleeding in addition to being soaked and chafed, he arrived at the edge of the clearing. He had come in near the southwest corner, where there was no watchtower. It was also, conveniently enough, closest to the building where he believed the colonel dwelled. The journey had been long and difficult, but the truly hard work was about to begin.

Lincoln set his pack down on a fallen tree and retrieved a container from inside it. Corbett had given it to him, and it contained grease used on his plane. He set it aside and found a small paper bag—soaked through, now—that held a dozen steel S hooks. Those he set into the eyelets in his web belt. He had carried an AR-30 down from the village, along with plenty of ammo, but had not had to use it. He would leave it here—it would only get in his way. He would take two grenades, and he would take a suppressed Elling 9mm pistol. If having overwhelming firepower became an issue, he was dead anyway. He was counting on stealth, not lead, to get him in and out. He would adopt the techniques of North Vietnamese sapper attacks, which often became suicide missions, and use them against the Laotian allies of the NVA.

He peeled off his wet clothes, dipped his fingers into the grease, and spread it over his legs, torso, and arms. His dark brown skin would hide him, but the grease would help, and it would also keep him warm. Then, leaving on only his underwear and the knife at his ankle, he strapped the belt around his waist, with the holster, grenades, a single ammo pouch, and the S hooks attached.

Hoping the cleared area had not been mined since the earlier attack, he started across it. He doubted it—the attack had been repelled so easily, the Pathet Lao were probably convinced that their defenses were adequate. And the only real damage had been from mortar rounds and RPGs, which land mines wouldn't protect against.

Between the darkness and the rain, his skin color and the grease, he felt almost invisible as he approached the fence. He could see a handful of cigarettes glowing, but only in protected areas; under the roofs of the towers and close to the barracks buildings. He didn't think many soldiers, if any, were at the machine gun emplacements or patrolling the wire.

The fences were as he remembered them; chain link outer, concertina wire along the ground, then ten strands of barbed wire. He could cut through with wire cutters, but that would leave him exposed, and the clicks might give him away. Instead, he would use the mud and the grease to his advantage.

Reaching the first fence, Lincoln went down to his knees, then to his belly. The ground was soft enough here that he was able to scoop it away with his hands, making a space under the chain link. It would be a tight fit, but he thought he could do it. He pushed himself under, arms first, then turned his head and skidded through the cold mud on his left cheek. When it came to his shoulders, he had to burrow deeper, like an animal, but the grease helped him slide through. Once his shoulders were clear, the rest was easy; he had only to swim forward, using his arms to propel himself, until he scooted all the way through.

So far so good. The concertina wire would present problems of its own, but he had a plan for that, too. Approaching the first coil, he took the wire in between the razored barbs and lifted it to a coil above. Then he slipped an S hook from his belt—he had lost a couple going under the chain link, he realized, but he still had plenty—and hooked the two lengths together. He moved down and did the same a little more than a foot from the first, and it gave him the clearance he needed to slide beneath.

On the second row, he miscalculated slightly and felt the razor wire bite into his shoulder. It stung, but he knew the grease and mud would fill the wound and keep it from bleeding too much. He repeated the S hook trick on the third and last row, giving himself a little more space. When he had to beat a hasty retreat, knowing where the openings were would give him an advantage over the Pathet.

Finally, he was at the barbed wire. The strands were taut, but he was able to lift the first one to the height of the second and clip them together with the S hooks, then lift the second almost to the third and clip those. It didn't give him full clearance, but with the soupy mud beneath, it should be enough. A few more cuts were a small price to pay.

Another swim through the muck and he was inside the line. So far, no alarm had been raised. He couldn't see a soul from here and didn't think anyone could see him. Even if a light fell on him, all they would see was a pair of eyes floating through the night.

He stopped long enough to check the pistol, ensuring that its barrel hadn't become packed with mud. It was cleaner than he expected, so he shoved it back into the holster.

At a crouch, avoiding illuminated areas, he cut across the camp to what he had come to know as the parade ground, though it was too small for any real parades. It was an inky pool near the center of the camp. In it, he stopped once more, checked his pistol again, and unsnapped the strap around the knife's grip. The colonel's quarters sat dead ahead—or at least Lincoln thought that was where Phan could be found. If he was wrong about this, then the whole mission would be a pointless exercise, probably ending in his death.

But he didn't think he was. A Pathet Lao colonel—one known to the CIA as a "warlord"—wouldn't share lodging with his men. He would want his own place, and the smallish, square building was the only one that qualified. The fact that there was a jeep, or the Chinese equivalent thereof, backed up close to the door also testified to the occupant's importance.

Besides, he saw now, there was a guard outside it. He was huddled under an overhang that probably didn't keep him very dry. He was smoking, and he appeared to be shivering. Chances were, keeping an eye out for a single intruder was the furthest thing from his mind.

The guard wouldn't hold still. He was probably trying to stay warm while wearing a uniform every bit as oversaturated as Lincoln's had become. He was twitchy, turning this way and that, sucking down smoke and hoping for warmth, then lighting another cigarette from the tip of the first. Lincoln moved closer, slowly, staying low. If the man kept up the same pattern, Lincoln knew when his chance would come.

Luckily, the man was true to form. As his cigarette shortened to a stub, he reached under his slicker for another. At that moment, Lincoln charged across the remaining distance. The guard didn't react until one of Lincoln's feet hit a puddle and splashed, but his hands were inside his coat and he couldn't reach his gun. Lincoln leapt, got one hand on the guard's face and another around his chest, and snapped the man's neck. When Lincoln released him, he crumpled to the mud with a rustle that was barely audible over the rain pelting the roof.

Inside, there might be another guard and there might not. If the opportunity had presented itself for Lincoln to watch longer, he might have known for sure. But he hadn't had that opportunity, and at this point, it didn't matter that much. Guard or not, the man he wanted was inside there, so he was going in.

The door wasn't locked. It looked like there was light around its edges, which could be a problem; if he opened it and light spilled through, anyone watching in this direction might be alerted. On the other hand, for all he knew people came and went all night long, and no one would give it a second thought. Lincoln had no way to tell and no alternative way inside anyway.

He opened the door as narrowly as he could, slipped inside, and closed it again.

The inside was more luxurious than he had expected. At the front of the room was an ornate desk, with an inkwell and a blotter and a leather desk pad. Two straight-backed chairs for visitors stood close by.

Behind that was an Oriental trifold screen, and behind the screen, Lincoln found Colonel Phan. He was asleep in a bed covered in silken sheets and pillows and protected by mosquito netting bunched at a central point overhead. Not far from the bed, an electric floor lamp burned—the source of the light. Apparently the colonel was afraid of the dark.

As Lincoln crossed toward the bed, a floorboard squeaked under his foot. Phan stirred at the sound, then opened his eyes. After a beat, they flew open wide.

Lincoln almost felt sorry for the man. From what seemed to be a sound sleep, he had awakened and looked up to see a nightmare in black, coated in mud and grease, coming directly toward him with a pistol in his hand. The sight must have been horrifying, Lincoln thought.

Phan certainly found it that way. He pawed at the bed, trying to rise to a sitting position. He had a holstered pistol and a sword Lincoln knew as a *dha* on a low table next to the bed, and panicked, he flung a hand toward them. Instead of the gun, he found the *dha*, yanked it toward him, and drew it from its scabbard.

Lincoln didn't hesitate. He cleared the space in a single bound, landing on the bed and dropping the gun. One knee smashed into Phan's chest, forcing the wind from him so he couldn't cry out. Lincoln ripped the *dha* from the colonel's hand, spun it around, and drove its point up through Phan's throat and chin and out the top of his head.

It took only seconds for the colonel to die. Lincoln studied the scene, wanting to remember every detail. The sword's blade tapered away from the grip, then widened again near the end, where bits of gray matter dangled. The cylindrical grip and scabbard were both black lacquer, with rattan strips on the scabbard and a cord baldric to suspend it from a strap. The end of the grip was capped by a coin stamped "Indochine Francaise."

The colonel was a whip-thin man, the skin of his face so tight every detail of the musculature seemed to show through. His teeth were yellow and in terrible shape, and the thrust of the sword through his mouth had pinned it open to display them to their worst. Blood was running out the corners.

Lincoln hoped that, in his final seconds, Phan had known that it was an American who had come to snuff out his life.

Satisfied that he had accomplished what he came for, he retrieved his pistol and started toward the door.

He had taken two steps when it flew open wide.

29

Two dripping-wet Pathet soldiers stood in the doorway, as surprised to see Lincoln as he was to see them. He guessed they had spotted the body of the guard outside and come in to investigate. One had an AR in his hands, which he was swiveling around toward Lincoln. The other held his loosely, by the barrel, as if he hadn't expected to use it any time soon.

Lincoln raised the pistol and fired two shots. The first powered through the forehead of the soldier who was about to fire, before he could take aim. He dropped as if his legs had been knocked out from underneath him. The second shot caught the other man in the jaw, cutting bone and tendon so that his mouth fell open. Lincoln rushed him, snatching up his AR-30 and driving him against the doorjamb.

He stepped outside. Three more soldiers were running toward him, from different directions. One shouted something in Lao.

Lincoln wasn't getting out of the camp unscathed, it seemed. If he got out at all.

He reversed the borrowed AR, settled it against his shoulder, and fired three quick bursts. All three of the men went down. But the screams and the gunfire would bring more, in a hurry.

Now he had a choice to make and not much time to think it over. He could stick to his original plan and head out through the openings he had left in the fences. That would require him to dive down into the mud and squirm through, though, during which time he could be easily picked off.

The other choice was right outside—the colonel's jeep. Assuming it would always have its ignition key in place, Lincoln grabbed the second soldier's AR-30, ran to it, and jumped in behind the wheel, tossing both weapons onto the passenger seat. The key was there. He cranked it, slammed the gearshift into place, and stomped on the accelerator.

The rear tires spun, flinging mud against the colonel's wall.

Lincoln downshifted, tried again. It budged a little, then slipped back into the trench it was busy digging. Over the din of the racing engine and the spinning wheels, he heard the camp coming to life.

A shot *spanged* against the jeep. Lincoln hadn't seen the shooter, but he picked up one of the ARs and fired a burst toward where he thought it had come from. Then he hit the gas again, and the jeep's tires finally found purchase. The vehicle lurched forward.

Lincoln cranked the wheel, making a quick right. His rear tires fish-tailed into the parade ground, but the front ones caught again, and he headed, slipping and sliding, toward the main gate.

As he neared it, he snapped on the headlights. They showed him nine or ten Pathet soldiers in his path, all aiming weapons his way. His path was straight, and he needed momentum to break down the gate—they weren't likely to open it for him. He couldn't afford to backtrack, and he was being fired on from behind.

He took up both of the ARs he had acquired and held them tight against the wheel to keep the vehicle on a steady course. Smashing the pedal to the floor, he opened fire as he drove, twitching the guns this way and that to hit when the communists tried to dodge.

The plan almost backfired when he slammed into fallen bodies, but the mud was wet enough that the jeep's wheels pushed them down into it, giving him the traction he needed. His front end crashed into the gate, and it swung wide. He was out of the camp—but on a road that went only one way from here—toward the north.

And behind him, he heard the rumble of trucks in pursuit.

He kept the pedal floored. The road here was slick, just as muddy as it had been in the camp, and at every turn the jeep fishtailed and threatened to flip, or slide sideways off the road. He couldn't keep going north indefinitely, and he didn't know how long he could outrun his pursuers. He needed to get off this road, but there didn't appear to be any others. A few clicks ahead he would hit the intersection of routes 7 and 13—the one he was supposed to take, with his Hmong soldiers—but he didn't know if he could hold out that long, or where he would go when he got there.

No, he had to take decisive action sooner than that.

He rounded a curve. Now he had put at least three turns between him and those chasing him. Not much distance, but for the moment, at least, he couldn't see them, which meant they couldn't see him.

He slowed and turned the wheel, swerving left and then intentionally skidding the jeep off the right side of the road and letting it come to rest up against the trees, with the rear as far out into the road as he could get it. Then he jumped out, taking the ARs, careful to cross the road in the tire tracks he had left. He dashed into the trees on the left side, then hurried as fast as the brush would allow, back in the direction he had come. After a few paces, he crouched and waited.

He didn't have to wait long. The trucks came barreling around the last turn and hit the brakes when they saw the empty jeep partly blocking the way. The front truck shimmied all over the road, shuddering and threatening to spill over.

Lincoln helped the process along with one of his two hand grenades. He tugged the pin and tossed the grenade out to where the truck was about to wind up when it finished its slide, just feet behind the end of the jeep. The grenade exploded behind the left front tire, blowing the wheel off and throwing engine parts through the hood. The truck lurched sideways and came to a halt half off the road, leaning precariously.

Two more trucks had been roaring along behind it, too close to stop suddenly. The nearest slammed into the first truck, and the next driver, trying to avoid a pileup, cranked his wheel to the left. Bad idea. The truck's wheels locked and it slid toward the others, then tipped over and skidded into the first two, ramming them with its tires. Lincoln threw the second grenade into the mess of buckled steel and dizzy, disoriented Pathet Lao. The explosion touched off spilled gasoline, magnifying its effect.

Lincoln didn't stick around to enjoy the fruits of his labors. He stayed in the shelter of the trees until he had passed the third turn, then took to the muddy road. Progress was difficult there, but not quite as slow as it was in the jungle. He cut back into the trees to give the fort a wide berth, then circled around to where he had left his clothes and pack.

He was shivering uncontrollably, possibly close to hypothermic from the rain and mud and grease coating him. His eyes stung from the gun smoke, and his ears were ringing from the noise. But he had killed Colonel Phan and delivered a blow to the camp that would take a long time to recover from—if they ever could. He considered the mission a success. All he wanted now was to get home to Vang Khom, to shower, and to sit near a fire while Sho tended to his wounds.

He felt like he deserved a little TLC.

30

They were driving through River Row in Lincoln's Samson Drifter at night, following a van packed with furs and three men—a driver and two others on the bench seat beside him—who they had to assume were armed, given the value of their cargo.

"Not so close! They'll get suspicious!"

"Jesus, Giorgi, this isn't my first job!" Ellis snapped. "I know how to tail a mark!"

He wasn't happy about being here, in Lincoln's car, on Vito Scaletta's turf, about to rob a man who funneled a lot of money into his girlfriend's organization. But he had no choice. And he fucking *hated* not having choices.

"I'll follow just long enough to make sure they're taking the same route your guys say they always take, then we'll break off and get ahead of them so we can lie in wait at the ambush point." The van mostly stuck to well-traveled roads, but River Row was an industrial area, and the warehouse it was headed for was on the other side of a section full of vacant buildings; going around would have been safer but would also make the trip that much longer, and the driver apparently thought what he made up for in time was worth any associated risk.

Giorgi's scouts had identified a spot where they could cut off the van in between two of those vacant buildings, and a couple of guys already in position could push some dumpsters into place behind it to keep the driver from backing up. Then they could pick the truck's crew off at their leisure and take the van to one of Sal's warehouses. *Fastoche*.

It was a good plan, really; all the better for its simplicity. No one would get hurt, and the donor would never know what—or who—hit him.

But Ellis had pulled jobs with Giorgi and Danny before. He knew there would be some kind of hitch, no matter how good the plan. There was *always* a hitch.

"Okay, okay. I'll back off and let you do your thing. No need to be so damned touchy about it. We'll be done and back in time for Danny to get it on with Boobs McFarland."

"Fuck you, man, her name is Wanda. And we'd better be. She doesn't like it when I'm late, and it's not like a girl like her doesn't have other options."

"Hell, Danny, she's not the only one with options—you need to remember that. Besides, maybe you grab one of the furs out of the van to give her as a little present. She'll forgive you for being late then. Probably do you right then and there and not care who's watching."

As Giorgi and Danny tried to imagine exactly what lewd form Wanda's gratitude might take, Ellis peeled off down a side street and headed for the ambush spot. He was almost there when red lights flashed in front of him and a long, low whistle sounded.

"What the fuck?" Giorgi spluttered, taking notice of their surroundings for the first time in a while. "A fucking *train*? Why didn't we know there was going to be one at this time? Didn't you check the schedule once you saw our route was crossing railroad tracks?"

Ellis hadn't, but he wasn't about to admit that to Giorgi.

"These damn things are never on time; you should know that. Maybe it will be a short one."

It wasn't. Ellis counted 212 cars plus a caboose before the arm went up and they were able to cross the tracks.

"Well, hell. Now what?"

"Now we have to do this the hard way," Giorgi replied. "We go to the warehouse."

• • •

Ellis hadn't memorized the route to the warehouse, since he was never supposed to have to drive that far, so Giorgi guided him there. This area was better lit than where they'd planned to hit the van, but the warehouses on either side appeared to be closed up tight; apparently they didn't get shipments at night.

The van was sitting in the loading bay in front of an open roll-up door. One man stood sentry beside it; there was no sign of the others.

"That's a huge building," Danny said, "Is the whole thing full of furs? Maybe we're thinking too small."

Giorgi shrugged. "Fucker owns a whole chain of stores across the southeast, so maybe it is all his. You've probably seen his ads—calls himself the King of Furs, wears a half-assed crown. But if he just rents space here, then the rest of the place will be locked up, maybe have its own guards. That's why I didn't want to come here." He glared at Ellis when he said it; Ellis took the glare and gave it right back. No way was Giorgi laying this one at *his* feet. *He* hadn't wanted to do the job at all.

"Well, come on. Let's get this over with."

Giorgi led the way toward the open bay, keeping to the shadows along the side of the building. They approached from the side of the van opposite from where the guard was. It meant he couldn't see them coming, but they also couldn't see what he was doing; he could appear from either the front or the back of the van at any moment. And they still didn't know where the other guy was. Or the driver, for that matter.

They reached the van without incident. Giorgi motioned for Danny to go around to the far side and take care of the man there while he and Ellis crept into the warehouse through the open roll-up door.

As Giorgi had predicted, the place was sectioned off with chain link fencing, behind which were a myriad of different goods: furniture, bicycles, elaborate lace-and-pearl wedding dresses in plastic. Some partitions held boxes stacked almost to the ceiling with no hint of what might be inside them. Ellis thought there must be millions of dollars worth of merchandise in here. Maybe Danny was right; maybe they were thinking too small.

Then they heard footsteps, and he and Giorgi had to hurry and duck around a corner of the dress-filled partition as the other man came strolling into view.

"Yo, Jimmy! I did something to my back—it's killing me. Why don't you take this next load?" There was a pause. "Jimmy?"

Ellis and Giorgi looked at each other. Ellis nodded, and they moved out from behind their white frilly cover. As they crept up on the man, he drew his gun, his attention focused on the open bay door and the nonresponsive Jimmy.

Giorgi had his own gun out, pointed straight at the guy's aching back, but Ellis drew his own gun, reversed it, and, moving in before Giorgi could take the shot, he slammed the butt of the weapon down against the base of the man's skull. The man dropped to the concrete with a grunt and a clatter, his own gun falling from his hand. Ellis knelt and picked it up, stuffing it into the waistband of his pants as he stood. When he straightened, Giorgi was glaring at him again.

"What? We don't know who else is in here. You fire that thing, you could bring a whole mess of shit down on our heads. You can shoot him later, once we know the building's clear, if you really want to. It's not like he saw our faces or anything."

Giorgi glared for a moment longer, then shrugged, either unable or unwilling to refute Ellis's argument. Danny appeared from around the van, having used Ellis's tactic on the other guard.

"Let's get these guys tied up before they come to," Giorgi said to Danny.

"What's he going to do?" Danny protested, pointing at Ellis.

"I'm going to make sure there aren't any other guards in the building," Ellis answered. "So your skinny white ass doesn't wind up in prison. Then I'll bring back the other furs Jimmy's buddy here already unloaded, so we can get the hell out of here."

Ellis gave a mock salute with the barrel of his gun and headed down the aisle the second guard had come from. He didn't really expect there to be any other guards; he just hadn't wanted Giorgi to kill the man for no reason. Vanessa was really starting to rub off on him. There were ways to get what you wanted that didn't include violence or even the threat of it. There were ways to live that didn't include crime, he was learning. Maybe not for him—he was who he was, after all, and that would never change. But Vanessa was having an effect on him that he hadn't anticipated, making him look at the world in a different way.

He rounded a corner to find one of the chain link sections open and the furs hanging inside, along with hundreds more. For a moment, he considered taking more than what had been in the shipment—it would give him seed money to start a new life with Vanessa—but he quickly discarded the idea. If she knew where the money had come from, she wouldn't want to have anything to do with him. Instead, he loaded the new furs in their clean plastic onto the empty cart sitting next to the rack and left the furs in the dusty plastic hang where they were. He was just placing the last of the furs on the cart when a voice called out from behind him.

"Who the hell are you? Where's Chuck?"

Ellis spun, gun raised, to see a heavyset white man in a dark suit standing in the doorway to the partition. His complexion paled when he caught sight of Ellis's weapon.

"I'm the guy who's robbing you. You're the guy who's going to come over here, kneel down, shut up, and stay out of my way, if he knows what's good for him."

The man moved into the partition where Ellis motioned and knelt on the concrete floor.

"Take your tie off."

"Are you going to kill me?"

"Pretty sure I told you to shut up."

The man closed his mouth and took off his tie. Ellis moved over to him and grabbed the tie, intending to truss him up like a Christmas turkey.

"I know you," the man said suddenly, his eyes narrowing. Ellis felt his heart jump into his throat. "You were with that Marcano boy. I see him all the time at the yacht club, holding court with his slimeball of a father. Never thought I'd see him doing something decent at a civil rights rally. Now I know why he was there."

"Listen, you need to forget you ever saw him, or me, or anyone associated with the Marcanos at that rally," Ellis warned. "Say you never got a good look at the robbers, collect your insurance money, and be done with it."

"Yeah? Why should I do that?"

Just then, a shot rang out in the distance, followed by two others. Then there was an ominous silence.

"Because that's what the Marcanos do to people who recognize them when they don't want to be recognized. That was Jimmy, and Chuck, and the driver of the van, and if you don't want it to be you, too, you'd best do as I say."

Ellis knew he should just shoot the guy, but he couldn't. Visions of Vanessa kept swimming in front of his eyes, an accusing and disappointed look on her face. What would she think of him if he did something like that? Killed a man in cold blood when he didn't have to? When he could scare him into not talking?

He heard footsteps approaching.

"Look, I'm really sorry about this," he said, then took the butt of his gun and slammed it into the man's temple. The donor slid soundlessly to the floor. Ellis quickly tied him up, then searched him for keys.

Giorgi and Danny rounded the corner. Giorgi's gun was still in his hand, and Ellis figured he was the one who'd done the shooting.

"Who's that?" Giorgi asked.

"The owner," Ellis said, grabbing the cart and pulling it out of the partition. He pulled the door shut behind him.

"Wait, what about all those?" Danny demanded.

"No time. Owner said something about a second shipment. We need to get out of here before it arrives."

He padlocked the door, then went through the keys until he found the right one and locked the donor in with his furs. Then he turned and threw the key ring as far into the warehouse as he could.

"All right, let's blow this joint."

They hurried through the warehouse and loaded up the van with the rest of the furs, Ellis trying hard not to look at the three dead bodies lined up just inside the roll-up door as they did. Then Danny climbed behind the wheel of the van and took off, and Giorgi and Ellis closed the loading bay door, headed for Lincoln's car, and did the same.

"You done good tonight, Ellis." Giorgi said, holding out his hand. "I don't know how I could've done it without you."

"You couldn't, Giorgi."

"We're even, man. More than."

Ellis took his hand and shook it.

No, Giorgi, he thought. *We're not even. Not even close. You're my friend, and you'll run the Marcano family someday, but you'll always be a trigger-happy punk. I'm going to be someone who deserves to be with Vanessa.*

31

The next time Corbett came to Vang Khom, Donovan was with him. Corbett left the unloading to the Hmong and disappeared into Mai's hut almost immediately. Donovan chatted with the Hmong for a while—they were still delighted to see their old friend—then took Lincoln aside. They strolled up to the well and stood by the windmill, which creaked in a breeze blowing in from the east. It had been a couple of days since the last rain, but clouds were piling up again.

"You caused a hell of a stir at the Pathet base," he said.

Lincoln couldn't tell from his casual tone how he felt about that. One of the problems of conversing with a trained spy, he thought—they kept their emotions close to the vest.

"Yeah, I guess."

"Killed the colonel and a bunch of other soldiers, too."

"That's the idea, isn't it?"

"Yes and no," Donovan said. "Killing the Pathet Lao is okay. But we need to have plausible deniability. If a bunch of rogue Hmong attack a Pathet base, that's not a problem. Everybody knows they're in Laos. They're entitled to be. And if they have problems with the commies, nobody's going to bat an eye."

"There's a 'but' coming, isn't there?" Lincoln asked.

"A big one. But, when someone assassinates a Pathet Lao colonel with his own sword, then kills nineteen more men escaping the scene like Steve McQueen or John Wayne or some goddamn thing . . . well, let's just say that doesn't come across as indigenous resistance."

"Nineteen?"

"But who's counting? Point is, the Pathet Lao complained."

"I thought this was a war," Lincoln said.

"It's a war, but there are fucking rules. And we're breaking them just by having you here. Calling attention to that fact is a problem."

"I didn't mean to cause any problems, Donovan. I just wanted to kill that warlord motherfucker. And I did."

"That you did. If I wasn't here to give you a hard time about it, I'd say well done. You really kicked some ass, and I just wish I could have gone in with you. But I have to give you a hard time, because the Laotian government gave Washington a hard time and threatened to invoke the Geneva Accords, so Washington came down on me. The Laotians don't believe one man caused all that chaos, and they want assurances that we don't have ground troops in Laos."

"Which I'm sure Washington gave them, right?"

"Of course."

Lincoln was proud to have been the source of so much consternation and surprised to be getting heat from Donovan over it. "Do we know what the fallout's going to be? Are they abandoning the base?"

"No such goddamn luck," Donovan said. "They're expanding it."

"Expanding?" Lincoln wasn't sure he'd heard right.

"You can't just take out their head guy and expect them to fold their tents and go home, buddy. There are plenty of officers in the north who are champing at the bit to come south and prove their mettle. And the Plain is too important to them to walk away—just like it is for us. Since they suffered such an ass kicking, they're going to put a bigger force down here—maybe double the size. The new man in charge is named Colonel Sun Youa. He's an old war-horse, a real hard-ass." Donovan reached into a side pocket of his blazer and pulled out an envelope. "Here are the latest aerial shots, showing the expansion."

Lincoln sank to the ground, sitting with his back against the windmill frame, and thumbed through the photographs. "Jesus," he said. "I fucked up, didn't I?"

"Lincoln, you killed Phan. You gave them a hell of a scare. If it was just me, I'd be clapping you on the back and pinning a fucking medal on you.

I kind of thought I'd get here and you'd tell me it was you and ten other Green Berets. You've vastly exceeded my expectations."

Donovan paused while he took a cigarette from a pack and lit it, offering one to Lincoln at the same time. Lincoln declined with a shake of his head.

"But it's not just me," Donovan said. "We have to take a big-picture view. That attack the Pentagon ordered didn't do the trick, and your escapade made the situation worse, not better. Now we need to think strategically."

"Meaning what?" Lincoln asked.

"Like I said, you can't just take out the top guy. There's always another one waiting in the wings. If you want to put an operation out of business permanently, you have to work from the bottom up. You go after the infrastructure that props up the top guy. You dismantle his operation piece by fucking piece. Then, when he's got no support structure, no one to stand with him, you go after him. Do that, and the Pathet will decide it's too much trouble to keep a post down here. At least, that's the theory. I'm not big on theories, but killing a bunch of fucking reds sounds like a good idea anyway."

Lincoln shook his head. *With my sixty men?* he thought. *Less than, now.*

But he didn't say it. His mind was already racing ahead, trying to puzzle out how he could accomplish the task Donovan had set before him. He would need help, but he could get that.

Suddenly, it didn't all seem so hopeless after all.

• • •

When Corbett came out of Mai's, he was wearing a broad smile. Donovan was off visiting with Kaus, and Lincoln was sitting in the shade outside his longhouse, looking at the new aerial photos and mentally plotting out his next moves. Corbett beckoned him with a twitch of his hand, and Lincoln tossed the pictures inside, then joined him for the walk back to his U-10.

"Have a good time?" Lincoln asked.

"She's a great girl, man," Corbett said. "I'm starting to see the appeal of Oriental chicks, after all. She said you and Sho have been going at it pretty hot and heavy, too."

"I've never known anyone like her," Lincoln admitted. "She's beautiful and sexy, but it's way more than that. Deeper. It's like she can see my soul, and it don't turn her off. That's something I've never experienced."

"I guess we're both lucky guys, then. Thanks for introducing me to Mai."

He started for the plane, then stopped again, touched Lincoln's arm. "You probably think I'm a hypocrite, being with her after all that racist shit I said before. I just want you to know I didn't mean none of that. I say that crap when I'm flying, to distract my passengers, is all."

Lincoln just nodded.

"We cool?" Corbett asked. He seemed like he genuinely wanted Lincoln's affirmation.

"Sure," Lincoln said. "We're cool."

At the plane, Corbett opened the copilot's side door and removed a leather satchel from under the seat. He unbuckled it and took out two small bundles wrapped in brown paper bags and taped closed. "Here's the payroll for your men," he said, handing over the first one. The second was thicker, and he held on to it for a moment longer before putting it in Lincoln's hands. "And here's your cut of the product sales. It's great stuff. Super strong, which is what the customers like."

"Isn't that more dangerous to use?" Lincoln asked.

"That's not our concern, man. Junkies gonna use what they use. Important thing is we get our piece of the action."

"I guess." Lincoln wasn't opposed to drug use, but he couldn't help wondering what Sammy's reaction would be if he knew Lincoln was making money from the sale of heroin.

"Pleasure doing business," Corbett said. He looked around the airstrip. "You know where Donovan is?"

"Last I saw, he was in with the chief. Want me to check?"

"Yeah. We need to get going. Miles to go before we sleep, and all that." He held out a meaty paw, and Lincoln shook it. "Catch you next time, brother."

32

After the plane had left, Lincoln called Koob into his longhouse. Together, they sat at Lincoln's table and divided up the cash Corbett had brought. The payroll went to the men in equal increments, with a bonus to Koob for his leadership and translating effort. The poppy money went into a general village fund, managed by Koob and Kaus. Lincoln had already skimmed off his slice.

"You've gotta send runners to all the nearby villages," Lincoln said after the finances had been dealt with. "We need more men, and fast."

He spread the photographs Donovan had given him on the table. "The Pathet Lao are expanding their base and bringing in more soldiers. We need to take the place apart at the seams, and we need more people to do it. We have more guns on the way. Mortars, grenades, RPGs, all the supplies we need. Tell whoever you send to show some cash around, let the people in the other villages see that soldiers are well paid here."

"I'll send them," Koob promised. "Tomorrow, they'll go." He grinned. "Soon we will have too many soldiers!"

"No such thing," Lincoln said. "We'll have to clear some more forest and get busy building new houses for them. Your village is about to get a lot bigger, Koob. And a lot richer, too."

...

Koob was as good as his word. The next day, men from Vang Khom spread out to all the villages in the area, to bring the good word about opportunities to oppose the communists and earn some money. Those left behind started cutting down trees and burning brush to make room for the expected newcomers. The smoke roiled into the village, stinging Lincoln's eyes. The smell was everywhere, inescapable. Lincoln knew it could be seen for miles and miles and wondered if it would attract the attention of the Pathet Lao. So far, his attacks against their outpost had not drawn retaliatory action against the village. But it was the nearest Hmong village to the camp, and he fully expected that they would show up sometime. If they did, it would be a slaughter. The village was barely defended, and its warriors were few. Now that they were bulking up their force—if indeed, people came from other villages to join their effort—maybe he would be able to improve Vang Khom's defensive capabilities. Fences and land mines at the very least would be a good idea.

Lincoln wasn't sure what to expect of the Hmong men's recruitment efforts. He braced himself for disappointment, and during the hours he spent alone, studying the Pathet Lao camp's expansion and trying to formulate a battle plan, he included in his calculations ways to attack effectively with no more men than he already had.

So several days later, when the first man returned—accompanied by more than a dozen hardy males from another village—he was surprised. Another pair came back to Vang Khom leading a procession of thirty or more men, plus the women and children who had chosen to accompany them. When everyone Koob had sent away had arrived, Lincoln's army had grown to almost two hundred. Over the next several days, more trickled in, having heard about the effort.

He radioed Donovan a coded message with the news and added a plea for increased payroll. The response came almost immediately: a promise that Corbett would bring more cash on his next visit.

Like it or not, Lincoln was forced back into the roles of trainer and drill sergeant. This time, he had more than a handful of men to instruct. But he had advantages he had lacked earlier, including a rudimentary knowledge of the Hmong language—which Sho was helping him with every night—and more Hmong who knew some English.

As before, he instructed them in basic military discipline and standard hygiene, as well as in the arts of war. He drilled them mercilessly on the weapons available to them. He taught them hand-to-hand combat techniques and made them practice on one another until every one of them was bruised and bloody. He was less hesitant than he had been earlier about using live fire in his drills. He knew now that they would face enemy soldiers who would try to kill them and would succeed in some cases. They had to be prepared for a battle in which real bullets, and worse, would be coming at them.

He identified some of the men who had a modicum of medical training, or what passed for it in remote mountain villages, and showed them what modern techniques he knew. He taught them what everything in his medical kits was for and how to use it. He would need more medics than just himself, with a force of this size.

He let up on the drilling only when he and Pos made another scouting trip to see the camp's expansion in person. They took a different route in and discovered that the original game trail had been mined and the sides of the trail booby-trapped in other ways.

The post was indeed larger than before. The fence came all the way out to where the original cleared ground had been, and many more structures—mostly barracks, Lincoln judged, but also storehouses and bunkers and an enlarged motor pool area—were tucked behind it. A large swath had been scraped clean all the way around it, killing ground for the towers—one at every corner, now—and weapons emplacements positioned throughout. The road leading up to the camp had been paved, as had roadways inside.

It would take a massive frontal assault to dislodge the Pathet Lao now. Even with his new recruits, Lincoln didn't have a force nearly large enough for that.

But since his last conversation with Donovan, that wasn't the plan. A victory that couldn't be won with direct action could still be achieved in other ways. For his attack on Colonel Phan, Lincoln had adapted techniques common to North Vietnamese sappers, and they had worked. Guerilla tactics were the only ones that had a chance of success in an unconventional war like this one. And there was no law saying the communists were the only ones allowed to practice those.

Seeing the camp in person, in its expanded size and scope, gave Lincoln the inspiration he needed. He knew what to do now. He just needed to be able to pull it off.

33

When Lincoln got back to Vang Khom, he saw that at least a hundred more Hmong had arrived, including more women and children. The village was bursting at the seams, and it couldn't continue. He pushed through the crowd to find Koob holding court outside his house.

"We have to talk," Lincoln said. "Inside."

Koob apologized to the assembled crowd and waved Lincoln in ahead of him.

"There is a problem?" he asked when they were both seated on the floor.

"The problem is we're getting too many people here." Lincoln waved a hand toward the throng outside. "I wanted more soldiers. We've got those, but we're also getting their wives and their kids. Others are coming without their families, which means their own villages are underdefended. We've got to find some kind of balance."

Koob gave him a blank look. "Too many people," Lincoln simplified. "Maybe I was wrong about how to recruit more."

"You are not wrong," Koob said. "You are very smart."

"Not always," Lincoln admitted. "I don't want all the other villages around to be emptied out while we take in everyone here. We need to send some of these people home."

"But you said—"

Lincoln raised a hand, cutting him off. "I know what I said before. Trouble is, we can't support that many people. And we need the Hmong scattered around, so they can attack the Pathet from different sides." He didn't want to give voice to his biggest fear—that with the regional Hmong population concentrated only in Vang Khom, the Pathet Lao could wipe them all out with a single assault on the village. "You should pick some of the men who have been well trained and know their stuff. Have them train the newcomers, then send them back to their own villages. We can give them radios so all the villages can stay in contact easily, so we can coordinate our efforts. But they can't all just live here."

"I will tell them to go," Koob said. He looked disheartened.

Lincoln didn't want him to think the problem was his fault. "I should have been more careful, should have set some limits," he said. "I didn't think so many people would come."

"Everyone wants to kill the Pathet and VC," Koob explained.

"That's a good thing. Everyone will get their chance. They just can't all stay here, and I don't have time to do all the training and drilling for everyone. Set up some training schedules for the new ones, and get the ones who've already been trained back to their own villages."

"I will," Koob said.

• • •

That crisis handled, at least for the moment, Lincoln headed back to his own longhouse. Sho was inside. Some familiar bundles rested on the table, along with a few letters.

She jumped up at his approach, wrapping her arms around him and kissing him. After a few minutes, they pulled out the chairs and sat. "Corbett came," she said. "To see Mai. He brought money and mail."

"I see that. I didn't know he was coming. I guess now that he has Mai, we'll be seein' more of him."

"Mai loves him. She says he is not always nice to her, but she loves him."

"Not nice, how?"

"He argues. Sometimes he slaps her. But then he makes love to her."

"She shouldn't put up with that." Even as he said it, he knew that plenty of women back home put up with such treatment, too. Corbett hadn't learned that behavior in Southeast Asia, he was sure.

"She loves him."

"Maybe she should have better taste in men."

"I am glad you're not like that, Lincoln," Sho said.

"Never."

He flipped through the mail. There was a letter from Sammy, one from Father James, and one from Ellis. He opened Ellis's first. It was brief and to the point. When he was finished, he set it aside. "Speaking of love, Ellis has himself a girlfriend."

"Your brother?"

"That's right. He's dating some girl named Vanessa. Sounds like she's a keeper."

Sho's eyes welled with moisture. "What's wrong, baby?" Lincoln asked her.

"I wish you would never go. I want to be a 'keeper,' too."

"Sho, you are a keeper. You're like nobody I've ever known."

"But you will still go. Leave me here."

He had been giving a lot of thought to that issue lately. Maybe there was a way to take her home. First he would have to smuggle her into Vietnam, but Corbett would be willing to do that. Then he'd have to falsify a Vietnamese identity for her and marry her there. Donovan could help with that.

He couldn't marry a Hmong woman from Laos, a country he had never officially set foot in. But a Vietnamese wife? Nobody could stop him from bringing her back to the world with him.

"There might be a way you can come with me," he said. "I have to think on it some more, and talk to some people. I think we can work it out, maybe."

"Really?" Sho asked, bolting from her chair and falling to her knees beside him. The tears continued to slide down her perfect cheeks, but judging by the beam she projected, they had changed to tears of happiness. "Oh, Lincoln, you would really take me with you?"

"I said maybe. I'll try. It's complicated, but I think there's a good shot."

"That makes me so glad," she said, laying her head on his thigh and snaking her arms around his waist. "So, so glad."

"Me, too," he said. He stroked her hair, dried her cheek with his thumb. "Whatever makes you happy makes me happy."

34

"What's eating you, boy?"

Ellis looked up from his untouched beer to see Father James sliding into the seat next to him at the bar. Sammy's was empty at this time of day, and he was surprised to see the priest here.

At his look, Father James chuckled.

"Don't worry, I'm not turning into a lush. Came by to drop off a letter for Lincoln. Plain to see something's troublin' you. Want to talk about it? It's kind of what I do for a livin'."

Something *was* troubling him. He'd been mulling it over ever since the fur job, worrying on it like a dog with a thick bone, and he'd finally come to a decision.

He wanted out. He wanted to be free of the Black Mob, free to live a normal life, one that didn't revolve around guns and heists and fast girls and faster cars. He wanted what the Average Joe had and thought wasn't enough.

Above all, he wanted Vanessa.

And he had no idea how to tell Sammy.

"Have you ever made a decision you knew your folks wouldn't be happy about, even though you knew it was the right path for you?"

Father James laughed.

"I've had troubles of my own, with the law and otherwise, Ellis. Yes, I've got a pretty good idea what that's like."

"How did you tell them?"

Father James grew serious.

"Just what is it you're wantin' to tell Sammy, Ellis?"

"I think I want out of the family business," Ellis said. It was the first time he had vocalized it, and it sounded stupid to him even as he said it. Give up everything he had, for a girl?

Not just any girl, he reminded himself. *Vanessa*.

"Oh," the priest replied. But then Ellis's words seemed to sink in. "Oh," he said again, more gravely this time.

"Exactly."

"I can't say as that's something I'd ever expected to hear coming from you," Father James said. "What's prompting it? Did something happen?"

"No, not really. Nothing like that." Ellis took a deep breath. "There's this girl."

"Ah."

"No, you don't understand. She comes from a good family, one that makes their money straight. And she's really involved in the movement, and she's gotten me turned on to it, too. And I'm starting to see there's ways to make things happen that don't involve puttin' the beatdown on somebody, or threatening to. And maybe that's a better way to live, you know?"

"There's not a lot of money in that way of life for most people. Most folks are just scraping by, paycheck to paycheck. It can be a hard life, Ellis. Much harder than you're used to."

Ellis blinked. "Are you trying to talk me out of it? You're the one person I figured would be all for me going straight!"

"I *am* all for you giving up the life of a criminal, Ellis. But you mentioned a young lady, and I imagine your plans involve her, no? So you have to be realistic. You have to know you have the means to support yourself *and* her—legitimate means. What skills do you have that don't involve running numbers and shaking people down for money? You need to think about that. There are a lot of jobs out there for unskilled laborers, but they don't pay much and it's hard work. You have to know what you're getting into, and be prepared for it. Otherwise you'll be back here in a week, begging Sammy to take you back."

Ellis hadn't thought about that, but he realized the priest was right. He had more to consider before he had a sit-down with Sammy. He needed to have a plan in place, or the old man would shoot him out of the water, just as Father James had done.

"You're right, Father. You've given me a lot to think about. Thank you." And he got up from the bar and headed out to find the nearest newspaper, leaving the priest staring after him, bemused.

• • •

"And why are you dressed in your Sunday best, drinking my 'shine at three o'clock in the afternoon?" Sammy asked as he walked into the bar to find Ellis bellied up to the counter with a glass in his hand, a folded-up "want ads" section under his arm.

"Just got back from an interview," Ellis said proudly.

"From a what now?"

"An interview. For a job." Clerking over at the K&B. Not a job that was going to make him rich by any means, but an honest one, and there was potential to move up into management.

"And why on God's green Earth would you be needing to do that?"

Now that the moment had finally arrived, Ellis wasn't as nervous as he thought he would be. Maybe it was because his interview had gone so well. Maybe it was because he had a plan in place that he knew Sammy couldn't find fault with. Maybe it was because he knew deep down he was on the right path at last. Whatever it was, he faced his father with a calm exterior and an interior that mostly matched it.

"Because I'm getting out of the business. I'm going straight."

Sammy burst out laughing.

"Well, if that ain't the damned funniest thing I've ever heard. Ellis, you want a job, you should take that act on the road. You'll have 'em all in stitches!"

"Laugh if you want, old man. I'm serious. I want out."

Sammy's smile faded.

"You want out, you say. To do what? Wait tables? Wash cars? Lay pipe? Dig ditches? What sort of work is that for a son of mine, eh?"

"It's *honest* work," Ellis replied.

"Honest?" Sammy echoed. "It's *cheap*. It will get you none of the things you want, none of the luxuries to which you are accustomed. You will live hand to mouth, just as your grandparents did. Why do you think I have worked so hard to rise to this position, if not to keep you from that sort of life, huh? And now you want to turn your back on all I have offered you? And for what?" His eyes narrowed. "This is because of that girl, n'est-ce pas?"

"What's so wrong with wanting to live a life free of violence? Free of crime? We could do that! With your connections, we could make legitimate money, give up the numbers running, all the rest. Go straight with the bar and the nightclub and whatever else—maybe a restaurant. Grand-mére had the best recipes—"

"That's enough," Sammy said. "Look around you, Ellis. We are only a few generations removed from slavery, segregation is still rampant, the Southern Union still runs the wealthiest part of this city. The only freedom to be had for the black man is in cold, hard cash, and the only way to make that money is under the table, by violent means. We may not want it to be that way, Ellis, but that's the simple truth of the world right now, and none of your marches or Freedom Rides or 'I Have a Dream' speeches can change that fact.

"No, Ellis. Having money is the closest we can get to having freedom. Maybe things will be different for your children or your children's children, but for you and me, that's the way it is. You want to consign those future children to more years of virtual slavery to white masters, you go ahead and leave. That's not what I want for you or for them—*I* want you to be *free*—but I can't stop you. You're a man now and you make your own decisions. Just stop and think hard about what you're giving up when you walk out the door before you go. And that it's not just yourself you're making that choice for but for every Robinson who comes after you."

Sammy had come over to stand beside Ellis while he spoke; now, he clapped his son on the shoulder once, twice, then turned on his heel and left the room, leaving Ellis as unsure about what he should do as he had ever been.

He'd never thought about it from Sammy's perspective before, but the old man made a lot of sense. Money *was* freedom in New Bordeaux, especially if you were black. And he'd never make enough of it as a drugstore clerk—or even a manager—to have the kind of life Sammy was talking about. The kind of freedom he dreamed about sharing with Vanessa.

Damn it! Why did everything always have to be so complicated? He downed the rest of his 'shine and poured himself another glass, wondering if he'd find the answer to that question at the bottom of the bottle, or maybe just a respite from having to think about it. Determined to find that much, at least, he set about getting good and drunk, and it wasn't long before he wasn't thinking about anything at all.

35

To take down an organization, cut it off at the knees, Donovan had said. Lincoln had heard Sammy Robinson give similar advice. Lincoln hadn't taken it to heart before, but his failures against the Pathet Lao had caused him to reconsider.

The post had grown extensively. That meant it relied more than ever on shipments from the north—of food, medical supplies, weapons and ammunition, uniforms, men—all the stuff that a modern army lived on. He needed to target those things, in order to make life hell for Colonel Sun.

That was where he would start. The convoys would be guarded, but they would also be far more vulnerable than the fort itself. And he had experience hitting trucks, from his New Bordeaux days. He and Ellis and a couple of the guys had once taken down a truck delivering TV sets, three weeks before the Super Bowl. They'd made a killing selling them on the streets.

This one would be a little more complicated, but the basic idea was similar. He sent Pos and a few other scouts down the mountain to determine whether trucks arrived on any regular schedule. While they were gone, he had Koob pull together a platoon of a hundred of their best men and they rehearsed the plan Lincoln had come up with, over and over until they had it down. He contacted Donovan for some additional supplies. By the time the scouts returned with their report, Lincoln felt fully prepared.

There was a schedule, it turned out. The next convoy would be arriving in twenty-two hours. That didn't leave much time to get into position, but the men were ready to go. They double-timed it down the mountain, Lincoln knowing all the while that coming back up would be a considerably slower process. Bypassing the camp completely, they went to a spot Pos had identified a few kilometers up the main road.

Other than military traffic—units from the camp going up to patrol around the intersection and convoys coming from the north—virtually no one used the road. Lincoln had no way to guarantee that they wouldn't be surprised from the south, which would turn into a much bigger fight than he was looking for. But if the scouts were right about the convoy schedule, they shouldn't have to be here for long, mitigating the risk of surprise.

Lincoln liked the spot Pos had picked out. It was just after a blind curve in the road, with the forest pressing in on both sides. As soon as they arrived, they felled several large trees and positioned them across the road, about thirty yards down from the turn. The men in the convoy would recognize it as an ambush as soon as they reached it, but by then it would be too late.

While they waited for the trucks, Lincoln sat on the newly paved surface with Koob and Pos, smoking cigarettes and chatting. "You men have really made a big difference," Lincoln said. "You've helped take us from a ragtag bunch of clowns into a real fighting force."

"Clowns?" Pos asked. "What is that?"

Lincoln pondered ways to explain what clowns were but then shook his head. "Never mind," he said. "Too complicated."

"I understand," Koob said. "Not clowns, but the rest."

"I just want you both to know that I appreciate everything you've done. You and your friends, the other Hmong. They make me look good to my bosses."

"You are the boss," Koob said.

Lincoln laughed. "Not hardly. I'm just an enlisted schmuck."

"Your boss is the president of US?" Koob asked.

"He's one of them," Lincoln said with a chuckle. "Most of them are officers with brass on their shoulders, but some of them wear suits. The president is one of those."

"You know him?"

Lincoln shook his head and held out the backs of his hands. "In

America, most people don't get to know the president. People with my skin color don't often spend time with people like that."

"There are many colors there?" Pos asked him.

"A few. White, black, brown, yellow. No green yet, but maybe someday the Martians will come."

"Yellow?" Koob asked. He pointed to some of the wildflowers that had sprouted along the road during the monsoon season. "That's yellow, no?"

"Not yellow like those," Lincoln explained. He touched the back of Koob's hand. "Like you. This is what we call yellow skin."

Koob and Pos both started laughing, lightly at first, then hysterically, spitting words in Hmong to each other when they could. Lincoln couldn't catch what they were saying but assumed they were making fun of the concept of their nut-brown skin being called yellow. Then again, he had differentiated between black and brown, knowing full well that his own skin, and that of all the other black folks he had ever seen, was really brown. So was the skin of the Mexicans and Puerto Ricans he had known.

With that realization, he started laughing, too.

They were still at it when they heard the rumble of trucks, coming closer.

Instantly, everyone scrambled for their assigned positions. Weapons were checked. Lincoln took a last look before heading for cover in the trees and was pleased to note that he couldn't see any of the men, even though he knew where to look for them. When it came to hiding in the brush, the Hmong were masters.

He took his position and waited.

The first truck rolled into the curve, then around it. The driver was intent on regaling his passengers with what must have been an entertaining story and didn't even see the fallen trees until one of the passengers cried out. The driver slammed on his brakes and the truck shuddered to a sudden stop. It started to reverse, but the next truck was following closely, and by the time it stopped, there was no space. Only the fourth and last truck was able to try backing up, to get headed north again, but by the time it did, the Hmong had come out of the trees and blocked the road.

The front and rear trucks were filled with men, presumably to guard the convoy. They hopped down from the trucks, but gunfire from the trees cut them down before they could use their weapons. RPGs sliced through the air and disabled the trucks. Within five minutes, every man in the convoy was dead or close to it, and there hadn't been a single Hmong casualty.

Knowing that the noise of battle could have been heard from the Pathet Lao post, Lincoln wrapped up the operation in a hurry. It didn't matter what had been in the cargo trucks—whatever they might have held was in flames. Lincoln and his men melted into the woods and split up, knowing they would reunite at the jars before starting up the mountain again. Any would-be rescuers from the camp would find only burning trucks and corpses.

36

A week later, they hit the supply convoy again. This time, the government in the north had sent more trucks and more men. Lincoln moved the ambush point up a couple of kilometers and also brought more men. His side had two KIAs, but on the Pathet side there were no survivors.

Ten days later—the Pathet Lao having altered their delivery schedule—they took down another one. Still more trucks and more men, but with essentially the same results.

Three days after that, still another convoy came through, this time with a dozen trucks and a few hundred men. It passed without incident and went to the camp.

But while it was there, Lincoln and his men cratered the road out with heavy explosives. When the convoy tried to leave, it was unable to. Until the road could be repaired—a dangerous proposition, thanks to Hmong snipers who made it so—all the additional soldiers who had accompanied the convoy had to be housed and fed at the camp.

Lincoln had to laugh. Once the idea had occurred to him to become an insufferable pest, it had seemed like a stroke of genius.

By now, Lincoln had contacts in Hmong villages ringing the entire Plain of Jars. Scouts from the northern villages kept an eye on the road and alerted him or Koob whenever a convoy was on the roll, giving them a day's warning before it would reach the camp. On the night before the next convoy's arrival, Vang Khom's own scouts—who kept the post in sight almost all the time—reported that a couple hundred men had gone up the road, getting in place to disrupt any ambush attempt.

Lincoln didn't plan any more ambushes for a while, though. Instead, this was the moment he was waiting for. He sent a half-dozen well-trained sappers through the wire, using techniques similar to the ones he had used to kill Colonel Phan. With so many soldiers out on the road, security was sparse. They set timed charges at each of the eight generators that powered the camp, the backup generators, and the underground storage tanks for the motor pool's gasoline supplies, and slipped out of the place before their presence was detected. At precisely two o'clock in the morning—Lincoln was waiting a few clicks south, checking his watch every couple of minutes—the bombs went off. Lincoln covered the distance quickly and saw that with the exception of the not-yet-extinguished fires, there wasn't a single light in the camp.

The immediate result wasn't disastrous for the camp. But the effect was meant to be psychological, not physical. Some soldiers would have died in those blasts. Worse was the knowledge the survivors had, that those who had perpetrated the attack had been inside their fences. The new, larger force, the expanded security measures, all meant nothing. They would be demoralized and frightened.

Being without electricity would be inconvenient for a few days, until they could rebuild generators or get new ones. Being without fuel for their vehicles would be worse, and it meant the next convoy would have to include fuel trucks. That might make for an interesting target, Lincoln thought.

Was it too soon to start hitting convoys again?

Probably so. Except one thing made the fuel trucks an especially tempting target.

With that in mind, he drew together three hundred of his Hmong warriors and set up an ambush a couple dozen kilometers north of the intersection—far from where any would be expected, based on past history. He let the first convoy pass through unmolested, because there were no fuel tankers in it. It had probably been on the move, or close to it, before word of the sapper attacks reached the north.

The next convoy, though, included four tanker trucks full of gasoline. This one, Lincoln stopped. A brief firefight ensued, and both sides took casualties. But when the smoke cleared, a dozen Pathet Lao vehicles and about a hundred and fifty Pathet soldiers were dead, and Lincoln's people were behind the wheels of the four tankers.

It wouldn't take long for word of the ambush to reach the camp or headquarters in the north. But Lincoln's plan didn't require much time.

The camp's water came from a river that cut through the Plain of Jars, on its way from the Laotian mountains and into Vietnam, then to the sea. The road passed over the river about four clicks from the camp. A little too close for comfort, if the garrison was responding to the ambush. Lincoln didn't think word would have reached them that quickly, and the action had taken place too far away for them to have heard anything.

He drove the first truck, and trusted drivers—there were not many among the villagers, few of whom had ever piloted big rigs—handled the other three. They left the road before the bridge and steered them into the river. Once the vehicles were all in place, they opened the tanks and ruptured them where they could without causing sparks or explosions. Fuel spilled into the river water. Within minutes, the smell was too powerful to bear, and Lincoln and his Hmong scattered back to their individual mountain redoubts.

The gas probably wouldn't poison the water all the way into Vietnam, Lincoln figured—it would be diluted in time—but it had to affect only the people in the camp. Either they would drink it and get sick, or they would avoid it and become dehydrated. When the next rain came, they would capture what they could of that, but without dedicated storage tanks, it would provide only brief respite.

Again, the idea was psychological warfare. Lincoln wanted the soldiers to know that nothing was safe—not their defenses, not their electricity, not their drinking water. Soon, he hoped, the desertions would start.

To speed up that process even more, he started sending Hmong squads out to the post at night with mortars. They would lob in a few rounds, do whatever damage they could, then fade into the darkness. It was another tactic borrowed from the VC, designed to keep the men inside the wire anxious and scared. By the time the soldiers could react to the incoming rounds, those who fired them would be gone. The next night, they would wonder—will it happen again? And it would, but not on any set schedule. Sometimes four or five nights would pass without any attack. Sometimes it would happen every night for a week, then stop.

After a few days of that, Lincoln's scouts reported that they had seen soldiers slipping away from the camp during the night. Others went out on patrol, then slipped quietly into the jungle while their comrades weren't looking and never returned. First it was a trickle, then a stream, and finally a flood. Whether they went north or south or into Vietnam was of no concern to Lincoln—they were no longer threats, and that was all that mattered.

Little by little, he was knocking the pins out from underneath Colonel Sun.

Soon, it would be time to finish the job.

3 7

Vanessa was quiet after the rally, though this one had been rowdier than most, with a group of antiwar protestors running naked through the middle of it, high on God knew what, their bodies painted with peace symbols, flowers, and "Make Love, Not War" slogans. There had been cops in attendance at this rally, though they had just been observing, making sure things didn't get out of hand. They chased down the nudists and hauled them off, much to the amusement of the other rally-goers. Ellis had thought the whole thing was pretty funny himself and was trying to elicit a smile from Vanessa with his exaggerated retelling of the tale.

". . . should hire some hippies to do that at every rally, just to keep the cops busy," he finished up. "We could even start charging admission for the show. Be a good source of income for the movement."

Vanessa blinked a couple of times and looked away, not responding. They were back at the park in her neighborhood, just a block away from her house, and whatever she saw outside the window of Lincoln's car seemed far preferable to what she saw inside it.

"Hey. Hey," he said, reaching out with one hand to grasp her chin and turn her face back toward him. "What'd I say? What is it? What's wrong?"

She just shook her head, whether to indicate there was nothing she wanted to talk about or to dislodge his grip, he wasn't sure, so he pulled his hand away.

"Look, there's something I wanted to talk to you about. I know you don't approve of my lifestyle, and I understand why—it's fast and violent and not the sort of environment you can raise a family in. I get that. That's why I'm getting out—"

"Ellis, we can't see each other anymore," she blurted, the tears she'd been holding back coursing down her cheeks like a dam had broken behind her eyes.

"What? What are you talking about? Is it your parents? I was just trying to tell you, I got a job at the K&B, I'm going straight, they don't have to worry—"

"No, it's not them. They don't even know about your background—I never told them. They would have forbidden me from seeing you in a heartbeat if they knew."

"Then what? What happened? What did I do?"

She turned and looked at him then, disappointment and accusation written plain on her tear-streaked face, and he knew. That imagined visage had haunted him ever since the fur job, despite everything he'd done to make sure he never had to see it. Now here it was, his worst nightmare made flesh.

Vanessa knew about the warehouse. Despite Ellis's warning, the donor had talked.

But he knew only about the Marcanos' involvement—he didn't know Ellis by name. Maybe there was still a way out of this.

"Why did you do it, Ellis? Why did you and your friends rob our biggest donor? Now he's withdrawn all his backing from CORE and the other groups, saying we've shown our true colors and aren't worth his support, let alone his money. And . . . you *killed* three men in the process?"

"That wasn't me!" Ellis protested. "That was Giorgi. It was all his idea, once he realized who your donor was and how rich he was."

A hard look came into Vanessa's eyes.

"Don't lie to me, Ellis. He saw you. He didn't know your name, but he told Oretha all about 'the black boy who was hanging around with the button girl.' I was the button girl that day, Ellis, and you were the only black boy hanging around me.

"How could you? I thought you believed in the cause, in what we're trying to do, and how we're trying to do it."

"Those guys are my friends, Vanessa! And I owed them. I pay what I owe, whether it's a favor or anything else."

"And that's the whole problem, isn't it?"

Ellis didn't have an answer to that.

"Tell me, was it all just a ploy to get me to sleep with you?"

"What? No! Of course not. Vanessa, I love you!"

He hadn't known the words were going to come out of his mouth until they were already spoken, and then they just hung there in the air between them, like a white flag raised on the field of battle after the war had already been lost.

"That doesn't matter now," she said after a moment. "You killed people, or you were involved in it. It's probably not the first time, and it certainly won't be the last. Violence is in your blood; you can't escape it. I didn't understand that before, but I do now.

"I can't live like that, Ellis. I won't. There are some things love can't conquer. This is one of them." She grabbed the handle of the car door, opened it, and climbed out.

"Vanessa, wait! I—"

"Good-bye, Ellis," she said, and closed the door. And all he could do was watch as she walked away, into the darkness and out of his life.

• • •

Ellis drove around aimlessly for a while before heading back to Sammy's. Where else was he going to go?

Besides, he needed the old man's advice. Sammy had always been straight with him, even when they disagreed on something, which was more often than not these days. He needed to know if he should go after Vanessa, which every fiber of his being was screaming at him to do, or let her go.

She hadn't said she loved *him*, after all.

But, then again, she hadn't said she *didn't*. Just that it didn't matter, because she thought he'd killed people.

But it wasn't just the killing, he knew. It was the robbery, it was paying off the cops, it was everything associated with the lifestyle. It was who he was, down at the core.

Vanessa thought Ellis Robinson was a mobster, through and through. And maybe she was right, because right now all he wanted to do was kill somebody, and he didn't much care who. He had only been fooling himself, with that nonsense about getting a straight job and leaving the life. She had shown him that there was a different way to live, and it had filled his head with mirages that could never be true. Not for him.

Giorgi was not only Ellis's friend, he was his future. He could see that now. Giorgi would take Sal's place one day, and Ellis would take Sammy's. The two of them would run New Bordeaux. There would be no shortage of women. Not ones like Vanessa—she was one of a kind—but she could never be his. He would have to accept that and make the best of who he was and what he had.

When he got to the bar, Sammy was involved in a late business meeting. Ellis hung around outside the old man's office, hoping it would be short and he could talk to his father before he went to bed. So he could hear bits and pieces of the conversation Sammy was having, and it didn't sound like it was going well.

". . . it's high-quality stuff, man, and I've got a steady supply from Southeast Asia. More than I can sell in my current markets, so I'm looking to expand. What I've heard, New Bordeaux is the perfect place for it, and you're the perfect man."

"Well, then you heard wrong," Sammy's voice snapped back, annoyed and affronted. Ellis could just imagine his expression. He wondered what kind of "stuff" the other man was talking about. Drugs, obviously, but what? Southeast Asia . . . that meant opium. Heroin? No wonder the old man sounded so pissed. Ellis almost laughed. Wherever the other man had gotten his information, he'd been seriously misled. Sammy wanted heroin in the Hollow like he wanted a hole in the head. Wasn't happening.

"Maybe you're not hearing me right. We're talking a thirty percent cut. I'm taking all the risk getting the product out of the jungle and into the States. All you have to do is move it."

"And worry about my people getting busted for possession and distribution. In case you haven't noticed, this is a black neighborhood. If there's

215

anything the police like to arrest blacks in the South for more than drug-related crimes, I'm not aware of it. And don't even get me started on what your 'product' does to its users. We don't need that kind of poison here in the Hollow—not to use it, and certainly not to sell it. I'm afraid you've wasted your time."

"You're turning up your nose at the deal of a lifetime," the other man said, and Ellis didn't like the warning tone in his voice.

"I've said 'no' to better offers, for less cause. Now, if you'll excuse me, I have real business to attend to."

"You can pretend you're acting in the best interest of the people in your district by refusing to deal, but the truth is, you just want to control which vices they get to indulge in. You're not a mob boss with morals; you're just a lousy hypocrite."

"Fuck off," Sammy replied calmly. "And get the hell out of my office."

"With pleasure," the other man said, and Ellis flinched as the door he'd been listening at was flung open and a big, dark-haired white man in a Hawaiian shirt stormed past, muttering angrily to himself.

When he was gone, Ellis stepped inside Sammy's office.

"That didn't go so well."

Sammy looked up at him.

"Eh, it was nothing. Some fool wanting to sell heroin in the Hollow. I set him straight."

"I heard."

Sammy chuckled.

"What are you doing here so late? You're not out with that girl?"

Ellis cringed.

"She broke up with me."

"Ah." Sammy patted the seat the drug peddler had just vacated. "Come. Tell me."

Ellis came and sat in the chair while Sammy leaned against the edge of his desk.

"She found out about the job we pulled to settle up with Giorgi for paying the cops off at that rally. Giorgi capped a few guys during it and she thought

I was involved in that part, said violence was in my blood. That I can't escape it. Do you think that's true?"

"I think that's exactly why I do what I do. So someday you—or your children, or theirs—*can* escape it. With enough money, anybody's blood can be purged. Anyone's slate wiped clean. That's what freedom is, Ellis."

"I don't think she sees it that way."

"Most people who don't have to fight for what they want don't. She's black, so she still has to fight for the same rights we all do, but her family's well off, so she's never had to fight for basic necessities, for her very survival. She doesn't know what it's like to be truly down, so she doesn't understand what it takes to claw your way up. She never will, son.

"Maybe there'll come a time when we're rich enough to leave this life in the past, but until then, violence is part and parcel of who we are. It has to be—that's the only way we survive.

"You need a woman who understands that, like your mother did. She knew what it took to make it in this life, and she was willing and able to do it all, God rest her."

"But . . . but I loved her."

"Maybe you did, son, but love will come again. And next time, maybe it'll be for a woman who can handle what being loved by a Robinson means—the burdens *and* the boons. When you find *that* woman—then you'll know you've found the one who deserves your love, Ellis. And I'll be looking forward to the grandchildren you two make together, eh?"

Sammy clapped him on the shoulder.

"Come on, now. All this talk of business, love, and life has made me thirsty. Let's go get a drink. The good stuff tonight. I'm buying."

"Easy enough to offer, since it's already yours, old man," Ellis said with a laugh.

"Exactly, Ellis," Sammy replied with a smile. "Exactly."

38

This time, there was no attempt at a surprise attack.

Four days earlier, Donovan had dropped into Vang Khom with an urgent message. "This is about to go to shit, Lincoln," he'd said. They had been sitting inside Lincoln's longhouse, having sent Sho out to get some privacy.

"What do you mean?"

"There's a major force moving down from the north," Donovan explained. "Seven to ten thousand, according to the intel we're seeing. They're sweeping this way, wiping out Hmong villages as they go."

"Why?" Lincoln asked.

"Because they know the Hmong want them gone. They suspect the Hmong are harassing them, not just here, but all over the Plain of Jars. You've heard about Sherman's March, right? Carving through the South, burning towns as they went? This is the fucking Pathet Lao version of that."

"And they're headed this way?"

"They're going to reinforce that camp. They need that intersection before the end of the rainy season, so when it's dry again they can move into Vietnam. But it's likely that they'll also keep hitting Hmong villages, and that'll include Vang Khom. They're not going to stop until the Hmong are extinct." He paused long enough to shake a cigarette from a pack and light it. "I told the Pentagon to just drop some fucking bombs on them, but they basically told me to go fuck myself. I swear, one of these days I'll have a trophy room in my house, and I'll have some old, white, shit-eating heads and shoulders mounted on the walls."

"Shoulders, too?" Lincoln asked.

Donovan blew out a puff of smoke. "So I can count their goddamn stars."

The idea that the Pathet Lao would wipe out Vang Khom had never been far from Lincoln's thoughts, but at the same time, he had been able to convince himself that if it was going to happen, it already would have. Up here on this mountain, he had felt safe. He wouldn't be able to live with himself if everyone he had come to know here was killed, because of things he had done or not done.

Sho especially.

"What can I do?"

"If you're going to take that camp, you've got to do it now," Donovan said. "If they know they've lost the intersection for good, they might back off. Take another path into Vietnam. But only a significant goddamn loss is going to be convincing enough to change their plans. And I'll warn you—even that might not work. Saving Vang Khom might be a lost cause."

"Might be," Lincoln repeated.

"Nothing's for sure until it's for sure. Except this—if you want to give this village a chance, you've got to raze that fort to the fucking ground. And you've got to do it now."

• • •

By all reports, a couple hundred Pathet Lao soldiers had already deserted the camp. Those who remained had to know the end was coming soon. Lincoln expected a ferocious response—men fought hardest when the stakes were highest. But his hope was that some number would favor surrender to death, so he wanted them to see what they were up against.

His Hmong irregulars had no uniforms, and their weapons and accessories were an odd assortment of bits and pieces from practically every country under the globe except the United States. What was Donovan's phrase? *Plausible deniability*, Lincoln remembered.

He had upward of six hundred men, and he was the only American in the bunch. If that wasn't deniability, he didn't know what was.

In their loincloths and loose pants and colorful shirts and headbands, the men gathered for the fight. Lincoln heard laughter and shouts, but he also heard quiet words of inspiration and fear. The faces of his men were somber, scared, at peace, excited, anxious, jovial. They were here to kill communists; some of them would die in the bargain, and every one of them knew that. They had come anyway.

The feelings welling through Lincoln as he walked among his warriors surprised him. He felt honored by their presence here. They had come at his bidding, willing to put their faith in his guidance and leadership, trusting his decisions. They would follow his orders to the death. No greater sacrifice could be asked. Lincoln Clay was just an orphan kid from New Bordeaux, abandoned, a punk who had grown up on the streets and in the embrace of a mob family. Life had not prepared him for this kind of responsibility.

But it was here, and it was his, and he was determined to live up to it. He would see this through to the end.

He just hoped that when it did end, he would still be around to know it.

Instead of attacking by night, under cover of darkness, they came during the daylight. Lincoln took up a position near the camp, hidden by the trees, because he wanted to see their approach the way the Pathet Lao would.

It happened just as he had planned. The Hmong came silently, from every direction, melting through the trees like floodwater through grates. One moment they weren't there, then they were, then there were more of them, and more, and still more.

Lincoln heard the alarms being raised throughout the fort. Even though he didn't understand the language, the tension was electric. The Hmong men moved like ghosts, manifestations from the spirit world. They hadn't even pointed their weapons yet, and the Pathet Lao were already terrified of what they faced.

Then Lincoln gave the order.

Mortars thumped from the forest, and explosions blossomed at random points inside the wire. RPGs arced into the camp, targeting the watchtowers and the soldiers amassing for battle.

Finally, the Pathet Lao screwed up the nerve to strike back. Their machine guns raked the trees, but they were met, round for round, by machine guns carried in by the Hmong and set up in strategic spots.

Infantrymen inside the fences opened fire. So did the Hmong, many of whom had trees to shield them.

Lincoln couldn't simply watch any longer. Bloodlust was as real as any other kind, and seeing his men fall to the Pathet bullets, he needed to be part of the action. He had two ARs, one in his hands and the other strapped onto his back, in addition to his other weapons. Now he opened fire with the first of them, spraying a long burst at the soldiers who lined the fence nearest his position. Some of them hit home, and he was gratified to see the carnage that resulted.

He emptied that magazine and switched guns, letting the first cool for a spell. In that way, alternating weapons, he powered round after round through the fences. On the inside, bodies started piling up, and some of the Pathet soldiers lay down behind their dead comrades, using them for cover as they kept firing back.

From deep inside the camp, Lincoln heard a rumble that was at once familiar and strange. He knew what it was but hadn't known there were any here, hadn't heard one in many months. It took only a few minutes for the tank to emerge from behind some buildings, still half-draped in the camouflage netting that had disguised it from the air. It was at least a dozen years old—a Soviet-made T-54/55, Lincoln thought. But it was a tank; one thing his troops didn't have and couldn't match.

An RPG jetted toward the tank and exploded against it, seeming to not even scratch the paint. The turret swiveled, like the head of a fat, ungainly bird seeking its prey. With a burst of flame and a loud boom, the tank fired. Trees blew apart, and human beings with them, engulfed in a blast of fire and smoke.

Having fired, the tank didn't hesitate. It rolled down the pavement toward the front gates, which Pathet soldiers were swinging open for it. Lincoln started in that direction, shouting orders as he wove through the trees. He needn't have bothered—the Hmong in that area were already doing what he wanted: shooting at the men at the gate.

The gatekeepers were cut down before the tank had cleared the gate, but it didn't matter; the massive vehicle crashed through, tearing fences from their moorings. The turret turned, and it fired again. Then its machine guns opened up, clanking and spitting lead that splintered trees and tore through flesh. It plowed forward on enormous treads, following the pavement until it had passed the minefield, then turning into the trees. Trunks shattered before its weight, and men scattered or were cut down by its guns and ripped asunder by its shells.

Instead of running away, Lincoln hurried toward it.

Up close, it was like some mythical beast, a dragon or a T. rex restored to awful life. Its sinister look and the sound of its roar inspired terror, even without acknowledging its terrible destructive power. The flash when it fired was almost blinding. Lincoln knew the thing could alter the tide of the battle if it wasn't stopped. Grenades had proven ineffective; bullets just bounced off its steel hide.

Its machine guns, fired from within, lacerated everything in their path. Lincoln had to swing wide to avoid them, then angle in toward the right rear corner. Soviet tanks were made for taller crews than Chinese-made ones, and although the disadvantage of a small interior compartment wouldn't be a problem for the Pathet Lao soldiers inside, he hoped their lines of sight were hampered by their small stature.

That was just a hope, though, not at all a certainty. Charging toward the rattling, clanking, roaring beast was one of the scariest things he had ever done.

He had to do it, though, if this day wasn't going to be a repeat of the last attempt on the base. And he had already decided that it wouldn't be.

It turned out that approaching the tank was only the second scariest thing, because leaping onto it was far more terrifying. Lincoln's left foot slipped off its body and touched the tread, and he yanked it away, knowing that to be snagged in that would guarantee that he'd be pulled under and run over, spread all over the jungle floor like jam on toast.

Then he stopped thinking about what could go wrong. No more time for that. The hatch opened as he was reaching for it, and an angry face showed behind a gun barrel. Lincoln pulped it with a burst from his AR. The soldier fell away, and the hatch cover dropped back into place. Lincoln let the weapon dangle from its strap as he tugged two grenades from his belt. He pulled the pins, held them for an almost unbearable few moments, then kicked open the hatch again and tossed them in.

Without worrying about where he would land, or on what, he leapt from the tank. He hit the splintered remains of a tree, feeling wood jab into him like knives, but he yanked himself free and ran. Another thing he knew about the T-54/55 series was that their internal ammunition supplies weren't shielded.

One grenade flew into the air and exploded harmlessly in the tree canopy. Presumably no one could find the second, or in their rush to get it out the soldiers inside the tank collided, because it went off, sending a jet of flame out the hatch. The secondary explosion—the tank's ammo stores—was much, much larger. Fire shot up into and through the canopy, and the tank almost seemed to swell from the force of it. The turret dislodged, and the main gun drooped. From the Hmong forces, a cheer went up that almost shook the jungle floor.

The tank's death breathed new life into the attack. Hmong fighters kept up their positions encircling the camp, but the larger mass of them pushed toward the destroyed gate. Flowing from the jungle onto the pavement meant they could safely avoid the land mines.

Pathet Lao soldiers surged toward the gate to plug the gap, but that only meant that a furious firefight broke out. The Hmong had numbers and momentum on their side, and it wasn't long before the Pathet fell back. Another cheer rose from the Hmong as they swarmed through the gates and were finally inside the Pathet fences.

Lincoln wasn't cheering, though. Progress was progress. But the soldiers inside would be desperate now, cornered beasts fighting for survival.

The worst, he knew, was yet to come.

39

Lincoln joined the throng heading through the gates. He saw Pos and tossed him a grin, but all he got in return was an ashen look. The man's cheeks were wet. "What's wrong?" Lincoln asked.

"Koob," Pos said. "He's killed."

At first the words didn't register. Watching for signs of Pathet resistance, Lincoln's attention was divided, and whatever Pos had said didn't sink in. Then Lincoln looked at his face again, the tracks tears had cut through the dirt caking it. "Koob?" he asked. "Where the hell is he?"

Pos pointed to the area struck by the first tank round. "Back there."

Lincoln was torn. The enemy was ahead of them. But the closest thing he had to a friend—besides Sho, thankfully safe in Vang Khom—was behind, dead or badly hurt. He wasn't sure he wanted to take Pos's diagnosis as fact.

"Listen, you be careful in there," he said after considering the dilemma. "I'll be right back."

With that, he turned and dashed against the stream, to the denuded area Pos had indicated as Koob's resting place.

It took a while to find his friend, because there wasn't much left of him: strips of gray flesh hanging off a broken body, his torso burst open like a red-and-yellow meat sack. Lincoln recognized what he could see of Koob's clothing and his hair, strangely intact even though it was attached only to a string of scalp and face, dangling somewhere around Koob's midsection.

Lincoln's gorge rose in his throat. He was no stranger to violent death—hadn't been even before the war—but this was gruesome, and it hit home in a very personal way. He had trusted Koob with everything, just as Koob had trusted him. He usually kept Koob close by, in case he needed translation assistance. He could have been standing next to the man when the tank round hit.

He was glad he had killed the tank crew. He wished he could go back in time and do it again, knowing as he did what he was punishing them for.

The staccato rattle of automatic weapons fire reminded Lincoln that he was living in the now, not in the past. He had to rejoin the battle and perhaps take some additional revenge for the death of Koob—and so many other Hmong warriors—at the same time.

He raced toward the gate. His Hmong soldiers recognized Lincoln and parted to let him through, some slapping him on the back in encouragement as he passed. At the front of the advance, the Hmong gunned down fleeing Pathet Lao. Some of the Pathet soldiers returned fire from behind whatever cover they could find, but the attackers outnumbered them and quickly swarmed their positions. Lincoln was impressed that the Hmong soldiers seemed to have no fear of death. If one fell to the Pathet bullets, others moved into the same space their comrades had just vacated. The defenders couldn't kill them all.

In just minutes, the Pathet Lao fighters were gone.

Lincoln knew that didn't mean they were all dead. But they had gone to ground, which would make them harder to find and to kill.

He moved into the front of the pack, trying to show his men that he was equally fearless. There had been many times in his life that he had been sure he was going to die—even, in his early days at the orphanage, before he really understood what that meant. But he hadn't died then, and he figured that if he had survived the upbringing he'd had, there must have been a reason for it.

The Pathet Lao camp was surprisingly quiet for the moment. Lincoln's men listened for signs of the enemy, but the enemy was laying low. Then a single crack sounded and a round streaked so close to Lincoln's cheek, he thought he could feel the heat. It landed harmlessly in the dirt behind him. One of the Hmong soldiers pointed at a ground-level window in a nearby building—presumably a basement. It was open just a crack, but wide enough for a rifle barrel.

Lincoln fired a burst into the window, to discourage a second attempt, then sprinted to it. He stood to the side, stuck his AR's barrel through the shattered glass, and sprayed lead inside. An abrupt cry made him think at least one of his bullets had found its mark.

"Spread out!" he called to his men, wishing Koob were beside him to translate. "Eyes open! The Pathet could be anywhere."

Some of the Hmong seemed to understand, and they shared with the rest. The pack broke apart, men going in every direction. Soon Lincoln heard doors being kicked in, and sporadic gunfire indicating that hidden soldiers had been discovered.

He entered a barracks, a long, narrow building with twin rows of bunks. Sunlight slanted in through windows lining one side. All appeared still, but the dust motes floating in the bars of light close to one window danced madly.

Lincoln lowered himself to a crouch and eyed the spaces under the bunks. His gaze could only go so far on the left side, because at a bunk there—directly across from the window where the dust had still not set-tled—a footlocker had been dragged from its space at the end of the bunk and turned sideways between two. Peeking out from behind it, Lincoln saw a trembling boot.

"You can surrender," he said, aiming his weapon at the footlocker. "Or you can die. Your choice."

He waited. He had not really thought about what to do with prisoners of war, if there were any. He would have to have the Hmong hold them for the Laotian army, and he would have to make himself scarce when they were collected. But where they could be held was another question. Vang Khom had no jails, and he doubted if any of the other villages did. They might have to turn this camp into a prison camp and appoint Hmong warriors as jailers.

The man hiding behind the footlocker hadn't responded, and Lincoln's patience was growing short. "I'll count to three," he said. "One . . . two . . . two and a half . . ."

At that moment, the Pathet Lao soldier's rifle barrel swung into view around the other side of the footlocker from the boot. Lincoln opened fire the instant he saw it. The Pathet soldier screamed and lurched to his feet, his right hand mangled and bleeding. He tried to raise the weapon with his left, and Lincoln finished him with a quick burst to the midsection.

All around him, he heard the sounds of similar encounters. A shot here, a volley there. He guessed things were being wrapped up. But he still had a last responsibility to address.

Back outside, he worked his way toward what had been Colonel Phan's headquarters building. The camp had grown considerably, but he didn't think that structure had been repurposed. If he was going to find Colonel Sun, it would be there.

• • •

The level of resistance Lincoln met convinced him he was on the right path. Not all the Pathet Lao soldiers had given up or gone into hiding; close to the headquarters building they still held ground and acted as if they planned to keep it. Lincoln had to advance little by little, taking out opponents where he could. He took a bullet in the left arm, a through-and-through that cost some blood but would hurt more later than it did in the moment.

He hurled a grenade into that pocket of soldiers and kept going. More popped up from behind sandbags. He dropped them with a spray from his AR and continued forward through the billowing smoke. The entire camp seemed to be veiled with smoke from all the guns and fires, and he knew he would smell it for days, that and gun oil and the metallic tang of spent brass and spilled blood.

Lincoln fought until no one stood between him and the building. He didn't know what waited inside, but he was bone-tired and ready to finish this task, whatever it took. He kicked open the door and stepped aside, expecting a burst of fire to come his way. It didn't. Was he too late? Had Sun escaped?

Cautiously, Lincoln peered inside. Only one man stood there, in full officer's uniform, his spine ramrod straight. He was short and squat, and under other circumstances Lincoln might have thought him a small-town butcher or perhaps a middle manager. His face was open and might have seemed friendly, though at the moment it was composed, without obvious expression.

He held a pistol in his left hand, but if he had any other weapons, Lincoln couldn't see them. The pistol was held loosely at his side, not pointed at Lincoln. Lincoln didn't make the same mistake—he centered his barrel on the officer's midsection.

"Come in," the man said in English. "You are the American, yes? The one everyone talks about."

"I didn't know people talked about an American," Lincoln said. He wouldn't commit to his identity, even if it were just the two of them here. He couldn't be sure they weren't being recorded or perhaps transmitted to the north.

"Of course. We know all about you. We wait only for verifiable evidence before broadcasting your illegal presence to the world."

"You're Colonel Sun, I take it?"

"I am. And you are Lincoln. Like your president."

That surprised Lincoln even more. He tried not to let on, to keep his face as settled as the colonel's.

"I'm offerin' you the chance to surrender," Lincoln said. "And to tell the rest of your men to surrender, too. If they don't, the Hmong will kill them all." From outside, another volley of shots sounded. "Better do it fast."

"We don't surrender," Sun said.

"Plenty of your men have deserted in these last couple of weeks."

"They were cowards. They are not fit to serve."

"One way to look at it, I guess."

"You are going to shoot me?"

Lincoln shrugged. "You don't surrender, I don't have much choice."

"There is one other way," the colonel said.

"What's that? I'm not surrenderin' to you, if that's what you have in mind."

Sun smiled briefly and held up his pistol. "This."

It took Lincoln a moment to understand what he meant. "What about . . . oh. You'd rather do it that way?"

"Yes," Sun said. He nodded toward the door. "A moment's privacy?"

Lincoln was torn. Walking out the door and leaving an armed enemy alone seemed like a bad idea. But he couldn't think of anything it could hurt. If Colonel Sun had wired the camp with explosives and had a detonator hidden inside, he probably would already have used it.

Finally, he shrugged, checked outside to make sure it was safe, then stepped out and pulled the door closed.

He was there for only seconds before he heard a gunshot from inside the building, followed by a rustling slide and a thump. He threw the door open again.

Sun was crumpled by the wall where he'd been standing, a spray of blood and brains on the wall and ceiling above him and a streak down the wall he'd left on his way to his resting spot.

Outside, the sounds had changed from sporadic gunshots to celebration. The camp had fallen; the Hmong were in charge. With that victory, the crucial crossroads was back in friendly hands as well.

Lincoln went out again and was hailed by his Hmong warriors as a hero. He let himself relax, allowed a smile to cross his face.

It wouldn't last long.

<u>40</u>

Lincoln left a small force of men at the former Pathet camp to defend it and bury the dead, and headed up the mountain to Vang Khom with the rest. There would be feasting, drinking, the slaughter of buffalo. Women who had lost their men would wail their sorrow, but those cries would be drowned out by the celebrating. Lincoln guessed he would have to requisition more ammo, not just because of the battle but because the men would fire off whatever was left as they partied late into the night.

When they reached the village, a light rain had started to fall, though the massing of dark clouds in the near distance warned that it would get heavier.

Lincoln broke into a jog. It had been too long since he had seen Sho, held her. He'd had moments during the fight when he wondered if he ever would again. But he had survived, and his house was just ahead. He was a little surprised she hadn't come out when she'd heard the sound of the returning army, but then he thought about some of the things that could signify, and they mostly had to do with her being naked and waiting for him. He ran faster and burst through the door. "Sho!" he called. "I'm back!"

The inside was dark, and his eyes needed a few moments to adjust after climbing in bright sunlight. There was a strange, coppery smell, but he thought that was him; his sleeve was drenched in blood from his arm wound.

It wasn't, though.

She lay on the bed, her clothes torn, her head tilted back, her arms and legs splayed out, her beautiful brown eyes open but sightless. Her throat was a gory red slash.

"No!" he cried, falling to his knees and scooping her into his arms. "Sho! Sho!"

She was already cool; life had been gone from her for a while. He pressed his forehead against her, his tears splashing onto her supple flesh.

He didn't know how long he stayed like that, releasing great sobs that racked his spine and made his chest ache. After a while, his thoughts turned in a darker direction. Who had done this, and why? Somebody would pay, and pay dearly.

Finally, he tore himself away from her and went outside again. People had gathered in the rain, drawn by the sounds he'd made. Worried faces turned up toward his.

"Sho's been killed," Lincoln said, struggling to keep his voice even. "I want to know who did it. Someone here knows."

A couple of English speakers translated for the rest, and within moments, loud, wailing cries soared up toward the heavens. No one came forward with information, though.

"Who did it?" Lincoln thundered. He came down from his house and went to the next one, kicking out one of the stilts from beneath a front corner. "I'll tear this fuckin' piece-of-shit village to the ground, piece by piece!"

"No, Lincoln!" It was Pos, shoving his way through the growing crowd. "Do not hurt the village! We'll help! We'll find the killer!"

"I want his ass in front of me now," Lincoln said. "Right now. Whoever knows who it is better fuckin' turn him over."

Pos said something that Lincoln assumed was a desperate appeal for information. He saw only people looking uncertain, confused. No one volunteered anything useful. He kicked over another stilt, and the whole house lurched forward. The door swung open and contents spilled onto the ground: cookware, rubber sandals, a jar of water that trickled into the dirt.

Lincoln knew he was threatening the wrong people—most of these men had been in the battle with him, and the butchery done to Sho didn't look like a woman's work. But he was out of ideas, too frantic to think clearly.

Finally, he turned away from them and stormed toward Mai's hut. She was Sho's best friend; maybe she knew something.

By this point, word had spread throughout the village. Everywhere he went, people eyed him with pity or fear or something in between, and they whispered among themselves as he passed. "Mai!" he called as he neared her place. "Mai!"

Nobody answered. He yanked open her door and stepped inside without waiting for an invitation. She was on the bed, curled up in an almost fetal position, and for one horrible instant he was afraid she had been killed, too. Then he saw her back and shoulders hitching, heard her soft sobs.

"Mai, damn it," he said. He grabbed her shoulder and pulled her around, onto her back. She tried to writhe away, but he held her down. "What the fuck is going on around here?"

She relaxed a little, lowered her hands from her face.

That's when he saw what had become of it. Her lips were mashed and pulpy. She had a black eye, and the left side of her face was a mass of bruises. He wasn't sure, but he thought her cheekbone might have been broken on that side. Bruises encircled her throat, and more stood out on her upper arms.

"What happened to you?" Lincoln asked. "What . . . Sho is . . ."

He couldn't finish his sentences. Sho and Mai, both brutalized. It was too much. He didn't understand. He said the only words he could manage, asking the only question that seemed important. "Who did it?"

She wrenched out of his grip and turned back toward the wall. Less gently than before, Lincoln grabbed her and turned her around again. "Goddamnit, Mai, who did this? Who killed Sho?"

Mai exploded into loud sobs and curled into his arms. He held her, realizing he would have to wait until she calmed enough to remember her English. Every now and then he prodded her, stroking her head or drying her tears with his fingers. "I know, I know," he said quietly. "I feel the same way. Whoever did this is gonna fuckin' pay, Mai, I promise you that. I promise you."

After a long while, she got hold of her emotions. "Corbett," she said softly.

Lincoln wasn't sure he'd heard right. "Corbett? Corbett hurt you?"

"Yes," Mai said. "Corbett."

"But why? He loved you!" But even as he said it, he remembered what Sho had told him. Corbett hit Mai sometimes. He had a violent temper. "What happened?"

Mai sniffed, wiped her nose on her dress. "He say . . . he said he would kill Sammy when he goes back to U.S."

"Sammy?" Lincoln echoed, confused. "Sammy who?"

"Sho said Sammy is your father."

"He's gonna kill my father? Why? He doesn't even know my father!"

Lincoln realized abruptly that he didn't know that for sure. Corbett made regular trips back to the world, usually to sell heroin. He had asked Lincoln about his family in the past. He knew Sammy's name and his position in the New Bordeaux underworld.

"He knows him," Mai said. "He said Sammy talked to him like he was a child. Said Sammy insulted him. Nobody insults Corbett, he said. He will go back and kill Sammy."

"I still don't—where does Sho fit into all this? And why did he hurt you?"

"After he told me that, he hit me some, then got drunk. Fell asleep here in bed. I worried, so I told Sho what he said. Sho said Sammy is your father, that she had to tell you. When I came back here, Corbett was gone. I was glad. After a little time, his plane went away."

"So he didn't leave right when he woke up? You came back here and he was gone, but it was a while before he left? How long?"

"Not a long time. But not short."

"So you think he killed Sho?"

"Maybe he heard me talk to her? Hid until I come back here, then killed her, then left?"

It had probably happened in just that way, Lincoln thought. Corbett hadn't been as passed out as Mai thought. When she left the house, he followed. The bamboo structures were far from soundproof, and Corbett spoke Hmong. He could have hidden by Lincoln's longhouse and listened to the conversation. He would have known that Sho would tell Lincoln as soon as he returned to the village but would have also believed that, since he had already brutalized Mai and killed her best friend, she wouldn't dare say anything to Lincoln, or anyone else. Besides, killing Mai would have cast even more suspicion on him. Once he had murdered Sho, he would have wanted to get airborne in a hurry, in case someone found her.

But where would he have gone from here? Vang Khom was usually in the middle of his rounds, not the beginning but far from the end. Not only did he have to make more official stops before returning to Saigon or Vientiane, he would want to pick up more poppies and distribute more heroin money, too.

Would murder have changed those plans? Lincoln didn't think so. He believed Corbett to be utterly amoral. Snuffing out the life of a Hmong woman wouldn't seem like much of a crime, particularly compared to killing Lincoln's adopted father. Corbett could probably do both murders, then come back to Vang Khom acting like Lincoln's best friend.

Lincoln could wait for his return and take his vengeance then.

But that would risk Sammy's life. And he didn't want his revenge served cold. It burned inside him, like he had swallowed coals straight from the fire.

He wanted his hands on Corbett's throat, now.

"I'll be back," he said. He ran from the hut and toward the village center, calling for Pos. In another few moments, he was explaining his plan. "Get on the radio," he said. "Find out where Corbett landed after he was here, and if he's still there, let me know. Immediately!"

Pos nodded his understanding. Lincoln would rather have trusted Koob with this, but he had no reason to think that Pos wouldn't do his best.

Waiting was the hard part. He couldn't be sure how much time had elapsed since Sho's murder and Corbett's departure. Even the few Hmong who wore watches didn't seem to pay any attention to them. Lincoln had, for a while, admired a life that was at once so busy and so slow that the passage of time hardly mattered. Now, he felt like every minute was an eternity, because every second that passed meant Corbett might be getting farther away.

As it turned out, Pos came back with the information after only about fifteen minutes. He named a village that wasn't too far away—along the spine of their mountain range and downhill a ways, it looked down on a more central section of the Plain of Jars.

"Is he still there?" Lincoln asked.

"Yes! He is there! He still is!"

"Make sure he stays there," Lincoln instructed. "Have someone disable his airplane. They'll get a big reward. Lots of cash."

"'Disable'?" Pos asked.

"Break the engine. Slash the tires. Pour dirt in the fuel tanks. Burn the fucking thing, I don't care. Just make sure Corbett can't leave in it. I'll pay you, too. You and whoever in that village destroys that plane."

"I will," Pos said. He scurried back toward his hut.

Lincoln couldn't wait around to hear what the outcome of the conversation would be. He needed to be on the move. Once Corbett's plane was wrecked—if it was—he would be on his guard. Lincoln had to get there before he was able to get out of the area, because once he knew Lincoln was gunning for him, he might never come back.

41

Lincoln had already been tired, already operating on no sleep. But the image of Sho's mangled corpse gave wings to his feet and new energy to his lungs. He quickly gathered what he would need and set off across the mountains. The path wasn't straight or level—several times he had to climb a peak and then descend on the other side, only to find a taller one waiting.

He forced his legs to keep working, carrying him forward. His arms and shoulders ached, his lungs burned with exertion, his stomach felt like it would gnaw through his insides.

Still, he pressed on.

The sun went down. There were tigers in these mountains and snakes that could swallow a human being whole. All he had to light his way was a right-angle flashlight, and its batteries died halfway through the night. He threw it aside, glad to be rid of its useless weight.

The darkness made him want to lie down and rest. If Corbett was still in the village now, he would be there tomorrow.

Instead, Lincoln kept going. One foot in front of the other, ignoring the pain and the exhaustion that threatened to drop him at any moment. Branches ripped his clothing and tore his flesh, and the wound in his left arm throbbed. It was probably infected by now, he guessed. Smelled bad, anyway. He couldn't let that slow him down.

He reached the village before first light, but not by much. The landing strip was much like the one at Vang Khom, a narrow gash in the jungle on the edge of the mountain. A pilot would have to be a madman to fly in and out of places like that. Lincoln guessed Corbett qualified.

His U-10 sat at the end of the strip. Lincoln saw at a glance how someone in the village had disabled it: Both blades of the propeller had been snapped off, and the tires had been slashed to shreds.

In case Corbett was inside, Lincoln approached it cautiously, his AR-30 at the ready. When he worked his way around to the cockpit, a motion inside startled him and he almost fired, but as his finger closed on the trigger he realized the face looking at him was Hmong, not white.

He held his fire, and the airplane's occupant opened the door, dropping lightly to the ground. "Lincoln!" he said. "I broke the plane, like you said!"

"That's great," Lincoln replied. "Where's Corbett?"

"Pos said you would pay a reward."

Lincoln sighed, nodded, and reached into the pocket where he had stuffed a wad of Laotian currency. "Here you go. Where's Corbett?"

The man shrugged. "He left."

"Where? When?"

The man shrugged again, and pointed in the direction of the Plain of Jars. "Down the mountain."

"In the dark?"

"Before dark," the man said.

So Corbett had a big head start.

But he was on foot and headed into the Plain.

Corbett was a skilled, experienced Special Forces soldier who had survived some of the most dangerous action the Korean War had seen. It wouldn't do to unde-restimate him.

But he was a dozen years older than Lincoln, and if he had spent time in the Plain, he hadn't said anything about it.

If Lincoln could catch him down there, he could kill the man. He was sure of it.

Anyway, he had to try.

• • •

Lincoln lost Corbett's trail a couple of times before the sun rose. Each time, he managed to find it again, but without a flashlight it was a time-consuming process. With every minute Lincoln spent on his knees, looking for sign, Corbett was getting farther away.

Once the sun had cleared the horizon, tracking was easier. Corbett had done a fairly good job of covering his trail, but he had made some mistakes, and he was heavier than Lincoln, so he left impressions in the rain-saturated ground. Sometimes he had left the existing pathways, but then he'd had to cut through jungle, leaving broken branches and disturbed undergrowth in his wake.

Whenever Lincoln caught a glimpse of the Plain, he stopped and scanned with binoculars, hunting for his prey. If his willpower flagged, all he had to do was remember Sho's face and that ragged wound across her throat. That image was burned into his mind, and it provided all the motivation he needed.

Finally, with the sun sinking low, Lincoln most of the way down the mountain, he caught a glimpse of movement across the Plain. At first he wasn't sure if it was a human being or an animal, some kind of deer or antelope, maybe. The figure was moving toward the northeast, which seemed like a strange direction for Corbett to go. Eventually it would take him into Vietnam, but the farther north he traveled, the more he risked running into VC or NVA or Pathet Lao troops.

Lincoln broke out the field glasses and found the figure again. Focusing in, he recognized Corbett's shape, his gait, and a bright flash of color that could only be his distinctive Hawaiian shirt. How long could Corbett last in a war zone wearing that?

Lincoln didn't want someone else to kill Corbett, though. He had set that task for himself, and he didn't intend to share it.

The pilot was miles ahead of him and moving along at a brisk pace. Lincoln would never catch up at this rate.

So he had to pick it up. He took a couple of deep breaths and began to run.

He moved along at a steady jog, not so fast that he winded himself or so slow that Corbett outpaced him. He covered ground quickly and steadily, and he felt like he could run this way for days without tiring.

Of course, he knew that was an illusion. He was fueled by sorrow and fury. While those were inexhaustible resources, given the situation, at some point his muscles would simply refuse to work.

He had to catch Corbett by then, or at least get close enough to shoot.

42

Every time he reached high ground, Lincoln scanned for Corbett. The rain had softened the ground enough to make tracks impossible to hide, but at the same time, it filled and distorted them, so he couldn't tell how much time had elapsed since they'd been left. He caught glimpses of his prey now and then and knew he was gaining on him. Whether it was enough remained to be seen.

Corbett's trail still trended northeast, but at one point it made a seemingly abrupt swerve due east, across the road that edged the Plain and into the jungle beyond. Lincoln swore. On the open spaces, he could make good time, but in the jungle he couldn't run, couldn't move much faster than Corbett. His only advantage would be that Corbett had already cut a path for Lincoln to follow, so at least he wouldn't have to pick his way step by step like the pilot did.

The understory was heavy here, dark and dripping rainwater in a kind of constant shower. Lincoln pushed through, becoming ever angrier with every scratch and cut and bruise he endured. What advantage could Corbett gain from this? His escape was slowed as well. Unless he had a particular destination in mind—maybe a village where he had friends, or some sort of defensible bunker. Did he even know Lincoln was after him? He had to assume that, or he wouldn't have run. The instant he saw the damage to his plane, he'd have known who was behind it.

His mind racing with these thoughts, building rage, and the difficulty of progress through the thick forest, Lincoln didn't see the trap.

A wire stretched across his path, hidden by carefully placed fallen leaves and branches, caught his ankle. He stumbled forward, arms out to steady himself in case he fell. He caught the trunk of a small tree and kept his balance. Further enraged by his own carelessness, he charged ahead, straight into a sharpened bamboo shoot positioned at gut-level. The other end was wedged into the crotch of a tree, so it had nowhere to go when Lincoln ran into it. He spotted it at the last second and tried to halt his momentum. Too late, though, the makeshift spear sliced through shirt and flesh.

"Fuck!" he shouted. That was a mistake, a momentary lapse in judgment. Corbett had set this trap, so he knew that Lincoln was dogging his trail. He might have stayed close, to finish his pursuer off once the bamboo stake had weakened him.

Gritting his teeth against the pain, he backed off it, carefully. Blood flowed at once, running down his belly and into his pants. He listened for any sign of Corbett's approach. Hearing none, he shrugged off his pack and sat down, panting heavily. There was a first aid pouch on his belt, and he pawed through it for the benzalkonium chloride tincture. Swabbing some of that on the wound and wincing at the sting, he slapped a bandage over it and wrapped gauze around his midsection to hold it in place. When that was done, he allowed himself a couple of swallows from one of his canteens.

Still no sign of Corbett. Lincoln lurched uneasily to his feet—the wound hurt like a son of a bitch—and continued on his way, sidestepping the bamboo spear and watching more cautiously than ever for more booby traps.

Eventually, the pilot's trail wound west again, and Lincoln saw the end of the jungle ahead. Beyond it lay the Plain. So all of this had been meant to slow Lincoln down, draw him into that single trap? It didn't make sense.

He paused at the edge of the trees. Out there, on the Plain of Jars, the rain had stopped but the sky was low and leaden and ominous. They had reached another jar field, one Lincoln had never seen—he had never been so far north, and he wondered where they were in relation to any Pathet Lao elements. The jars were arrayed over rolling hills like an army on the march, more than he could begin to count.

Once his vision had acclimated to the brighter world beyond the jungle, he stepped out from the trees. Still a little unsteady from his wound, his boot slipped in the mud and his balance shifted to his right.

That probably saved his life.

The shot came from somewhere out among the jars, but Lincoln didn't see where. The bullet whipped past his left ear and crashed into the trees behind. He darted back into the cover of the forest and hit the dirt, facedown in the mud. More rounds pelted the trees, but they flew over him. When they finally stopped, he rose to a crouch, AR at the ready. He scanned the jars, breaking the space ahead into imaginary squares and studying each one, front to back and side to side.

No sign of Corbett.

He didn't want to use the binoculars. That would take both hands, and if Corbett did appear, he wanted to be able to shoot. Besides, any stray sunlight on the glass could give away his position.

All Lincoln could see were the jars. Corbett was out there somewhere, taking cover behind one or lying flat on the ground, sighting toward the spot where he had left the jungle, knowing that was where Lincoln would emerge as well.

Lincoln had very nearly fallen into that trap. Now he had to fade back into the jungle and work his way north or south, in order to leave the forest at a point Corbett couldn't anticipate.

He decided to try north. With every kilometer they progressed in that direction, they were heading into more dangerous country. For that reason, he figured Corbett would expect him to backtrack to the south instead.

Unless Corbett had reasoned in the same way and so knew Lincoln would choose the unexpected northern approach. That was the trouble with going up against someone who'd had the same kind of training; if the more experienced Corbett knew every move Lincoln would make before he made it, there would be no way to beat him.

Instead of relying on his Green Beret training to make decisions, then, Lincoln had to forget everything he had learned since his days on the mean streets of New Bordeaux.

Screened by the trees, he moved north as quickly as he could, pausing only occasionally to eye the jars, looking for Corbett. When he felt like he had gone far enough from the site of the pilot's ambush, he approached the tree line again. This time, he waited and watched for long minutes before showing himself. He would have to cross a road and thirty yards of open space before he reached the first of the jars, and he knew that would be Corbett's killing ground. Speed and stealth would be his only allies here.

Taking one long, last look and seeing no sign of the pilot, Lincoln dashed as fast as he could at a crouch, holding the rifle in both hands in case a target presented itself. Every second felt like it might be his last. The sodden ground made running even more difficult, and the sucking sounds made silence impossible.

Still, Corbett didn't shoot. Had the man moved on? When his first two traps had failed, had he given up and chosen instead to put more distance between them?

There was only one way to find out. Lincoln had to work south, staying among the jars for what cover they could provide, and find Corbett's tracks again. Or better yet, the man himself.

Then he spotted the brilliant red of Corbett's Hawaiian shirt. This time, he had spotted Corbett first. It was the advantage he needed to put an end to the chase.

43

The pilot had not left the area. He was hunkered down behind one of the jars, watching the tree line. He clearly didn't know that Lincoln had already emerged. Lincoln was surprised; he had hoped for more from Corbett's years of experience.

It was going to be a long shot, and most of Corbett was hidden by the jar, but enough of his shirt showed that Lincoln thought he could hit his target from here. He rose to his full height, shouldered the weapon, and sighted on that stupid red shirt. Corbett hadn't budged. Lincoln breathed in, then blew out the breath and squeezed the trigger.

His gunfire seemed incredibly loud on the quiet plain. The rounds streaked across the distance and found their mark, shredding the shirt and knocking Corbett over. Probably not dead yet, but badly injured anyway, so Lincoln would have to approach cautiously.

Lincoln took a few steps closer. Corbett hadn't moved. Maybe he was dead?

Dropping to a squat, Lincoln set down the AR and pulled the binoculars for a closer look.

Through the glasses, he found Corbett's red shirt—and the jumble of sticks that had been inside it.

He dropped the glasses and grabbed for his gun, but too late.

Corbett bolted out from behind a jar upslope from Lincoln, slashing at him with a machete.

Lincoln scrambled away from the attack—and his rifle—his feet failing to gain purchase in the mud. Corbett—shirtless and barefoot, his face and torso streaked with mud like war paint, wielding a machete with a twenty-two-inch blade—looked like a demon from the nether reaches of hell. Lincoln's feet went out from under him and he fell onto his back, then quickly rolled to his hands and knees. Corbett had closed the distance, though. As Lincoln tried to stand, he reached for the pistol on his belt. Corbett's machete sliced toward the holster, and Lincoln had to move his hand or lose it. The machete bit into the holster and gun, which was a good thing, or it would have taken a big chunk out of Lincoln's hip.

It stuck there for a moment, giving Lincoln the chance to snatch at the pilot's arm. He caught it, but the mud made it too slippery to hold. Corbett lurched back, tearing the machete free.

When he did, Lincoln made another grab for his pistol. Once it was free of its holster, Lincoln saw that the hammer had been damaged by the machete, and the barrel was packed with mud. It might fire, but it might just as easily blow up in his hand.

Instead of risking it, he hurled it at Corbett. The pilot swatted it out of the air with his free hand—Lincoln was pleased to see the gun open a cut on the ball of his thumb. It bled just a little, but he was tired of being the only one bleeding.

The throw only bought him an instant's respite. Then Corbett was coming at him again, blade swiping through the air. Lincoln yanked his knife from its sheath and sprang to his feet. As Corbett charged down, Lincoln pushed up to meet him. He ducked under Corbett's swing and thrust the knife forward.

The point jabbed into the meaty part of the pilot's upper thigh. Corbett screamed and flinched away, bringing the machete down in a series of wild strokes to keep Lincoln at bay. The knife was still stuck in his leg. When he tugged it free and hurled it aside, blood spurted from the cut, and Corbett seemed to swoon a little.

"Listen, man," Corbett said, his voice shaky with pain. "There's no need for this shit. We're on the same team, man. I'm sorry about that chick, but you know, business is business. You can find another slant chick anywhere. You can have Mai, brother. She's a good lay. You'd like her."

"Fuck you," Lincoln said.

"Come on, Lincoln, be reasonable. I mean, you got no weapons left. I used all my ammo on you and missed, but you're already hurt—you're bleeding bad from the gut, man—and I still got my steel. So let's call it a draw and get the hell out of here. We can be rich, the two of us, if we work together."

Lincoln saw the jars standing in disorderly rows behind Corbett. If he were to die here, in a country where he had no official presence, in which no one would acknowledge that he had ever set foot, he supposed that in the midst of ancient funerary casks left behind by strangers like himself was as good a place as any.

"Fuck," he said. "You."

With that, Lincoln attacked, forging uphill, dodging the ever-wilder slashes of Corbett's blade. He had to get that machete away from the pilot or die trying.

The weapon glanced off Lincoln's right shoulder, cutting flesh but not doing serious damage. Lincoln pushed past the pain and got inside Corbett's arms, where the machete could do no damage. He charged forward, hoping to bowl over the pilot. But even on the muddy ground, even with his thigh gushing blood, the man held his position. Lincoln's fingers clawed at Corbett's throat. Corbett got his left hand between them, the butt of his palm against Lincoln's chin, and pushed, trying to bend Lincoln's neck backward. At the same time, Lincoln could hear him trying to reverse his grip on the machete, so he could stab inward.

Then Lincoln's foot slid on the muddy slope, and his hand released the pilot's throat. Corbett completed his grip change and cut toward Lincoln's back. Lincoln altered his strategy—instead of going for the throat, he slammed his fist down, hard, on Corbett's injured thigh.

The pilot screeched in pain and rage, and his leg gave way beneath him. His face was dark red, his long hair caked with mud. He still had a grip on his weapon, and he struck wildly at Lincoln, catching him glancing blows from time to time.

But he was down on one knee, his other leg bent, his balance precarious. The more he swung that blade, the more he threw off his own center of balance. Lincoln waited until the blade had swished past, then stepped in, throwing a punch with all the force of his shoulder and back. His fist smashed into Corbett's mouth. He felt teeth break under its weight, and when he stepped back again, blood bubbled up and ran from the corners of Corbett's lips.

Corbett was still mostly upright, though he was listing. Lincoln stepped to his left, dodging the machete, then sent a fast snap-kick into the pilot's good leg. He wasn't sure if Corbett's tibia snapped, but the blow knocked that leg out from under him. Corbett went down on his back in the mud, and the machete flew from his grip.

Weaponless, Lincoln dropped onto Corbett's chest, forcing the wind from him. Corbett protected his throat, but Lincoln hammered his face, landing punch after punch. His fists tore the pilot's right cheek, splitting it to the bone. He smashed the other cheek, and Corbett's left eye spilled from its socket. Pain shot up from Lincoln's fists from every blow, but he kept picturing Sho on their bed, her throat slashed, and he kept swinging and swinging long after Corbett's arms had fallen limp at his sides, after the torso on which Lincoln sat rose and fell no more.

Finally, he rolled off the brutalized hunk of flesh that had been Brad Corbett, went to his knees in the mud, and wept for the woman he had loved. Above, the sky opened up and the rain came and washed away the tears and the blood and the gore. But it couldn't touch the memories, and those were what hurt the worst.

EPILOGUE

Three days later, Tommy Pinchot landed an Air America U-10 at the Vang Khom airstrip. Tommy stayed in the cockpit, looking glum, but Donovan climbed down. He wore a white blazer and a dark blue dress shirt and white slacks, and he looked more like a banker on vacation than a spy.

"We found Corbett's plane," he said. "Wrecked. Looks like it didn't make a landing at a mountain airfield and fell off the fucking side."

"Let's take a walk," Lincoln suggested. "I have a story to tell you."

They hiked up from the village and sat on two big rocks near the peak, Vang Khom below them to the south and the Plain of Jars to the north. Lincoln indicated the Plain. "He's down there."

Donovan had been about to strike a match, but he paused, eyed Lincoln, and raised an eyebrow. "You know that how?"

"Told you I had a story," Lincoln said. "Here's what happened."

He started from the beginning, told Donovan about his relationship with Sho, about Corbett and the poppies, about Mai, and about Corbett's final betrayal. He almost teared up when he got to that part, but he held it in check. He hadn't been back in the longhouse except to dress Sho and prepare her for burial, and to collect the cash he had tucked away in there. He was sleeping in the open because it was easier than being inside the place where he had found her.

Finally, he described the hunt for Corbett and the fight that had ended it.

"I tossed him in one of the jars," he said. "You could search for a hundred years and never find him. I don't even remember which one. I'd never been to that jar field before, and I wasn't really paying attention to where the hell I was at the time."

"You threw Corbett in a fucking jar?" Donovan asked, incredulous.

"He made a hell of a splash, too. Thing must have been half-full of rainwater." Lincoln considered how it must sound to Donovan and added, "Guess I fucked up, huh?"

"What do you mean?"

"I mean, Corbett was CIA, right?"

"He was a contractor."

"Whatever. He worked with you guys. He was an American."

"He was an asshole," Donovan said. "I can't believe he did that."

"Yeah, I guess he had it comin'."

"He sure did."

Donovan handed Lincoln the pack and let him light a smoke from the tip of his own. They sat on the rocks for a few minutes, both men staring off into the Plain. Lincoln couldn't be sure what was on Donovan's mind, but he knew what was on his.

When Donovan spoke again, it was clear he'd been thinking along the same lines.

"You want to stay?"

"In Vang Khom? Fuck no."

"Anywhere in Laos."

"Not really," Lincoln said. "Not at all, in fact. This place is fucked up."

"Like Vietnam's any better."

"At least there the people trying to kill you are the enemy."

"Usually," Donovan admitted. "Not always. Anyway, I can get you out of here. Vietnam, Germany, stateside, wherever you want to go. Just say the word."

"Vietnam's okay," Lincoln said. "That's where the war is."

"It's here, too," Donovan countered. "We're not done in Laos, you and me. I don't want to get on some goddamn high horse, but democracy's important enough to protect anyplace it's in danger, and that includes Laos. But you can go back to Vietnam for a while."

"What about Corbett? Will I face any charges?"

"Corbett died trying to desert to the north. In the process, he crashed the plane he wanted to trade for privileged status. He was a fucking traitor to his country, and he deserved to die."

"But that's—"

"Lincoln, the stories we tell about this place are what becomes the official version. Sooner or later, they become the truth. You see anybody who's going to contradict it?"

Lincoln looked out toward the Plain again. The ghosts of the ancient travelers, maybe.

But they had been quiet for a long time. They had seen a lot of death. They wouldn't say anything.

"Guess not."

"Damn straight," Donovan said. "Corbett will go down as a would-be Benedict Arnold, and when—if—Special Forces soldiers even mention his name, they'll spit at the memory. And I'll do whatever I can to help you out, Lincoln—here, and back in the world. We're a hell of a team, and it would be stupid to break that up."

"You sure?" Lincoln asked.

"You got any more dumb questions, soldier?"

Lincoln sucked down his last drag and squashed the butt under his heel. "Just one," he said. "How soon can we get off this fucking mountain?"

ACKNOWLEDGMENTS

The authors would like to thank the folks at 2K and Hangar 13 for creating the *Mafia III* game. Great appreciation also goes out to Mark Irwin and the gang at Insight Editions, and to Howard and Kim-Mei for their invaluable support. As always, thanks to the boys for putting up with us while we write, and to Catherine.

ABOUT THE AUTHORS

MARSHEILA (MARCY) ROCKWELL and JEFF MARIOTTE have written more than sixty novels between them, some of the most recent of which are the Shard Axe series, a trilogy based on Neil Gaiman's Lady Justice comic books (Rockwell), *Deadlands: Thunder Moon Rising*, and *Empty Rooms* (Mariotte). They've also written dozens of short stories, separately and together. Some of their solo stories are collected in *Nine Frights* (Mariotte) and *Bridges of Longing and Other Strange Passageways* (Rockwell). Their collaborations include the novel *7 Sykos* and short works "A Soul in the Hand," "John Barleycorn Must Die," "V-Wars: The Real HousewiVes of Scottsdale," "X-Files: Transmissions," "The Lottons Show," "Letting Go the Ghosts," "Son of Blob," and "A Single Feather," and the soon-to-be-published novel trilogy *Xena: Warrior Princess—Gods of War*. Other miscellaneous projects include Rhysling Award–nominated poetry (Rockwell) and Bram Stoker Award–nominated comic books (Mariotte). You can find more complete bibliographies and news about upcoming projects, both collaborative and solo, at marsheilarockwell.com and jeffmariotte.com.